DAUGHTER OF DISHONOR

I saw a wizened crone shrouded in funeral black, the dark fringe of her shawl giving an effect of tatters and ribands. Her gnarled hands and arms emerging from the folds of the shawl were waxen, a startling contrast to the gypsy-brown face capped by a cascade of slate-gray hair which fell almost to her waist.

The hunched shoulders straightened as she became aware of my presence, then she moved slowly toward me, head thrust forward, peering, a mad and malevolent scrutiny. I recoiled as the hag lifted her hand, the clawlike fingers almost touching my face. "I know you, I know you" came the hoarse, crackling whisper. For a second we stood transfixed, paralyzed, until she whirled away, and her voice rose to a scream.

"It's the murderer's daughter! The murderer's daughter has returned!"

There was nothing to protect Rochelle Dumont from the horrifying truth and its terrifying consequences at River Rising. Not even love. Especially not love. . . .

Big Bestsellers from SIGNET

☐ **THE HIGH VALLEY by Jessica North.**
(#W5929—$1.50)

☐ **KINFLICKS by Lisa Alther.** (#E7390—$2.25)

☐ **LOVER: CONFESSIONS OF A ONE NIGHT STAND by Lawrence Edwards.** (#J7392—$1.95)

☐ **THE SURVIVOR by James Herbert.**
(#E7393—$1.75)

☐ **THE FOG by James Herbert.** (#W6708—$1.50)

☐ **THE RATS by James Herbert.** (#W6460—$1.50)

☐ **THE KILLING GIFT by Bari Wood.**
(#E7350—$2.25)

☐ **WHITE FIRES BURNING by Catherine Dillon.**
(#E7351—$1.75)

☐ **CONSTANTINE CAY by Catherine Dillon.**
(#W6892—$1.50)

☐ **THE SECRET LIST OF HEINRICH ROEHM by Michael Barak.** (#E7352—$1.75)

☐ **YESTERDAY'S CHILD by Helene Brown.**
(#E7353—$1.75)

☐ **FOREVER AMBER by Kathleen Winsor.**
(#J7360—$1.95)

☐ **SMOULDERING FIRES by Anya Seton.**
(#J7276—$1.95)

☐ **HARVEST OF DESIRE by Rochelle Larkin.**
(#J7277—$1.95)

☐ **THE DEVIL'S OWN by Christopher Nicole.**
(#J7256—$1.95)

THE NEW AMERICAN LIBRARY, INC.,
P.O. Box 999, Bergenfield, New Jersey 07621

Please send me the SIGNET BOOKS I have checked above.
I am enclosing $_____(check or money order—no
currency or C.O.D.'s). Please include the list price plus 35¢ a
copy to cover handling and mailing costs. (Prices and numbers
are subject to change without notice.)

Name_____

Address_____

City_____State_____Zip Code_____
Allow at least 4 weeks for delivery

River Rising

by
Jessica North

A SIGNET BOOK

NEW AMERICAN LIBRARY

TIMES MIRROR

SIGNET TRADEMARK REG. U.S. PAT. OFF. AND FOREIGN COUNTRIES
REGISTERED TRADEMARK—MARCA REGISTRADA
HECHO EN CHICAGO, U.S.A.

SIGNET, SIGNET CLASSICS, MENTOR, PLUME AND MERIDIAN BOOKS
are published by The New American Library, Inc.,
1301 Avenue of the Americas, New York, New York 10019.

FIRST SIGNET PRINTING, MARCH, 1977

1 2 3 4 5 6 7 8 9

PRINTED IN THE UNITED STATES OF AMERICA

For Charles Shepherd and his friend Shirley

1

My mind, now that I can permit myself to remember all that has happened, returns always to the river, the great St. Lawrence pouring seaward from the cool heart of the continent, sweeping past the cities, farms and then that wilderness of Québec to merge with the Atlantic in that misty gulf whose reefs and shoals once made those waters a graveyard of ships and voyagers.

It was from the deck of a wooden sailing vessel journeying downriver that I saw the craggy headland and towering house known as the Rising, the place of my birth to which I now returned, a resentful stranger.

I was two years old when my mother took me from that huge house into exile, and a little more than twenty years had passed since them. I could not possibly have remembered those granite cliffs, the slashed foam where waves battered the rocks of Wind-Whistle Cove. Yet when the schooner *Etoile Filante* rounded an island and the scene burst into view, my astonishment was mixed with a strange sense of the familiar, as though memory of this land was implanted in my blood and I had unconsciously known that Rising, starkly beautiful, would loom from the shore at this exact place.

"Look!" I exclaimed. "That must be the Rising!"

The wrinkled, weather-browned steward of the *Etoile Filante* leaned against the rail beside me and nodded. *"Oui. C'est magnifique."*

Then, frowning, he muttered in accented English. "But it

has a dark history. An unlucky place." His disapproving gaze studied the churned spate of white water, the jagged rocks that could rend and grind the strongest hull. He shook his head at the sheer upthrust of the cliffs of the Canadian Shield, the oldest rocks and mountains in North America. *"Formidable."*

"You mean the rocks?"

"All of it. It is haunted, unlucky. There are stories about it. Many stories."

But the ship did not believe him. Like the shooting star she was named for, she plunged ahead, canvas booming in the freshened breeze. Sunlight sparkled on the water and the world that cool May morning was new-minted—jonquil weather, crocus weather.

Atop the cliffs, mansard roofs and gables of the ancient town gleamed above tall sycamores and firs shading and concealing the lower floors. Not knowing how I would learn to fear the whispering wind in those branches, I found myself thinking, Beautiful.

Grudging admiration. I had come filled with bitterness against the people who lived here, even though they were my own family, my only relatives. I did not want to like them or their country. Not *my* country! I told myself again. I had no country, no home.

Unfinished business had brought me here. That, and an unexplainable agreeing to do a favor for an old lady to whom I owed nothing. But perhaps there was a deeper reason for my coming. I felt rootless in the world. Not displaced, since I did not come from a home I loved, but placeless. Why not visit my mother's people? At least I could see for myself the cousins and the great-aunt who had done my mother such unkindness that for years she would not even mention their names. When she finally did, in her last delirious hours, it was to warn me against them. "Don't believe them, Rochelle! Don't trust them!"

Three solemn, slow bell strokes rang across the water, although I could see no church. The steward crossed himself, as though the distant bell were tolling, its deep notes echoing over the broad river, carrying an announcement of death to the far shore more than twenty miles away. Perhaps the three carefully timed strokes were really a way of announcing death, a Québec knell. Against my will, I suddenly thought of Dierdre Cameron, the pixie face, the mischievous eyebrows. The morning no longer seemed cool, but chill, the river a threat.

"Nonsense," I told myself. "Nothing has happened to Deirdre."

"*Quai Ste. Marie du Lac!*" shouted the steward, leaving my side. "*Quai Ste. Marie!*"

I looked once more at the great vista of cliffs, house and trees silhouetted against the sky, their beauty lulling me, deceiving me into believing that this moment, in spite of everything, might somehow be a new beginning for me.

It was not, of course, a beginning. The violence had already begun, the enemy had already struck.

Beginnings are hard to trace and recognize. They are like the St. Lawrence itself, whose waters seem to flow from the tip of Lake Ontario, although their true source is hidden a thousand miles away in the forests of Minnesota. The terror at River Rising had its wellsprings in the past, but for me it began without my knowing that forces from the past had reached out. The first move came not in darkness, but in the bright, crowded airport at Montréal only minutes after my arrival in Canada.

"Rochelle! Rochelle Dumont!"

Startled, I looked in the direction of the voice. My flight from the West Indies to Montréal had just landed and I had cleared customs. I now stood two steps inside Canada, and had paused to collect my wits and gather some first impression of my unfamiliar native country. But airports have neither nationality nor identity.

"Rochelle!" called the voice again. Who on earth? No one awaited me. Even if my great-aunt, Regina Armitage, had changed her mind and sent someone to meet me, it could be no one who would recognize my face. "I'll be right with you!"

Then I saw a girl my own age waving at me. She, too, had just passed through customs and was now fussing with the buckles of a canvas backpack that lay on a steel counter a few yards from me. Memories came back vaguely. College? Eastfield Hall? Yes, that was it.

She pushed past several people, the backpack dragging behind her, then threw her arms around me, exclaiming, "Rochelle, how wonderful! It's been ages."

"Deirdre Cameron?"

"Of course, Rochelle! I can't have changed in—how long is it? Three years."

"A little longer," I murmured. But it seemed as though a decade had passed since I'd left Eastfield at the start of my senior year to return home to Antigua. There had been my mother's final illness and death, the losing struggle to continue the day school she had owned, and at last selling it. Then several months in what seemed a vacuum, earning my living as organist in a local church, teaching piano to a handful of squirming, uninterested children, a time when life appeared to be held in abeyance.

"You haven't changed," I said. "Only you're wearing your hair longer, and it's even more beautiful." Deirdre's hair, now long and loose, was the same rich brown my mother's hair had been before it lost its luster. I had always thought Deirdre's name was lovely but inappropriate, for she had none of the ethereal saintliness of the legendary Deirdre of the Sorrows. Her face was elfin, she was a joyful Peter Pan.

"You've lost weight," she said, "and you look wonderful."

In college we'd known each other slightly, but had never become friends, having little in common except that we were the only Canadian students in a small New England school. This formed no bond, because I had no memories of Canada. Now the warmth of her greeting surprised me, even though I recalled that sudden, effusive bursts of affection were typical of Deirdre, who lived in a state of emotional vibration.

"Is anyone meeting you?" she asked.

"No."

"I'm alone, too. Let's have coffee at the snack bar."

I hesitated, appreciating her smile but feeling she was a figure from the past, a reminder of years I would gladly forget. But before I could refuse, Deirdre had captured a passing skycap and was loading him with our luggage, commanding him in French slower than my own to take the things to *Le snack bar.*

"Talk English, lady," he told her. "This is Montréal, not Québec City."

"Well, you never know in this province what language to use," she answered.

I retrieved a bright yellow shawl that had been lying on my suitcase.

"What's that?" she asked. "It's a beautiful yellow. Almost gold."

"A shawl. More a mantilla, I suppose. My Great-Aunt Regina made it and sent it to me. She wrote that it was to warm me in the Québec spring."

"What gorgeous crocheting! Like lace on an old valentine."

Taking possession, Deirdre draped it around her shoulders. Then I remembered another of her qualities. She loved to borrow or trade clothing. In college her eye had never fallen upon anything in my conservative wardrobe, but other girls had been constant victims of Deirdre's "Oh, may I just try it on?" Her childlike eagerness made it hard to refuse.

We passed through swinging doors and entered the main hall of the terminal, a place so crowded that it seemed a dozen flights must be arriving and departing simultaneously. A babel of languages surrounded us, not only English and French in various dialects, but other European tongues as well.

Deirdre preened in the shawl, running her fingers lightly over the fine stitchery, lifting her shoulders a bit. Anything new delighted her, but I remembered how temporary such pleasure proved. If the shawl had been hers, she would have quickly tired of it.

We were utterly unlike, I thought as we moved ahead. My silver-gray suit was what my mother had called "well-cut and sensible," or "appropriate for travel." It paled beside the flare of Deirdre's ankle-length skirt of rainbow-striped cotton. Her thong sandals scuffed the tile floor, and the sleeveless blouse, defying the cool morning, suggested a folk dance.

Our luggage carried the contrast even further. My plain leather suitcase was old but fairly expensive. Deirdre's canvas backpack, like her clothing, was deliberately cheap. As the daughter of a rich Ontario family, she could have anything that money could buy and the law would permit. She called her inconsistent and half-hearted attempts to wear a disguise of poverty "protest" and "rejection of our worship of objects." It struck me as silly but harmless.

We had almost reached the glass doors of the snack bar when a hefty man, obviously late for a plane, charged through the crowd. *"Pardon! S'il vous—"*

I stumbled against the wall, dodging his outflung attaché case. My ankle turned painfully and I felt the heel of my left pump give way, break off.

"What a rude, boorish—!" Deirdre sputtered angrily, then was kneeling beside me. "Are you all right?"

"I don't think it's a sprain, just a twist." Leaning on her, I hobbled into the restaurant and managed to get to a booth. "Is anything more awkward than walking on one heel?"

I asked the skycap to put my suitcase beside me so I could find another pair of shoes, and started to open my purse to tip him.

"No," said Deirdre. "He's mine. I caught him." She fumbled in her macramé bag, then my eyes widened when she carelessly put two thick rolls, actually wads, of money on the table. One crumpled stack was Canadian, the other American tens, twenties, fifties. Next she fished out a handful of coins of mixed nationality.

The skycap's emphatic "Thank you, miss!" attested her generosity. As she stuffed the bills back into the bag, I marveled that anyone could be so foolhardy. How much cash was she carrying? A thousand dollars? No, double or triple that amount. Hadn't she heard of purse snatching? Or of traveler's checks?

Just then I heard my name called the second time that morning. But now it was broadcast over the airport intercom.

"Miss Rochelle Dumont. Miss Rochelle Dumont. Please come to the information desk."

"I'll go for you," said Deirdre as the announcement was repeated in French.

"Really, I'm all right. If I can just find another pair—"

"It's at the other end of the building. Give that ankle some rest." She started for the doors, calling back, "Order coffee for me."

I unzipped my suitcase and then took out a pair of walking shoes. Who could be paging me? It had to be Great-Aunt Regina or some other member of the Armitage family. But Regina Armitage had been emphatic in her last letter. "We won't meet you. You must have a chance to meet Canada first." As though I cared about their frozen country! Or about them. Family concern from the Armitages was rather belated. Belated by twenty years!

I felt my ankle, finding it tender but not painful. I was determined to see as much of Montréal as possible this afternoon. After all, it was a vacation at Regina Armitage's expense, and while the family owed me nothing, they surely owed my mother a great deal. Guilt, I thought once more.

Regina Armitage, the *grande dame,* the matriarch, salving her conscience for all the years my mother had spent alone. Regina, in her first letter to me several months ago, had written vaguely of "this tragic estrangement," and seemed to assume I knew what she meant. Of course I did not. What had they done to my mother while I was still a baby? Some unkindness so painful she had never been able to speak of them.

As a small child I learned I was different from most other girls because my mother was a widow and I could not remember my father. Yet that was not so very unusual. My mother operated a private day school on the island of Antigua, and among her small group of pupils there were some from families broken by death or divorce. But later I asked questions about aunts, uncles and cousins.

"They're far away and you wouldn't like them," she said.

The flat words carried no emphasis, but I knew the terrible finality of that tone. Charlotte Armitage Dumont, my mother, could inspire awe, admiration and even fear, yet she had little power to evoke love. I felt myself an orphan who by an odd accident had a mother. An efficient, capable mother, never deliberately unkind, who made sure I was properly clothed, fed, and as soon as possible sent away to the United States for an adequate education. She never spoke of the past, but faced the present and future with a joyless courage. I could almost count the times I'd seen her smile with real warmth or burst into carefree laughter. My childhood loneliness would have been almost complete except for my music, which could hold me hour after hour in the brilliance of another world, and for the love given me by my mother's only friend, Paul LaFarge.

A waitress, pad and pencil in hand, came to the booth and I ordered two coffees. A moment later Deirdre arrived flourishing an oversized envelope with a red maple-leaf design. Two crimson ribbons streamed from the lower corners. "There was no one waiting, but they had this for you." She handed it to me.

My name, in block letters, was penciled on it. "Did they say who left it?"

"No. One of the skycaps brought it to the desk. Hurry and open it, Rochelle! It's a present of some kind. Don't you love unexpected presents?"

Slitting the sealed flap with my nail file, I looked inside, then murmured, "How strange."

"What's in it?"

"Nothing. It's empty."

"It can't be. Maybe there's something at the bottom?"

"You look." She did, and found nothing.

"Maybe my great-aunt's growing forgetful," I said. "But Regina Armitage sounded anything but senile in her letters."

Deirdre looked at me with new interest. "Armitage? You're not related to Morgan Armitage, are you?"

"I have a cousin named Morgan. Regina said he's a painter."

"A painter?" For a second Deirdre was speechless, then laughed. "A painter! Rochelle, your cousin may not be quite the most famous living Canadian artist, but most critics think he's the best. Didn't you know?"

I shook my head. "I don't know anything about my mother's family." Or my father's, either, I added silently.

"When I was thirteen I had the most terrible crush on Morgan Armitage," she went on, giggling. "I saw him just once, at the opening of an exhibition in Toronto. My mother—she's a culture-vulture—dragged me to it. I saw Morgan Armitage and went ga-ga. Maybe it was his eyes. They were hypnotic, almost amber or golden. He was the handsomest older man I'd ever seen. I mooned about him for a month, then got over it. You know how it is at thirteen. Weren't you in love with an actor or a musician?"

"No," I answered, but the sudden color in my cheeks gave me away.

Deirdre smiled. "Lying is a deadly sin."

"Well, there was an older man. A painter, too. He was from Martinique and his name was Paul LaFarge. But he wasn't famous or successful. Not even handsome. Just big and bearlike and rough and gentle at the same time."

Unwillingly I recalled Paul LaFarge's flaming red hair, the white duck trousers always paint-spotted, the kindness of his smile. My feelings toward Paul had been nothing like Dierdre's schoolgirl crush. There was no romance in what I felt for him—he was my mother's friend—but the happiest memories of my life were of those rare summer days when his unseaworthy houseboat was moored in the cove near our cottage.

When "Uncle Paul" was there, our world changed. My mother's firm lips seemed fuller and her smiles, while guarded, were honest. My love for him remained unchanged even during that terrible summer when I returned home from school in the United States and realized the truth: Paul LaFarge was secretly my mother's lover. He came to the house at night when they thought I was asleep. But sleep was impossible for me as I lay in adolescent torment. It was stealthy and dishonest, I thought. Ugly. Why wouldn't my mother marry him? The world might call him a failure, a drifter from island to island who, I was told, painted with the fury of a madman but hardly sold enough to buy new canvas. If my mother really cared for him, none of this would matter, I told myself.

Only when I was more mature, and long after Paul's death, could I force myself to admit that the fault may have been his—or perhaps no one's. Maybe he never wanted a wife, no matter how happy he seemed with us.

Eventually I realized that my feelings about "honesty" and "openness" were nonsense. If the affair had become known, scandal would have closed my mother's school in a week. The tourists who flock to the Leeward Islands might have taken a broad-minded view, but our livelihood did not depend upon them. The school was supported by conservative families of plantation owners, and my mother's position had been far more difficult than I had realized.

Now, as the waitress served our coffee, I forced my mind from the past and tried to listen to Deirdre as she chattered about the "Mystery of the Empty Envelope." She had changed more than I had first thought. Faint crescents darkened her lower eyelids, marks of lack of sleep, and her gaiety seemed forced.

"Tell me all about yourself," she said. "Are you still living in the Virgin Islands?"

"Not the Virgin Islands," I answered, keeping my voice even. "The Leeward Islands. Antigua, to be exact."

Deirdre, blushing, stammered, "Yes, of course. I get all those islands mixed up."

"Don't be silly," I told her. "I know about that college joke. At least three town boys in Eastfield used that Virgin Islands remark about me. It hurt at the time. I felt like a misfit. Now I know better. If I don't care to leap into bed, it's my own business."

"Of course," she agreed.

I was thankful she didn't go on to say I just hadn't met the right man yet. "I'm not living in the islands any more. I'm visiting Canada."

"You're not on a concert tour, are you?" she asked.

I shook my head. "That was a college dream. It turned out I don't have what they call 'an exploitable talent.' In other words, I'm not good enough."

She seemed honestly disappointed. "I remember that concert you gave in Eastfield," she said. "We all thought you'd be famous and we'd brag about having gone to college with you."

"I'm afraid not." I hesitated, then said, "I really haven't any long-range plans. I don't know what I'll do."

"That makes two of us." Deirdre, usually effervescent, suddenly looked woebegone. "I'm having a bad time, Rochelle. A very bad time." She avoided my eyes, carefully stirring coffee that contained neither sugar nor cream. "I'm on the run. Hiding out."

"Hiding out? Deirdre, for heaven's sake!"

"Not from the police. Oh, nothing like that! It's a personal thing I can't face." The brown eyes in her gamine face became misty as she held back tears. "Have you ever felt trapped, Rochelle? Really trapped?"

"I don't think so." A lie, of course. Sometimes it struck me that entrapment was the story of my life. Trapped by boarding schools, and so trapped by my mother's strict standards and steel discipline that the bars of the cage were invisible to my own eyes, although I knew they were there.

"I suppose it would be hard for you to understand my problems, Rochelle. I mean, you've always had everything. I used to envy you."

"You envied me!" Never in my life had I been more astonished. Deirdre Cameron, rich, attractive and carefree had envied *me*. It was preposterous. If there had been envy, it would have been on my part, not hers. "Why? I don't understand."

Looking up, she managed a wry half-smile. "At first because of things that aren't very important. I longed to have auburn hair like yours and those strong cheekbones. And when girls talked about how unusual your green eyes were, my own must have almost turned green with envy."

"Deirdre, you can't be serious," I said.

"But I am. The main thing I envied was that you were always so poised and sure of yourself. You always knew exactly what you were doing."

How little she realized. Either Deirdre had no perception at all, or the mask I wore was more effective than I had ever dreamed.

"It's what my father calls character," said Deirdre thoughtfully. "You have it, I don't. In college you always just went your own way. You were above all the crazy things we did."

Not above it, I thought. *Out* of it. Too serious, haunted by the feeling that my mother's keen eyes were watching from three thousand miles away. Couldn't Deirdre understand that this meant loneliness, missing the joy of being foolish, even if one had to face the consequences later?

"You'd never mess up your life and cause trouble the way I do," she said. "I hurt people I love. I don't mean to, but it happens. Afterwards I can't face things. I run away. If only I could manage myself!" She struggled hard for control now, her shoulders held rigid and her hands clenched tightly.

I had no idea of what she meant. Deirdre had been giddy but likable. I did remember a story about a broken engagement and I knew she had once narrowly avoided expulsion for vanishing from campus for several days. Had more serious things happened in the last three years?

"I haven't any right to burden you with troubles I've caused myself," she said.

"If it helps to talk, Deirdre——"

"It doesn't. I just want to get away. Forget everything. Far away where nobody can find me." Closing her eyes a moment, she took several deep breaths, then shook her head as though performing some ritual that instantly banished all troubles. The taut face relaxed, and she asked calmly, "What are your plans right now?"

I explained that I was going downriver to a village called Ste. Marie du Lac. It seemed odd to say "down" when on the map the village and lake were "up," north of Québec City. "I'm taking a ship. Regina Armitage arranged passage on the *Etoile Filante.*"

"Why, that's the old *Shooting Star*. What a wonderful way to see Québec!"

"You know the ship?"

She nodded eagerly. "I've made the trip twice. The *Star* is a real nineteenth-century sailing ship, but has engines for emergencies. It's been modernized for tourists, of course. People who just want to get downriver take the train or use the South Shore Highway. The *Star* is special." Pursing her lips, she thought a moment, then said abruptly, "I'm going with you. Maybe to Québec City, maybe all the way to the Gaspé Peninsula."

"But what about reservations?"

"No problem. Tourist season isn't here yet. I'm surprised the *Star* is sailing so early this year. I'm going right now to telephone."

I could have told her that Captain McCabe of the *Etoile Filante* was a friend of the Armitage family and that I carried a note of introduction to him. He might help with reservations, but I said nothing, having mixed feelings about the prospect of traveling with Deirdre. Regina Armitage wanted me to "meet my country" alone, no doubt a wise decision. Then, remembering Deirdre's blanched face, I felt guilty and unkind. She was in no condition to be alone, and what did a slight change in my plans matter?

A moment later she returned, elfin face glowing. "I've got a cabin. It's right next to yours."

"Lucky," I said, still uncertain about what kind of luck this might prove to be. Deirdre amazed me. Now that her future for the next two or three days was settled, all worry had evaporated like mist in sunshine. "How's your ankle?" she asked.

"Much better."

"Then I'll be your guide to Montréal. We don't sail until after ten tonight."

"It seems strange to start a sightseeing trip after dark."

"Rochelle, you're so unromantic. You'll see why later."

As we rose to leave, my glance fell on the big envelope with its maple-leaf design and gay ribbons. What had been left out when it was sealed? Something thin and flat, like a drawing? Odd that anyone would take the trouble of finding so special an envelope, and then forget to put anything in it. When I reached Ste. Marie du Lac and the Rising, someone, I supposed, would clear up the mystery. But in this I proved to be mistaken. The empty envelope became something no one wanted to talk about.

"Welcome to Montréal!" Deirdre said as our taxi sped toward the city. "Cultural, artistic and crime capital of Canada!"

"Crime?"

"A notorious underworld. We can boast the highest rate of bank robberies on earth and we also had the terrorism by the Québecois separatists. They've been quiet lately, but you never know."

I smiled. "That's what you're guiding me to? Crime and terrorism?"

"Not today. It's a fascinating city. But first we'll have lunch at Le Coq d'Or. That's a restaurant right at the wharf where the *Star* is moored. We can leave our luggage there until boarding time tonight."

The Montréal weather made no effort to welcome me. An overcast sky threatened rain, and thick but patchy fog shrouded the area near the river.

"We're in the Old Quarter now," said Deirdre as we passed docks and warehouses. Here and there I caught glimpses of buildings of dressed limestone, narrow-fronted structures with antique casement windows.

"Is that roof made of tin?" I asked.

"Yes. The old buildings all had metal roofs. A fire regulation. There were iron shutters, too. Not many left now, but you can still see the iron hooks they were attached to."

Restaurant Le Coq d'Or was either so self-effacing or so haughty that it did not deign to have any sign except a small brass plaque. Across the street I could see the masts and furled sails of the *Etoile Filante* rising above a wooden fence with closed gates.

"Mademoiselle Cameron!" An elegantly uniformed doorman appeared from the narrow entrance of Le Coq d'Or and greeted Deirdre enthusiastically in French so rapid that I suspected she caught only the gist of his welcome.

"Hello, Charles. Good to see you. Please put these things in the coatroom. We'll return for them tonight."

Inside, the restaurant was dimly illuminated by candles, ships' lanterns and deeply shaded lamps. I admired the huge fieldstone fireplace and the beams of rough-hewn cedar supporting the low ceiling.

The Maître d'hôtel and a waiter, as cordial to Deirdre as the doorman had been, ushered us to a table beside a front window, snatching away a card proclaiming the space reserved.

"Lunch, please, Armand." Deirdre waved the menus aside. "Whatever's best today."

"You're well known here," I said.

"I should be. I ate here at least twice a week for more then three months."

"You've lived in Montréal?"

She arched an eyebrow. "You might call it living. Another of my memorable foul-ups. I was out of college and . . ." She hesitated, then added, "I didn't graduate. The week before final exams I went to San Francisco. Maybe the fear of failing caused me to leave. I wandered around a while, then lived with my parents until I couldn't stand any more of their stuffy friends. There was a terrific row and I came to Montréal."

"What did your father . . . ?"

She tossed her head defiantly. "He couldn't stop me. I'd come into my own money. Besides, they didn't know where I was."

My liking for Deirdre was fading. I didn't know her parents and was aware there might be two sides to the story. Still, the line between shallowness and cruelty is a thin one. I began to understand what she'd meant about hurting people she loved.

"I joined a group and we shared an old house not far from here. We were into zen and yoga and macrobiotic food." She shuddered. "Soybeans! And things that tasted like stewed bark. So I'd slip away and come here for a good meal. I'm surprised they didn't make me eat in the kitchen, the way I looked and dressed then."

She was telling part of the truth, I felt, but certainly not all of it. I asked, "What made you leave?"

"I didn't really fit in. Besides, I got tired of supporting a dozen people. It was share and share alike, but I was the only one with any money. One night when everyone was at a rock concert, I left and went home. It was terrible afterwards. I got these threatening letters. Actually blackmail! My father went to the police. I didn't want to get anybody into trouble, but what could I do?"

The waiter, a young helper in his wake, presented a steaming tureen of soup. "Potage a l'Aurore," he whispered reverently.

Deirdre's gloomy memories vanished. Exclaiming with delight, she fell upon the soup so eagerly that she might still have been recovering from her soybean diet. I took my time, savoring the flavor, enjoying the glowing atmosphere of Le

Coq d'Or, candlelight soft on old silver and brass, the richness of thick linen and the sheen of plank floors. I loved the diamond-shaped panes of the casement windows beside us, and my gaze wandered to the street.

No color or quaintness there, except the top rigging of the *Etoile Filante*. A solitary pedestrian strolled slowly by, a sailor or a longshoreman, to judge from the dark corduroy trousers, turtleneck sweater and navy-blue knit cap.

His head turned sharply as he glanced toward the window. He hesitated an instant, then, deliberately looking away, slouched on. The sunglasses he wore were not just tinted glass, but had reflective lenses, small mirrors that completely concealed the eyes behind them, giving his swarthy face the unhuman appearance of a robot.

"Delicious." Deirdre sighed, swabbing her soup bowl with a crust of bread. Then she clapped her hands, childlike, when the waiter returned bearing Gaspé salmon poached in wine. "My favorite! My absolute favorite."

After the salmon course she said, "Excuse me. I have to congratulate Marcel. He's the chef." She was off to the kitchen, almost bounding, narrowly avoiding a collision with a startled busboy.

Her shifting moods were incomprehensible. A bowl of excellent soup was quite enough to lift her from depression to delight. And the restaurant held no unpleasant associations for her, although it was connected with a time of her life which must have been far worse than she said. She'd spoken of threats and blackmail, of stealing away in the night, as though held captive. For me Le Coq d'Or, charming though it was, would have been haunted if I had lived through Deirdre's experiences in this neighborhood.

I gazed idly at the street, my thoughts returning to the man wearing the knit cap and reflector sunglasses. Strange, the way he had looked in the window, then shifted his gaze so quickly. It had been furtive, not natural. Also, now that I considered it, how odd to wear sunglasses on a foggy, overcast day.

Nonsense, I told myself. There could be a dozen simple explanations, and very likely he'd hesitated to admire Deirdre. Her talk of escaping, of entrapment, threats and even the Montréal underworld had set my imagination running. I felt annoyed with her and more annoyed with myself. I was not a nervous type and I found it ridiculous to become uneasy because of one harmless glance from a passer-by.

Deirdre, her smile radiant, returned to the table but did not sit down. "Coffee? Or should we start sightseeing?" she asked.

"Sightseeing." I reached for my purse. "Let's pay the check and start."

"Nothing to pay. We just leave."

"But—"

"I took care of everything while I was in the kitchen. Now don't say one word, Rochelle! This is my treat, and I loathe arguments about money."

There was no chance for any such loathsome argument. She was already moving toward the door. "We'll stroll through old Montréal first. Place d'Youville and Place Royale."

Outside, the mist was like thin smoke. Deirdre hesitated, gazing up at the slate-gray clouds, trying to gauge the probability of rain. A block away I saw a pair of pedestrians, but not another person. The wispy fog softened the outlines of buildings, chimneys and the quayside fences, yet I could view the length of the street. "The neighborhood's deserted," I said. "Not even traffic."

"It's Sunday. Tomorrow this place will swarm with people."

Despite myself, the uneasiness I'd felt earlier returned, stronger than before, almost a sense of being warned. Because I could find no valid reason for my feelings, I seized upon the thought of Dierdre's purse. That was it, I decided. I had been unconsciously worrying about her carrying so much money.

"Should we have the doorman call a taxi?" I asked.

"Oh, no. You have to see the old town on foot. And look up all the time. Most ground floors have been modernized."

"Then let's walk." After all, Deirdre knew much more about the neighborhood than I did, and if empty streets did not bother her, I would certainly not hang back.

Excited by her new role as a tourist guide, Deirdre moved briskly ahead. The knotted purse, looped around her wrist, swung carelessly, and I found myself glancing from it toward the shadowed recessed doorways, the almost concealed entrances of service areas. We passed several parked cars and trucks, forlorn in the mist, as though abandoned forever. I kept wishing Deirdre would walk more slowly. I had been too optimistic about my twisted ankle. It was not yet really painful, but a dull aching had started.

"I'm afraid we'll have to take a taxi, after all," I said at last. "It's my ankle. I'll never make it."

"Oh, Rochelle! I'm sorry."

"It's not too bad yet, but a few more blocks and I'd be finished. Let's go back to the restaurant and call a taxi."

"No. I've already walked you too far. There's a public phone across the street at the corner. You stay here and lean or sit in this doorway. I'll go."

"All right. I'll wait here. Thanks."

She went on alone to the corner, and there turned to cross the street we'd been following. I noticed that the traffic signal was green her way as she stepped from the curb.

I will never know what made me look back at that exact second. I may have caught the sound of a racing motor, but I think the motor was almost noiseless. Perhaps it was only because of the wariness that had been growing in me. But I did look. Then I screamed, "Deirdre!"

A gray panel truck hurtled toward her, flashing past me even as I screamed. I knew the driver could never halt in time and I ran forward, shouting.

Warned by my scream, Deirdre had leaped back while the truck charged on, its driver ignoring the traffic signal. She had stumbled and now lay sprawled at the edge of the street. When I reached her, she was gasping for breath, feebly struggling to get to her feet. "Sit down," I commanded. "Here. Sit on the curb and lower your head."

Nodding weakly, she obeyed me. "My head hurts." Her voice was like a child's whisper. "The fender hit my hand."

My heart hammered, but I kept my voice calm. "Only a bruise, I think. You're all right. Your guardian angel was watching." The truck had missed her by only inches, and if it had struck at such speed—I refused to think about it, forcing away the picture of her broken body on the pavement.

"My fault, I suppose," she murmured. "But the light was green."

"Not your fault at all!" My fright and shock were suddenly replaced by anger. "No one expects a truck to speed through a crossing against the light. He was racing, too. And on a foggy day. That driver must be crazy or blind!"

Perhaps it was the word "blind" that caused me to re-member one fleeting impression I had from that terrifying moment. I had not really seen the driver, everything had happened much too fast. But hadn't there been a flash of light from the anonymous face? Reflector sunglasses? I was not sure. Had I seen a blue knit cap? Again I felt uncertain, yet I thought so.

Deirdre rallied, my anger seeming to arouse hers. "That man's a criminal! He should be reported and have his license taken away. If only we'd got the number."

"Yes." I struggled to remember. The truck had come from behind us, following the same street we had walked. I had no recollection of its front, but I had watched it lunge past Deirdre and speed to the next corner, where it had swerved sharply to the right, vanishing into the cross street. I could recall the shrill, harsh sound of tires resisting the sudden turn. But what had I actually seen? Double doors of gray metal. A rear bumper and a taillight. What else?

"There wasn't any license plate," I said slowly. "I'm sure of it."

Deirdre's eyes widened and she stared at me, bewildered. She seemed to struggle to find the answer to some question, some puzzle whose solution evaded her. Then her features changed, crumbled as though for the first time she fully realized how near she had been to death. Shuddering, she clutched the yellow shawl more tightly around her shoul-ders, and now her face was neither elfin nor mischievous, but puckered by fear, suddenly aged. When at last she spoke, her voice sounded strangled. "He meant to kill me, Rochelle. He must have!"

"Stop it, Deirdre! That's impossible." It was the only thing to say. But as I knelt beside her, trying to calm her, I felt a cold suspicion. Perhaps Deirdre was not mistaken.

2

─────●─────

We found our way back to the safety of Le Coq d'Or, a badly
shaken pair. Deirdre went quickly to a rear table, far from the
windows. "A brandy?" she asked.

"No. I don't think so."

But seeming not to have heard me, she ordered two
brandies. We sat in silence until the drinks arrived, then
Deirdre forced a wan smile. "I suppose all's well that ends
well. I mean, no real harm was done."

"Just the same, we should report the driver to the
police."

"The police?" The suggestion startled her. "Don't think
of such a thing! We haven't a license number or even much
of a description. We'd be questioned and could be delayed
for hours. You just don't know what the Montréal police are
like."

No, I didn't. But Deirdre, to judge from her reaction, was
altogether too familiar with the authorities. What had gone
on during those months she lived in this neighborhood with
what she, in calculated vagueness, described as a "group"?

She finished her drink, and the smile, less artificial now,
returned. "That stupid truck driver isn't going to spoil
your first visit to Montréal. We'll call a taxi and take a long,
slow drive through the city. You have to see Place d'Armes
and Notre Dame Church and . . ."

She was a marvel. Either Deirdre had iron nerves or, more
likely, she could banish any unpleasantness by looking the
other way.

19

I lacked this gift, and during the next hours I looked at the beauty of Montréal without really seeing it. The loveliness of Parc LaFontaine, the splendor of the cathedral were lost on me. Whenever we left the taxi, I found myself glancing sharply right and left with unnatural caution, unable to dispel my apprehension.

Deirdre's eagerness, real or pretended, irritated me as we climbed the steps of a baronial art museum. Could she think I wanted to concentrate on paintings or sculptures today?

"This is special, Rochelle. Something you can't miss." She moved quickly past a collection of old masters and a few French Impressionists, then halted. "Look!"

We stood before a large canvas in a simple frame, and as I gazed at it, my breath quickened. Color blazed at me, writhing golds, twisting greens with wild flashes of orange burning and fiery. There were no identifiable shapes, for the artist had painted only what he himself saw in the deepest recesses of his own mind. This was a portrait of pure emotion, astonishing and painfully beautiful. But its beauty conveyed terror, a sense of frenzy, the outpouring of a desperate man whose hurt and rage had exploded in color.

Moving nearer, I read the small plaque beside it. *Indian Summer by Morgan Armitage.*

"Glorious," said Deirdre, her voice, for once, hushed.

I nodded silently.

"You should be proud of your cousin."

"Yes." But I felt no family pride, the Armitages were only a name to me, and my admiration for *Indian Summer* was mingled with uneasiness at the prospect of meeting the artist, a man who must be possessed and driven by some private demon. It seemed impossible that this painter and my cool, emotionless mother shared the same background.

A middle-aged couple, proper English Canadians with black umbrellas, strolled by. The woman hesitated, glancing disapprovingly at the painting. "What on earth is that mess of splotches supposed to mean?" The tone was strident, almost blasphemous in the quiet museum.

Her husband peered at the title. "*Indian Summer.* The *Star* reported their buying this. It cost a good many thousands of dollars."

"For those smears? Outrageous!"

"Well, it's no Indian summer I ever saw."

They drifted on, oblivious to my glare. Unexpectedly I heard my own voice say loudly, "Any fool can draw a bottle. A real artist paints the taste of the wine!"

The departing couple did not glance back, and even if they had heard me they would not have understood. After all, there was no wine bottle in the picture. Only the taste, smell and pain of writhing heat, an inner-world captured at flashpoint.

"Did you just think of that remark?" asked Deirdre.

"No. I heard it somewhere. I can't remember."

As we left the museum the undefined yet meaningful shapes and masses of the painting haunted me. Everyone, I supposed, could find a personal meaning in the picture. For me, besides the feelings of pain and rage, it was the searing summer beaches of the Caribbean on those rare days when no breeze comes and the sands blaze under shimmering air. To my cousin it had been the flaming foliage of the Canadian autumn, if the title really meant anything at all. None of this mattered. I knew little enough about painting, but had no doubt that my cousin was a genius.

Perhaps I had seen greater works of art in other galleries, but never a picture that spoke so directly to me. In music I sometimes felt that the composer had written the melody or the counterpoint especially for my own hands touching the keyboard. Such moments were few and beautiful. *Indian Summer* had moved me in the same way.

"If your ankle's not too tired, there's one last place I want to go before supper," said Deirdre.

It proved to be an antique and curio shop almost across the street from the museum. I took a chair near the door while Deirdre gamboled among tables and counters.

"I'm buying this," she bubbled, displaying a music box encased in leather with a birchbark design. "Listen! When you lift it up, it plays 'Alouette.'" The tune of the most famous of all French-Canadian songs tinkled loudly and rather tinnily. Deirdre examined the box, puzzled. "How do you stop it?" she asked the clerk.

"Turn it over and set it down, miss," he said. "It's self-winding."

As we left the shop Deirdre was softly singing "Alouette" in English. "Pretty skylark, pretty little skylark! Pretty skylark, I shall pluck you now!" I had known the words since childhood. It had never struck me before that they were rather sinister.

At ten that night the gay lanterns of the *Etoile Filante* twinkled a welcome. We mounted the gangplank with a throng of fellow passengers, mostly youthful, who chattered happily in both French and English. Somewhere on board a concertina played a rollicking folk dance.

On deck, as our tickets and reservations were checked, Deirdre exclaimed, "We're going to have a wonderful time!" She glanced eagerly around, then her smile faded and she turned away. "Rochelle, I have to go ashore a moment. I'll be right back."

"What's wrong?"

She hesitated only an instant. "I forgot to tip Georges at the restaurant for taking care of our bags. Go to your cabin. I'll join you in a minute."

Deirdre rushed down the gangplank. Even if I had chosen to correct her, there would have been no time. I clearly remembered her handing a bill to the cloakroom attendant, doing it, as usual, before I had a chance to reach for my own money. Why did she bother to lie to me? If she wanted to go ashore, she owed me no explanation.

I remembered how suddenly her smile had vanished. It was as though she had seen something that put her to flight. Something . . . or someone.

Now there were only two couples on deck, teenagers gazing across the waters of the river dim in misty moonlight. Then I realized another person was present, a tall man whose white uniform almost blended with the painted mast he stood beside. His features were shadowed by the bill of the officer's cap he wore, then he lifted his head to inspect the rigging, and the lantern light revealed a dark face, bronzed by sun and wind. Could the sight of this man have sent Deirdre into sudden retreat? His firm mouth and the hard set of his jaw gave him an aloof appearance. But he seemed completely preoccupied with the rigging, unaware of any passengers on deck.

A steward was at my side, taking my valise. *"Suivez-moi, s'il vous plait."*

I followed him toward the companionway, passing close to the silent officer, who happened to turn, giving me an idle glance. Then, suddenly, his expression changed; I thought I saw a flicker of recognition in his dark eyes. Since he seemed about to speak, I automatically said, "Good evening."

My greeting went unreturned. The firm jaw tightened, he gave me the briefest possible nod and turned away.

Insolent, I thought, feeling foolish for having spoken first. Yet I was certain he had somehow recognized me, and I remembered Aunt Regina's letter saying she would mention me to her friend Captain McCabe.

"That officer on deck," I asked the steward. "Is he Captain McCabe?"

"*Non, mademoiselle. C'est le Capitaine Lachance. Un marin tres celebre.*"

Captain Lachance might be a famous sailor, I thought, but he would win no prizes for friendliness.

After the steward left, I inspected the small, charming cabin. Old brass running lights had been converted into electric lamps, and the polished planks of the walls were hung with engravings of great vessels, the *Cutty Sark* and the *Potosi,* their white sails billowing. Sitting on the neat bed, I tried to tell myself how comfortable the cabin was, how exciting the voyage downriver would be.

It was a useless effort. I felt only dread about going to River Rising, and the words my mother had spoken on the night of her death tormented me. She had been delirious, her fever-racked brain slipping into consciousness, then withdrawing. She mumbled my father's name, then I caught the words, "River Rising . . . Philip Armitage . . . Morgan . . . Regina . . ." She seized my hand, and for a moment her voice was clear and strong. "Don't trust them! Don't believe them. Rochelle, I'm sorry. I should have told you . . . so many things . . ." Then she slipped away again, leaving me bewildered.

I forgot about the puzzling words until months later when Regina Armitage's first letter arrived, then they came back strongly, as they returned again now: "Don't trust them! Don't believe them."

On the river a foghorn groaned, desolate and lonely. I rose quickly, as though in answer to a warning, and seized by an unexplainable impulse, reached for my unpacked suitcase, ready to run from the ship before it was too late. Ready to go—where? I could think of nowhere.

Then the decision was made for me. The *Etoile Filante*

shuddered, I heard the muffled clank of metal and the planks creaked as we weighed anchor. My future was determined.

A few minutes later Deirdre tapped on my door. "I'm in the next cabin, number eight." She frowned to see that I had changed to pajamas and a dressing gown. "Rochelle, you can't go to bed so early! Everybody stays up until all hours the first night. There's a band and dancing and lots of un-attached males and . . ."

"Go and attach one," I told her. "I want a hot shower, a long sleep and I'll wake up early to see the river."

She shrugged. "Your choice, I suppose." Starting to leave, she turned back. "Funny thing. I ran all the way to the Coq d'Or, and Georges told me I'd already tipped him. I guess we both forgot."

"Yes. Goodnight." So she suspected I had seen her give the tip earlier. Again I wondered why she bothered to lie to me. "See you in the morning."

Sleep came quickly but was not as unbroken as I'd hoped. Hours later I sat up suddenly in alarm, sure that someone had entered the dark cabin and was speaking softly to me. Then I realized that the partitioning between the cabins, which I had mistaken for heavy planks, was only thin paneling. Deirdre, at her own door, was bidding someone a prolonged and giddy goodnight. Then I heard water running, followed by rather unsteady footsteps as she prepared for bed. After that, welcome silence.

The chiming of the ship's bell awakened me in the morning. Either the bell or a sudden ray of bright sunshine streaming through the porthole, for I know my first thought was, This is a beautiful day.

The gloom and uncertainty of last night had been banished by sleep, and as I brushed my hair I smiled in the mirror. Perhaps my moods were as mercurial as Deirdre's.

At the head of the companionway I halted, transfixed by the panorama of sky, river and shore. The wake of the *Etoile Filante* cut a white swath through the blue water, and faraway forests of pine and birch clothed rolling hills. I moved to the rail, feeling that I had walked into a cool, bright dream, and gazed on the same landscape my own an-cestors had first seen centuries ago.

Then I heard singing, young male voices approaching rap-idly. Two long canoes swept into view, each with a dozen youths wearing the long, colorful caps of *voyageurs*, paddles flashing in perfect unison to the rhythm of the eternal rowing song, the song of Deirdre's new music box. *"Alouette, gentille alouette . . ."*

Only an appetite whettted by river air could have pulled me from the deck to the dining room, but even there the waiter led me to a table with a glorious view of the north shore, and I was still with the river.

I took my time over the huge Québecois breakfast, sampling Canadian smoked meat for the first time and wondering what I should do with the cruet of white vinegar the waiter brought.

"It is to put on the fried potatoes," he explained, surprised at my ignorance.

Deirdre had been right about most passengers staying up late and dancing during the first night while the *Etoile Filante* passed the industrial towns just downriver from Montréal. The dining room was almost deserted, but I was content to be alone with the river and shore for company, enjoying glimpses of clapboard villages with thin church spires. I saw farms whose fields stretched to the water's edge. Now and then the twentieth century intruded as a huge freighter or ocean liner passed us with a rumbling whistle.

A tent card on the table announced in French and English that we would make port in Québec City early this afternoon, "winds being favorable." Passengers would have the rest of the day to explore the ancient town, and the *Etoile Filante* would not sail until early the following morning so "the spectacular lower St. Lawrence can be seen in daylight."

I spent the next hour exploring the ship, which was divided into two sections, cabin class and a large area called Steerage, comfortable but with crowded dormitories for less affluent travelers, mostly students, who were only now appearing on deck after last night's revels. The passengers struck me as a strangely assorted group, ranging from elderly couples in conservative tweeds to unkempt teenagers with Union Jacks sewn on their faded jeans as artificial patches. The groups never mixed, and the older generation eyed and younger with a good deal of distaste.

I did not see Deirdre all morning, but she joined me at lunch, barricaded behind huge sunglasses, her hair tied in a kerchief. "You missed a wonderful party." She stifled a yawn.

"I wore a black wig and a beret, very Montmartre and dangerous-looking."

"Did you find that unattached male?"

"Several. Especially one. He's a Hungarian poet, a refugee. He recites the most beautiful verses."

"In French?"

"No, Hungarian. He lives in Québec City because it's the only place in Canada that has a soul. At least I think that's what he said." She pushed aside the steaming bowl of thick pea soup. "Are you getting acquainted?"

"Yes. With the river and with Canada." I hesitated, then said what I had strangely come to feel. "It's like coming home. I don't understand."

"You certainly look happier than you did yesterday."

"Do I? I don't know why this should feel like a homecoming. I don't remember this country from childhood, of course. Longfellow's *Evangeline* is all I know about this part of Canada."

Deirdre laughed. "You don't even know that, Rochelle. The *Evangeline* country is Nova Scotia."

"I don't care. Everything I've seen this morning has been *Evangeline,* and I'll keep on thinking that way."

Deirdre was not listening. She looked past me toward the doorway to the deck. Captain Lachance, a clipboard in hand, paused to make a note, then strode on. Today he was accompanied by a dog, a powerful German shepherd whose dark head was tilted as proudly as his master's.

"The *coureur de bois,*" said Deirdre, scorn in her voice.

"*Coureur de bois?*"

"The legendary Canadian woodsman. The strong, silent folk hero of Québec. Or so he thinks."

"Do you know Captain Lachance?"

"Is that his name? No, but I just don't like that arrogant type of Frenchman. And he spoiled a lot of the fun on board last night."

Nevertheless, when the captain passed again a moment later, I thought that Deirdre, behind the sunglasses, gave him a calculating look that was not without appraisal.

"Emil, he's the Hungarian poet, wants to show me his favorite spots in Québec City. Why don't you come along? I'm sure he has a friend. We can double-date."

"No, thanks. I want to be on my own this afternoon."

She sighed. "Oh, well. I just thought you might enjoy meeting some people."

In my cabin, I stood at the porthole and watched the mighty rock citadel of Québec loom into view, the sheer cliffs that General Wolfe's men had scaled in the night to surprise the French on the Plains of Abraham and change the history of the continent.

The gangplank had hardly touched the dock before eager passengers rushed toward waiting taxis and horse-drawn fiacres, but I delayed, giving Deirdre and her Hungarian ample time to leave. She was his responsibility now. One day had been enough for me.

I was soon to learn that everything I had read in travel folders about Québec City was true. Hiring a carriage, I explored hillside streets lined with fanciful stone buildings, their mansard roofs agleam with spring sun. I stood breathless on the broad terrace fronting the Château Frontenac, gazing down hundreds of feet to the magnificent river where ferries bobbing like toys plied from shore to shore.

Only once did I see Deirdre. My carriage passed one she shared with three young men, all rather lank-haired and chinless. "See you tonight!" she called cheerfully.

I did not return to the ship for dinner. Lured by a quaint restaurant on the wooden stairway to the Place Royale, I dined in unaccustomed luxury, lifting my wineglass in a silent toast to a wonderful day. No matter what lay ahead at River Rising, I had seen Québec and would keep it in my memory forever, a treasure that would always be mine.

The night had turned chilly. Shivering in the taxi that took me back to the *Etoile Filante*, I reminded myself to reclaim my yellow shawl from Deirdre. On board there was excitement and loud music. I learned the reason when I reached my cabin. "Folk dance in dining room. Join us. Armand wants to meet you. D."

Armand? Probably one of the vapid young men I'd seen in Deirdre's carriage. The perfect anticlimax to a glorious day.

I dropped the note in the wastebasket, and half an hour later, tired but content, I fell asleep. My last thought was a hope that Deirdre would return to her cabin quietly and without a party of folk dancers.

The nightmare seized me at some unknown hour, that

most terrible of dreams when one sees danger approaching but lies paralyzed, unable to stir.

Someone, I felt, was moving stealthily in my cabin, standing over me, then quietly moving back, while I fought against a soft inner voice that whispered, "Stay asleep. You are only dreaming." I think a sharper sound, like the thud of a fallen object, almost awakened me, yet I resisted, clinging to the false security of sleep even when I heard a snatch of music. *"Alouette, gentille alouette . . ."*

Slowly I forced my eyes open. The small cabin was black except for a faint glow of moonlight against the sailcloth curtain of the porthole. I sensed no presence, heard no quiet breathing. Were there footfalls in the passage outside? I could not be sure.

I found the light switch, there was a click and the darkness vanished.

"Only a dream," I said aloud. Turning off the light, I lay back, waiting for the nightmare sensations to leave me. But an uneasiness remained as I tried to remember, tried to reconstruct the dream. I felt I had dreamed many more sounds than I could now recall. Had I been frightened by a muffled noise of something dragged across the floor near my bed? And the music. Was that, too, only part of my dream or had I actually heard the tune of Deirdre's music box through the thin wall?

Flicking on the light once more, putting on slippers and a robe, I tiptoed to the door. The planks beneath my feet undulated slightly, but I knew we were still at anchor. I opened the door a few inches. To my surprise, no lantern burned either in the passage or at the head of the companionway. On deck a voice, sharp yet not loud, snapped, "Robicheaux? Robicheaux, where the devil are you?"

"Here, Captain Lachance."

"What happened with the lanterns? You're on watch here."

"Just switched off, I suppose. *Oui.*" The companionway lantern blinked on. "Some of those young people wanting a dark corner, I'd say." The man chuckled knowingly.

"If they want a dark corner, let them book a cabin." The captain's voice dripped contempt. "Now keep your eyes open, Robicheaux. Half the scum of Québec has been trying to board tonight."

"Right, sir. Peculiar characters."

"Peculiar? That's the least of it. Well, the *Etoile Filante* won't be every hippie's party pad while I'm in command. See to it, Robicheaux. *Tabernac!*"

I heard Lachance stride away. I knew he was angry, no mistaking that, but failed to realize the depth of his outrage. I had not yet learned that the word *tabernac* was the ultimate of Québecois blasphemy, the curse of curses.

Bolting my door behind me, I returned to bed, relaxed now because the obvious explanation had come to me. In sleep I had heard Deirdre moving about in her cabin. She must have picked up the music box. I drifted off peacefully, and even the weighing of anchor a little later hardly disturbed my rest.

I dressed quickly the next morning, having slept much later than I had intended and not wanting to miss a moment of my last hours on board. When I reached deck, we had already passed Ile d'Orléans and the St. Lawrence was broadening, sweeping out to the north and south, and now I saw the widest of all North America's great rivers.

After breakfast I went to Deirdre's cabin. She might want to sleep all day, but I wanted my shawl. It would be neatly pressed and I would wear it for my arrival at the Rising. No answer came when I tapped, then, just as I knocked harder, the *Etoile Filante* tilted to meet a swell and the unlocked door swung open.

"Deirdre?" I said, stepping inside. The bed was neatly made, no one had slept in it. My eyes traveled the room swiftly. No sign of clothing, no rucksack. Deirdre had vanished—and so had my shawl, I thought angrily. A quick search showed that no note, no explanation had been left for me. Only one sign of Deirdre remained: her music box, sitting on the edge of the dresser.

Irritation mounting, I returned to my own cabin, taking the music box with me, fumbling with it, then remembering to turn it upside down to silence its loud tinkling. Perhaps she had slipped a note under my door and I might not have noticed earlier. But there was nothing. I leaned against the dresser, taking several slow, deep breaths to get a grip on my temper.

Good riddance! I told myself. This, by Deirdre's own admission, was typical behavior. Changeable, irresponsible, forever obeying a whim. But the theft of the shawl—and I could think of no kinder word than theft—was peculiar. It was out of the question she could have forgotten who owned the shawl, and out of character that she should walk off with it. Irresponsible, yes. Thieving? I didn't think so.

Calmer now, I tried to make sense of the situation. Deirdre must have debarked in the middle of the night, probably with her Hungarian poet in Québec City. She would not have wanted to awaken me, not wanted to explain. So very likely Deirdre had left the shawl with a steward. No doubt I was accusing her unjustly.

At the head of the companionway I found the brown, elderly man in charge of this section. "M'sieur, did Miss Cameron in Cabin Eight leave a shawl with you last night?"

"Nothing was left with me," he answered. "Inquire at the purser's office, please. All such objects go there."

"Merci."

The purser, an elderly man with thick glasses and a green eyeshade, sat on a high stool behind a counter in his office near the wheelhouse. When I entered, Captain Lachance was leaning against a desk, examining what appeared to be a list of figures. He glanced at me but did not speak.

When I inquired about the shawl, the purser shook his head.

"Did Miss Cameron leave any message for me?" I asked.

Frowning, he glanced at the open register beside him, then spoke in a heavily Scottish accent. "Ye said Miss Cameron? I fear ye are mistaken, miss. No such passenger aboard."

"But of course my friend was on this ship. We boarded together at Montréal."

"On the contrary, Miss Dumont." A new voice spoke, the abrupt tone of Captain Lachance. "You boarded alone. I saw you. Quite alone." His English was perfect, but the shrug of dismissal he gave me was utterly French.

"Well, I meant we boarded at *almost* the same time. My friend went ashore for a moment."

The purser spoke firmly. "My register has full information. Cabin Eight is now occupied by Miss Annabelle Lee of New York." He withdrew a small card from a filebox. "Reservation by telephone, Montréal. Passage paid in cash after boarding. Destination, Gaspé. That's the full outbound voyage."

His manner, though too self-assured, was courteous enough, and the anger that surged up in me was not really directed at the purser but at insolent Captain Lachance, who appeared to be enjoying my confusion. "Cabin Eight is empty. I've looked myself," I snapped.

"You *entered* the cabin?" The purser was scandalized.

"I did indeed. I was looking for Miss Cameron, who was very much on board last light and is decidedly not on board now. And I don't care if the register says there's a Miss Lee in Cabin Eight. I've known Deirdre Cameron for years."

The purser scowled. "My register is kept with uncommon care."

No one was going to help me here. Whirling away, I started toward the door, but the captain's voice halted me. "A moment. Your friend has a name I seem to remember." The tanned face and keen dark eyes had expressed indifference and some distaste before. Now he had turned suspicious, almost openly hostile. "Mr. Andrew, give me File X, if you please."

The purser handed him a manila folder and he leafed through it, murmuring, "Abbot, Beauchamps, Cagner . . . Ah, yes. Cameron. Here we are." He read silently a moment, then returned the folder. When he looked at me again, I was startled by his taunting smile.

"Our mystery is solved. Your friend boarded the *Etoile Filante,* but not under her true name. That would have been impossible. She has a prominent place in our dossier of unwelcome passengers."

"Unwelcome?" I blinked, astounded. "In what way?"

Again the careless shrug of dismissal. "You say you have known this person for years. Then you are familiar with her character. It is distasteful to speak of such matters."

"What nonsense!" My voice carried more conviction than I felt. "Miss Cameron comes from a very good family. She's impetuous, but—"

"We will end this unpleasantness," he interrupted me. "I remember the case too well. A year ago. Captain McCabe was ill, as he is now, and I was in command. Miss Cameron and her friends caused serious disturbances. They were obscene and using illegal drugs. One of her friends tried to sell these drugs to another passenger. I put the whole repulsive crew ashore at Trois-Rivières. I regret I did not inform the police. Clearly, I should have done so." He stood up, as though to terminate the conversation. "So she has boarded again, using a false name, and you say she left the ship last night. *Bien. L'Etoile Filante* is well rid of her. It saves me the trouble of throwing her overboard. Although that, perhaps, would be a pleasure."

He glanced at his watch. "We raise Quai Ste. Marie du Lac in about two hours. I ask that you be ready to debark promptly. Ste. Marie is not a regular call for us. Captain McCabe arranged to have you put ashore there as a favor to your Aunt Regina, Miss Dumont. Please be prompt."

"Why stop at all?" I asked hotly. "Just throw me overboard. That sort of thing seems to give you enjoyment."

He hesitated, then his hard eyes met mine in a look that was at once a warning and a challenge. "Regina Armitage is a remarkable woman. I would call her a lady. Yes, a lady. Some women today fail to understand that word in any language."

"The word has a counterpart," I retorted. "A person known in English as a gentleman."

He brushed past me and left the office, touching his cap in what was either a quite unconscious salute or a final gesture of contempt. I was left standing at the counter, trembling with rage, yet feeling an utter fool. I had no doubt that Captain Lachance had spoken the truth, even if he exaggerated. Deirdre's peculiar behavior now made sense. She had not expected Lachance to be aboard, much less standing on deck when she arrived. So she fled, to return when he was not watching. Also, I now understood the outlandish sunglasses in the dining room and her wearing a black wig to the dance. Deirdre would have enjoyed this game of disguises thoroughly.

The purser muttered to himself as he painstakingly corrected his records. "Miss Deirdre Cameron, alias A. Lee, debarked at Québec City. Fare to Gaspé not refundable." He peered at me over his spectacles. "D'ye happen to know your friend's home address? I like complete records."

"I do not. And I just decided she's no friend of mine."

Returning to my cabin, I finished packing, annoyed with the music box, because any way I moved it, it began to play its monotonous melody. I heard "Alouette" at least four times as it slowly ran down inside my valise.

My anger at Captain Lachance had not cooled in the least. How did he dare lump me with Deirdre? Clearly, that was his opinion. Arrogant, self-righteous! Then a voice, which seemed suspiciously like good sense, whispered inside me,

"Well, you were traveling together. You announced she'd been your friend for years."

All right, I had given the captain reasons for suspicion. Still, there was no excuse for his high-handed behavior. "Deirdre Cameron, I could kill you!" The words, not meant literally, of course, and spoken only half aloud, suddenly rang in my ears. Less than forty-eight hours ago in Montréal, someone had tried to do exactly that——to kill Deirdre. We had both thought so, and our later pretense had been little more than hoping or perhaps wishful thinking.

I sat still, forcing myself to be calm, to consider carefully. I now knew that Deirdre's Montréal acquaintances had been far more sinister than I had suspected. I was not naïve, and I had assumed that whatever cult or commune she'd been involved with experimented with drugs. But the selling of them on a public ship was a bolder and more serious affair. No wonder Deirdre had feared her former companions, had fled them in the night. Then, almost a year later, the man in the mirror glasses had accidentally seen her and tried to take final revenge.

It fitted together logically. But could I connect this with Deirdre's unannounced departure from the *Etoile Filante*? I thought of the sounds that had caused my nightmare, the faint footsteps and the tinkling tune I now recalled with frightening clarity. Suppose it had *not* been Deirdre in Cabin Eight? Suppose that . . .

Nonsense, I told myself. The simple explanation was the one I'd accepted when I entered the empty cabin. Deirdre had impulsively decided to remain in Québec City, to study Hungarian poetry, I thought grimly. And I was a fool to worry about her. Maybe in a few days she would send me a postcard, or even have the goodness to mail the shawl, although I doubted it.

The most convincing argument for Deirdre's safety was that no one knew she was boarding the ship. We had not been followed in Montréal. I had certainly looked back enough times that day to be very sure.

I rang for the steward, who took my suitcase to the deck. Captain Lachance, I resolved, would not be delayed one extra second on my account.

In the dining room I found a table at a window, and once again the stark beauty of the shore overwhelmed me. So this was *my* country, this wild Laurentian coast.

I ordered lunch, then became absorbed in the view and did not realize Captain Lachance had entered the dining room until he took the chair opposite me.

"I will join you," he said, an announcement, not a request.

"The only possible reason would be to offer your apologies," I said.

"There are other reasons," he told me, and my glare seemed not to trouble him. "I will be blunt. Why are you visiting Ste. Marie du Lac, Miss Dumont?"

I looked at him in surprise. "I will be equally blunt. That's none of your business, Captain. Now kindly leave my table."

"On the contrary, it is very much a concern of mine. I have lived all my life there. I know your family well."

"Then since you're an old family friend," I replied coldly, "I'll answer. I'm visiting River Rising because I was invited."

He waved away my answer with an impatient hand. "I know you were. Regina discussed it with me. I have accepted her foolishness in inviting you. What puzzles me is why you should come."

"One good reason is the matter of inheritance."

This time he was the one astonished. "You are hoping to become Regina's heir? You flatly admit to legacy-hunting?"

"Yes, when the legacy is already my own. My mother's furniture is at River Rising. It belongs to me now and I have come to claim it. Now may we end this conversation?"

He leaned forward, his face intent. *"Tiens!* A room or two of old furniture. I will make you an offer. Stay on the ship until we reach Gaspé, then go back wherever you came from. I will buy these things and send you the money. Their exact value."

It took me a second to comprehend this ridiculous and unexplainable offer. "Why?" I asked.

"Let us say it is my act of kindness to everyone concerned."

"I think this ship is unsafe," I said. "It has a madman for a captain. And if you won't leave this table, I will."

He rose slowly. "You will regret this refusal, Mademoiselle Dumont."

"I think not. Goodbye, Captain Lachance."

"Unfortunately not goodbye," he said, shaking his head. "Merely *au revoir*."

An hour later I stood alone on the ancient stone pier of Quai Ste. Marie du Lac wondering what I should do next.

The departing *Etoile Filante* was gliding toward midstream, shearing the blue water, leaving a wake almost as white as the rushing Rivière Ste. Marie, a torrent in spate that poured into the St. Lawrence two hundred yards from the pier. To the north, an old corduroy road divided a forest of tall firs and birches. The steward had told me that the road led to the village. "How far?" Only two miles. Perhaps three or a little farther. Now I looked doubtfully at my heavy suitcase.

Three empty fishing skiffs, oars shipped, swung idly at their moorings. There were no buildings except two long, low structures that appeared to be boathouses, their double doors padlocked.

I dragged the suitcase to the head of the pier and sat down to wait on a stone bench. Surely someone would arrive before long.

I had known that Ste. Marie du Lac was in wilderness, but I had never imagined a place so utterly deserted, so silent except for the distant hammering of a woodpecker and the cries of jays. There were a few foundations of ruined buildings being reclaimed by the forest, forsythia and sapling birches pushing upward between fallen masonry. The village, I gathered, had turned its back on the river.

A long time had passed when I heard a creak of wheels and then the voice of a man singing loudly and drunkenly, his French so laden with the accent of the province that he had repeated the same chorus three times before I caught the words, which seemed to mean, "Pour me up some brandy, boys, I'm feeling cold and thirsty."

A home-built farm wagon rolled into view, a dapple-gray nag pulling it. I waved to the driver, a black-bearded giant, and he nodded his huge head. The parts of his face not concealed by whiskers and mustache were flaming red. The squinting, sunken eyes resembled two tiny black buttons sewn deep in tufted upholstery. Leaning from the wagon bench, he peered at me suspiciously.

"*Bon jour,*" I ventured.

He inspected me, tilting his head to one side, and at last slurred the words. "*Mais oui.* This is what the daughter looks like."

Swinging from the wagon, he hoisted my suitcase as easily as if it had been filled with feathers. Not eager to be lifted by him, I climbed aboard quickly, stepping on the axle

hub. He mounted the wagon, flicked the reins. "Go, horse!"
The horse went.

"Did they send you to meet me?" I asked in my most
careful French.

He shook his head, wagging a thick finger. *"Anglais, non.
No speak."*

"But I'm speaking French," I protested.

After deep concentration he decided this was so, and it
seemed to trouble him. "Do they speak French in Australia?" he asked.

"In Australia?" It was my turn to be puzzled. "Some
people do." There seemed no point in pursuing this, and I
glanced at him uneasily. Certainly he was half drunk, perhaps he was also half-witted. Although shirtless, he wore
woolen underwear, a faded pink. The sleeves had been
chopped off at the elbows and I saw that the garment had
buttonholes but no buttons. He had been stitched firmly into
it, for the winter, I supposed. But now it was spring. Was
there an official day when the backwoods *habitant* were
snipped from their B.V.D.s or Stanfields?

As the road plunged into the forest, daylight vanished. We
were in a perpetual dusk mottled with cool yellow where a
few rays pierced the leafy roof. Farther away I could make
out a thick green tangle of second growth where the land
had been lumbered off long ago. It looked impenetrable,
without paths or gaps.

But the tall trunks lining the road had towered here for
generations, woodland giants, their branches intertwining to
form a great vault of green and brown.

"How beautiful," I said. My companion gave me a sullen,
skeptical glance, and I decided that the forest, to those who
live on its fringes, might not be such a friendly place. Indeed,
as the shade grew darker, the creepers and lichens more
tangled, I realized that this was not the tame, gentle woods I
had seen in the United States or the sparse groves and
orchards of the islands. Here the forest was awesome, a
friend to no one except the hidden creatures that dwelt in it,
like the silvery doe I glimpsed as she darted through the
brush and vanished. This was surely the "forest primeval" of
Evangeline, replete with its whispering pines and hemlocks.

The man beside me said, "I'm Gilles. They had to hire me
to meet you. There was no one else. Everything is disarranged at the château." The château, I gathered, was River

Rising. "The police are searching for the criminal. The little girl was stolen last night. The little girl with the rag doll."

A kidnapping? I struggled to think of the French verb and failed. "Tell me about it. What happened?"

"How should I know? Ask the fine people at the château. It is no affair of mine." From under the bench he lifted an earthen jug, uncorked it and took a noisy gulp. *"Cidre?"* he asked.

"Merci, non." I tried again to pry information from him, asking when they had discovered that the girl was missing.

"This morning. It is not my affair."

Aunt Regina's letters had given me no clue as to who the missing child might be. Morgan Armitage had a stepdaughter, but Regina had described her as "almost a teenager," which would make her too old for a rag doll.

A kidnapping. No wonder the household was "disarranged." I was arriving at an unfortunate time. Could this be the reason for Captain Lachance's eagerness to keep me away from Ste. Marie du Lac? I had been completely unable to fathom his strange offer to buy my bit of inherited furniture. I decided quickly that there could be no connection. The captain had some hidden motive for trying to prevent my visit, but it could have nothing to do with an event that had happened only this morning.

We entered a covered bridge, a long barnlike structure in which the creaking wheels and the horse's hoofs echoed as in the hollows of a wooden cave, blending with the churn and hiss of swirling water below.

"Ste. Marie du Lac," Gilles said laconically as we emerged.

A rolling green meadow flecked with new daisies and daffodils spread before us. Behind the hand-split rails of a meandering fence, a herd of cows, khaki-colored, quietly enjoyed the fresh grass and when one lifted her head I heard the soft tinkle of a bell.

I had seen pictures and read descriptions of Quebec villages. Several I had observed from the deck of the ship. Some were clusters of run-down shacks, unpainted clapboard, while others had quaint European charm. But nothing had prepared me for Ste. Marie du Lac.

The inhabitants had placed their settlement in a valley, protected from the bitter winds, where hills and ridges rose forest-clad on every side. The pastures to the south sloped gently to a stream-bank hedged by willows and larches. To the north, stretched a narrow lake, milky blue.

Facing neither the river nor the highway, Ste. Marie du Lac had escaped time. An ancient church of wind-worn stone that one might have discovered on a road in Normandy stood a little apart, an ivy-wrapped spire guarding the village like a tall sentinel. There was one principal street, but the houses, twoscore or more, were scattered along lanes with no apparent plan, cottages of timbered stone, all of them boasting dormer windows with diamond panes and a comfortable chimney at each end of every building.

"Your town is lovely," I said.

Gilles shrugged. "I will stop for the mail. Then to the château."

Beyond the village and to the west a huge structure, walled and turreted, dominated a low rise of land. "What is that?"

"The monastery." Again he seemed surprised at my ignorance. "You should know that."

We drove slowly down the deserted main street, whose asphalt paving was the only denial that we were in another age, another world.

"The town seems empty," I commented. "Where is every one?"

"Spring planting. Who'd be in town?" Gilles tugged at the reins. "Stop, horse!" The animal halted in front of a large, low building, the most impressive in the village except for the church, and apparently the commercial hub of Ste. Marie du Lac, housing a tavern, a general store, a butcher shop and, at the corner, some small office of the provincial government.

Gilles slouched into the store, and I was left to wait. An unreasonably long time seemed to pass. Had he stopped to gossip? To get news, perhaps about the kidnapping? Then a warning raindrop splashed on my hand, and looking up, I realized the sky was changing, becoming ominous. A little way ahead a narrow road veered west to climb the slope and disappear into the woods. I supposed it led to the château. How far, I wondered, how long to get there? Ste. Marie du Lac seemed like a ghost village, without a soul on its streets. A pair of sleeveless arms reached from a nearby window and pulled dark-green shutters closed in preparation for the storm. When a flurry of raindrops sprinkled the street, I climbed from the wagon and followed Gilles, determined to make him hurry.

The interior of the general store was low-ceilinged and gloomy, tiny windowpanes admitting only feeble illumination. The naked bulb dangling over the counter seemed only to create more shadows. For a moment I lingered just inside the door, accustoming my eyes to the dimness. The shelves displayed bolts of cloth, cheeses, canned goods, hardware and countless other oddly assorted items. Apparently the store also served as a social center, for several men dressed in coveralls lounged at two round tables, sipping mugs of coffee and playing cards. Gilles, his back to me, lounged against the counter, talking in low tones with a broad-faced woman in a white apron.

I had a feeling that the room had been lively with talk only a moment before, and the utter silence was caused by my entrance. No one looked up, no one spoke a greeting, and even when one of the cardplayers spread his hand and gave a nod of victory, no one congratulated him. Silence hung like the clouds of tobacco smoke above the tables, and a sleek tiger cat, lazing atop a barrel, cast a doubtful glance in my direction, then closed its yellow eyes. I seemed nonexistent, invisible.

I took a few hesitant steps forward, passing a potbellied iron stove. The woman in the apron must have whispered something to Gilles, for he looked over his shoulder. "I am still getting the mail," he said mulishly. I saw an envelope thrust carelessly in the hip pocket of his cord trousers.

Behind me the door opened and one of the men muttered, *"Bon jour, Madame Jeanette."*

A rasping voice replied, *"Bon jour, Bardot.* I see you gave up fishing today. It's well. I could have told you you'd have no luck. The moon was unfavorable last night."

Turning toward the speaker, I saw a wizened crone shrouded in funereal black, the dark fringe of her shawl giving an effect of tatters and ribbands. Her gnarled hands and arms, emerging from the folds of the shawl, were waxen, a startling contrast to the gypsy-brown face capped by a cascade of slate-gray hair which fell almost to her waist.

The hunched shoulders straightened as she became aware of my presence, then she moved slowly toward me, head thrust forward, peering. Involuntarily I drew back, felt my hand touch the cold metal of the stove. Pale, enormous eyes stared from hollow sockets into my face, a mad and malevolent scrutiny, but I was too astonished to feel panic. The cardplayers leaned forward, tense and watchful as one man made a vague sign of the cross.

I recoiled as the hag lifted her hand in a strange gesture, the clawlike fingers almost touching my face. "I know you, I know you" came the hoarse, crackling whisper. For a second we stood transfixed, paralyzed, until she whirled away, turning to the startled men, and her voice rose to a scream.

"It is the murderer's daughter! The murderer's daughter has returned!"

3

The hag's outburst had come so unexpectedly that I stood stunned, understanding her words yet not really grasping their meaning. Nor could I make sense of the babble of backwoods French that followed, catching only the name "Madame Jeanette" repeated over and over as the cardplayers tried to calm her.

She gesticulated wildly, screaming a torrent of unintelligible abuse, and although the men's faces showed disapproval and shock, they cringed from her, apprehensive of some unknown power. Then, in the midst of the confusion, I heard a low, almost obscene chuckle and realized that Gilles, still leaning against the counter, was leering at me, his slack mouth twisted in a hateful smirk.

A flood of anger and outrage brought me back to reality. I spoke to the woman in the white apron so loudly that it silenced the other voices. "I am unfortunate, madame," I said. "I have met the village sot and the village idiot on the same day!"

Chin high, I marched from the store, deliberately passing close to the shrouded figure of Madame Jeanette, and then slamming the door behind me. Mounting the wagon, I undid the loosely tied reins, realizing that my hands trembled from sheer rage. When I exclaimed, "Go, horse!" the patient animal plodded forward. If Gilles came running in pursuit, I would go to the nearest house and ask for shelter. No matter what, I was not riding another yard with him. But no one followed, and the village, braced for the onslaught of the storm, lay shuttered and still.

Anger had taken possession of me so completely that I gave no thought to the fact that I had not held the reins of a draft horse since childhood in Antigua. Nor did I stop to think I might be going in the wrong direction. I wanted only to leave Ste. Marie du Lac as quickly as possible.

Why had Regina Armitage sent such a creature as Gilles to meet me? What could have been in her mind? Then I remembered the kidnapping. There must be complete confusion at River Rising, and rather unwillingly, I suspended judgment.

The graveled road wound upward and soon the wagon seemed engulfed by pine forest. *The murderer's daughter has come back.* Madame Jeanette's scream rang in my head, and I saw Gilles's contorted face, a sneer of malice that seemed to confirm her accusation. Ridiculous, I told myself. I was a fool to let the raving of a madwoman upset me when she undoubtedly did not realize what she was saying. Probably she should be pitied, but pity was the least of my feelings, and if I felt any at all, it vanished as a new thought struck me.

"An ambush," I said aloud. That was exactly what the scene in the store resembled. Madame Jeanette had arrived almost on my heels, although she had not been in the street when I left the wagon. Where had she come from in those few seconds? She had moved straight toward me to utter her outcry with perfect timing and not one wasted word. As though she had planned the whole thing, I thought.

It seemed impossible, yet I could not quite dismiss the suspicion that the scene had been planned. Yet, for all I knew, Madame Jeanette might well act out this performance with every stranger who came to the village.

The road was still rising steeply and flame birches were now mixed with the pines that hemmed it closely. Overhead, swirling in the thickening sky, wheeled hundreds of flocking crows, black wings flapping as they screamed taunts at one another. Their cries, mixed with the rasp of the wagon wheels, grated on my ears. *The murderer's daughter has come back.*

Could there be any meaning, any reality at all, behind the words? Some time-worn rumor or spiteful gossip? I could not push from my brain the memory of my mother's closed, masklike face whenever I had asked about Jean-Paul Dumont. "He's dead, Rochelle. Why force me to remember those days?"

Her silence had been caused by love, I told myself now as I had so many times in the past. She could not bear remembering the loss of her husband.

What did I really know of the stranger who had fathered me? He was born in France and had no close relatives. I also knew he was an architect who met my mother when both were students at McGill University. He died young, by drowning, a tragic accident. My mother kept no photographs of him, no souvenirs of her marriage, yet I was certain she had loved Jean-Paul Dumont deeply. Once a tactless acquaintance asked what her husband had been like.

"A good man," she said. "A man of great kindness and tenderness." There was fierce pride in her voice, then she turned away. It was the only time I saw tears in her eyes.

Lightning streaked the sky and I heard the roll of distant thunder. Twilight was fading rapidly, and I tried to urge the horse to move faster, but despite my flicking the reins, he held his dogged pace. Cold, warning raindrops struck my hands.

We passed two granite boulders that strangely resembled fallen columns, the road turned sharply as we reached the crest and then, silhouetted against the thunderheads, River Rising loomed stark and solitary, towering above the gray granite of the cliffs toward the even deeper slate of the sky.

The windswept height was scarred by upthrusts of rock, the stone knuckles of the Laurentian Shield. Unlike the valley of Ste. Marie du Lac, this was hostile ground, a place without pity.

We passed through open wrought-iron gates set in an arch. A marble plaque said "River Rising—1760—In Saecula Saeculorum." For all the ages? Winds of more than two centuries had eroded the chiseled words and the bold motto now seemed like an epitaph on an ancient tombstone. The words the steward had spoken on the deck came back to me sharply. "It is haunted, unlucky."

I had smiled then. But now, approaching the enormous house with its tall gables and shuttered windows, I understood why the Rising might inspire all manner of strange legends. Towering above its palisade of wind-whipped trees, the château stood awesome and forbidding. Lights glimmered palely behind only a few of a hundred blind windows and suddenly even these were extinguished as lightning split the clouds and the wagon seemed to shake in the explosion of thunder.

The last crows, now mingled with crying gulls, scudded for the safety of the trees, and even the horse quickened his pace, sensing that the full rage of the storm was about to burst. We had just reached the shelter of a lightless porte-cochere fronting the main entrance when rain poured in a deluge.

I hesitated on the wagon seat. The sprawling house, in blackness now, appeared deserted. Then, at a near window, I saw a moving light and a moment later the massive front door swung wide.

"Gilles?" A voice boomed.

A bearlike woman stood in the entry holding a lantern aloft. She had the bosom of a giantress and her head, topped by a map of grayish red hair, protruded above the globular shoulders as a turtle's head pokes from its shell. She lurched down the steps, broad hips swinging, her unlaced boots scuffing the stone.

"Mademoiselle Rochelle?" Her voice was as outsized as her body and seemed to echo from a vast inner cave.

"Oui."

"But where is Gilles?" She addressed me in English, the words clear despite a French intonation.

"In the village. Drunk," I told her.

"Mon dieu! Such a day! Ah, let me help you down. You're wet and shivering. *Zut,* that Gilles! I could tear his arms off."

Gilles, I thought, should beware. The woman had a strength that matched his own as she lifted me from the wagon with no apparent effort. "Hold the lantern while I get your valise."

"It's very heavy. Let me help."

"What help would a twig like you be?" Her laughter bellowed as she seized the valise, hefting it with one arm exactly as Gilles had done.

"Did I steal the horse or does it belong here?" I asked.

"This horse? *Tabernac!* Would we have this bone-bag at the Rising? The eye tells at a glance it belongs to Gilles, the monster. Gilles is my own cousin, but that is the crazy branch of the family. *Fou!"* She pointed a thick finger at her temple and rolled her eyes to stress the madness of her relatives. "He had to be sent for you. There was no one else. The horse will go home by himself when the storm slackens. Do not distress yourself."

Ushering me into a wide entrance hall, she lighted an oil lamp, then hung the lantern on a hat tree. "Let me see you!" She stared a long time, the small eyes keen and probing. Then her laughter bellowed again. *"Mais oui.* The tiny one has blossomed into a beautiful lady. You have your mother's fine Armitage cheekbones, but those lovely green eyes . . . Why it is as though Lady Judith had stepped from her frame in the gallery!"

"Lady Judith?"

My question was unanswered. She suddenly threw her powerful arms around me in a stifling embrace. I gasped for breath when she released me. "Welcome home, *poupée.* I am Tante Emma, as you have already guessed."

Aunt Emma? Surely I had no Aunt Emma. Perhaps she was a relative of my father's. No one so utterly Québecois could possibly be an Armitage!

The sharp eyes read my confusion instantly. *"Poupée,* surely your mother told you about me. I have been at River Rising almost fifty years as cook, nurse, and almost all else. When your mother stole jam as a child, who pretended to spank her? Tante Emma! Who rocked your own cradle?" She stopped abruptly and her face closed, deeply offended.

"She must have talked about you," I said, attempting to set things right. "But you know how children are. I may not have paid attention."

"It is of no importance." The disapproving set of her lips gave a clear opinion of the heedless young. Then her expression changed to one of surprise. "You spoke to me in French!"

"Yes. Not good French, I'm afraid."

"Splendid! When your mother took you away, I feared my little one would never hear our language again. Australia is so far from here."

Australia again. First Gilles, now Tante Emma. Had my mother deceived people by saying we were going to Australia? I remembered a line in Regina Armitage's first letter: "I would have written you and your mother long ago, but I learned your address only this month."

Tante Emma took the lantern in one hand and my valise in the other. "My foolish mouth babbles while poor Rochelle shivers in the drafts. Come, we will go up to the Captain's Country. I have prepared a fire in the hearth and another in the Boston stove." As we mounted the winding stairway, she continued talking. "The Captain's Country is still as your mother must have described it to you. Her things are there— your things now. The bed your grandmother slept in, the rocking horse your grandfather rode as a child."

I did not disappoint her by saying that I had no idea what the Captain's Country might be. Besides, other questions crowded my mind.

"Gilles told me something terrible happened this morning. I think it was"—I used the English word—"a kidnapping. A little girl was stolen."

"Kidnapping? *Zut!* I knew they could not teach you French in Australia. A painting was stolen, the portrait of a child."

"Thank heavens it was only that," I said. "I misunderstood."

We moved upward, the lantern casting a feeble circle of light in a sea of darkness. We reached a long landing, and I felt an icy draft from an open hall to the left.

"The old gallery," said Tante Emma. A floorboard squeaked loudly under her heavy foot and the lantern flickered. In the wavering light Tante Emma's enormous shadow swayed grotesquely, a titan dancing. "Not a kidnapping, but a dreadful thing." She paused, turning to me and lowered her voice as though someone might be listening in the shadows. "Your Aunt Regina surprised the thief at dawn this morning. She told us his face resembled a death's-head. No wonder my poor lady fainted and injured herself!"

"Is she seriously hurt?" Was it the eerie darkness of the stairwell that made me feel an unexplainable concern, deep and personal, for this great-aunt I had never met?

"I think not, but her wrist was very painful. Also, there was a bruise where her head struck the door casing. Monsieur Morgan insisted on driving her to the hospital. There was a great argument because of your arrival, but at last my lady consented." Tante Emma smiled rather grimly. "An astonishment. One does not win arguments with your Aunt Regina."

Tante Emma resumed the climb to the second floor, and I followed closely, staying in the patch of light from the lantern. "Then neither Aunt Regina nor my Cousin Morgan is here," I said.

"No. And Monsieur Morgan's wife also wished to consult her doctor. Because of the shock, she said." A trace of contempt entered her voice. "Madame Dorothy suffers ill health with great *noblesse*."

At the head of the stairway Tante Emma hesitated. "Take the lantern, *poupée,* while I find the key. We will have lights again soon. The electric system is maintained by idiots. The merest whiff of wind or rain puts us in darkness." She fumbled with a great ring of clinking keys.

"You said Aunt Regina saw the burglar who stole the painting?"

"Yes, poor lady. She could not sleep last night, she was so excited about your arrival. For an old one she has the ears of a rabbit, and she heard a noise in the front of the house. Of course, she did not think of a burglar, no one would here. She went to see that all was well. *Voilà,* there was the man with the death's-head mask!"

"How frightening."

"*Formidable!* She is not a lady given to faintings or imaginings. When I heard her scream, I thought assassins were in the house. I leaped from my bed and seized a poker, but I was too late. She was lying on the carpet with her arm twisted under her and the monster had fled with the painting."

She moved down the hall to an arched doorway. "So they are at the hospital in Rivière Bleu, but will return tonight or in the morning." Commanding me to wait, she unlocked the door and disappeared into the room beyond. I heard the scratching of matches, and despite the rather unnerving blackness of the corridor, I smiled to realize that Tante Emma was creating an entrance effect. Then the door opened wide.

"All is ready. Welcome to the Captain's Country, *poupée*."

Candles in pewter holders and two violet-shaded oil lamps suffused the large room with their glow, soft light blending with the brightness of flames licking the fieldstone fireplace. The paneling and heavy timbers of the ceiling might have made this room dismal, for the alcove windows and deeply carved casements seemed made to trap shadows. Yet the whole atmosphere embraced me, with warm friendliness radiating from the gay print canopy of the tester bed, from

the hand-hooked rugs. Even the sage voice of the grandfather clock chimed a greeting as I stepped into the room.

"It's like a museum!" I exclaimed.

"Not a museum. Your mother's room. *Your* room."

"That tapestry!" I pointed at the opposite wall. "I've never
seen more brilliant colors. What is it?"

"Porcupine quills woven by the Indians long ago. The
designs means sunlight and good weather."

"I love it. Why is this room called the Captain's Country?
It's a strange name."

Tante Emma shrugged. "For some ancestor of yours who
was a captain, I suppose. Many were." She gestured toward
a set of double doors. "There are two rooms, both large. The
other is the nursery." She sighed, shaking her head. "A long
time has passed without a child there. You were the last.
This is a sadness for me."

My mother's room, I thought, letting my gaze wander over
the butternut cabinet, the finely stitched quilt on the bed.

"The quilt has the bluejay design," said Tante Emma.
"Look at the corner."

I found an embroidered signature, "Charlotte Armitage,"
and a date thirty years ago.

"Your mother was clever with her needle. Twelve stitches
to the inch and never a pucker. She was a good child, loved
by everyone." As Tante Emma turned quickly away, I
thought I saw a tear on her leathery cheek.

"Was this also my father's room?" I asked.

"No." She bustled about, fluffing pillows, setting my valise
on a trunk rack. "Jean-Paul never lived at the Rising. When
he married our Charlotte, they moved to the village. But
she came back for you to be born here. All Armitages are
born at River Rising."

"I'm not an Armitage," I told her quietly. "I am Rochelle
Dumont.

"*Zut!* Does a last name matter? You are Charlotte's
daughter, a child of this house. When Tante Emma saw you
tonight, she could have wept for joy." Opening the double
doors, she gestured toward the dark adjoining room. "That
is now your sitting room. Once it was your nursery for a little
while. Your cradle is still there. A dozen Armitage children
have been rocked in it. Good children and bad ones, those
who lived and those God took young."

I took a step toward the sitting room, then drew back,

startled as I glimpsed a human figure in the dimness. Tante Emma chuckled. "A statue. We call her the Duchess of Glenway because she was the figurehead of a ship of that name, a ship lost on the rocks here." Tante Emma's face darkened. "The river claimed every soul but one. An Englishwoman, Lady Judith Crenshaw, reached shore. Her husband and baby were swept away."

"How terrible! Did you know her?"

"Child, Tante Emma is as old as a spider, but this happened two hundred years ago." She paused, staring thoughtfully at the slim figurehead in the shadows. "But many in this house have known her in nightmares. Not Tante Emma, who never dreams. Lady Judith lived here. She became Malachi Armitage's second wife, poor creature, and he was a wicked man. In the village they say that even after two centuries his soul has no rest."

Tante Emma spoke softly but hoarsely, and the small eyes had become wide with wonder or perhaps fear. I, too, gazed at the statue on its wooden pedestal, feeling it was not the figurehead of the *Duchess of Glenway* but Lady Judith herself who might suddenly step down and glide toward us. I sighed with relief when the electric lamps flickered, then flooded the Captain's Country with light.

"At last!" said Tante Emma. "Now change your damp clothing and enjoy a hot bath." She peered near-sightedly at a watch strapped to her strong wrist. "Dinner in an hour and a half. You will hear the gong."

Her glance darted around the room, making a final inspection. *"Oui,* all is prepared—" She broke off sharply, alarm in her face. I followed her astonished gaze to the bedside table, where a bud vase, filled with leafy stems and pale blossoms, stood beside a Delft lamp. *"Tabernac!* Who could have done this?"

In three swift strides she rounded the bed and seized the vase. *"Sacrebleu!"*

"What's wrong? What is it?"

"Monkshood. How can it be here?"

"Is it dangerous?" I was baffled by her outrage. "Like poison oak?"

"Not like poison oak," she said grimly. "In the woods it is harmless. But monkshood is unlucky in a house. It means . . ." She hesitated, then said, "Never mind. I will take it away."

"No, wait. I want to know the meaning."

"Monkshood means that an enemy is near," she said reluctantly, then gave a giant shrug. "Of course, that is ridiculous." As she started toward the door, holding the vase gingerly, Tante Emma added in a growling mutter, "That strange child must have done this. But how? The door was locked."

"What strange child?"

"Thalia. Monsieur Morgan's stepdaughter. She is an odd one, but you must pay no attention. Perhaps she thought to give you a gift. With Thalia one cannot tell. She may not have known what monkshood means." Before leaving, she turned back, still disturbed but forcing a smile. "Forget this small matter, *poupée*. It is a blessing that you have returned home at last."

Alone, I stood listening to the crackling hearth and the rain pelting the leaded windows. Ste. Marie du Lac must seethe with superstition. In the store the villagers had obviously regarded Madame Jeanette as some sort of witch. Tante Emma talked of restless souls, and a few harmless blossoms had caused alarm that for a moment had been almost panic. Even Regina Armitage, an educated woman, had fainted when she mistook a burglar's mask for a death's-head. But of course, Regina's experience had been different. An elderly, no doubt frail, woman had good reason to be frightened by a thief.

As I changed into a warm robe and finished unpacking, I thought about the isolation of the village and the long snowbound winters when Labrador gales must howl in the eaves, when the brief light would be grayed by frosty glass. Stories and legends would be told, and would grow with each retelling. Some black tale, I gathered, had been spun about one of my own ancestors, Captain Malachi, Tante Emma had said. An odd name. Malachi, I recalled, had been one of the more sinister Old Testament prophets, one who thundered about smiting the earth with a curse.

The Captain's Country, I thought, looking again at the room that seemed mellow with the love of generations. How could my mother have resisted describing her home to me? Why had she not talked about the grandfather's clock that now ticked comfortably for me as it must once have done for her. She, too, had known the gleam of firelight on the quill tapestry and on winter nights must have been grateful for the brass bedwarmer now leaning against the side of the mantel.

I had always felt an emptiness because I knew nothing of my father, and now I realized that my mother had been almost equally unknown to me, a mysterious stranger. Her secret, the causes of her strange silence were here at River Rising and soon, I was determined, I would learn to know Charlotte Armitage Dumont.

I sat on the bed, then leaned back against the fluffed pillows. Closing my eyes, I enjoyed the security of the ancient walls, strong against the storm outside, sealing off all that had happened in the last days. As I listened to the sounds of the night, a line of almost forgotten poetry sang softly in my mind. *"Who loves the rain and loves his home and looks on life with quiet eyes . . ."*

That, I knew, was what I longed for. I had to find a place for myself, a life that was real and was my own. In the past, music served as a partial substitute, helping to fill an emptiness in my existence that I felt but could not understand. The countless hours I spent at the piano, later the organ, and at last the harpsichord were journeys to another world, a world where I belonged. But always the music ended, and it was not enough, never enough.

To look on life with quiet eyes. My own eyes were forever searching, forever turning away. I had looked into so many different eyes in these last days. Deirdre Cameron's, alternately filled with gaiety and fear, the eyes of Captain Lachance, dark yet flintlike, their only gleam the flash of mockery. And the mad, dilated stare of Madame Jeanette.

That's quite enough reverie, I told myself, and although the words were not spoken aloud, they seemed to carry my mother's tone of finality. Rising, I prepared myself for dinner, enjoying a bath in a big porcelain tub that stood high on claw feet, and appreciating the warmth from what Tante Emma had called the "Boston stove," which proved to be a Franklin.

I inspected my limited wardrobe, and my eye fell on a dress I had worn only once before when I played a recital my last month in college. It was heavy cotton resembling velveteen, long and flared, with a tight bodice and sleeves. The gown had been a rash purchase because its antique styling, complete with fine lace at the cuffs and neckline, gave the impression of a theatrical costume. But I had been playing

Scarlatti and Vivaldi that night, and the gown seemed to harmonize with baroque music. Now I felt it blended with the atmosphere of River Rising, and the color, a deep maroon, pleased me with its soft richness.

Just as a gong sounded far away in the house, I heard a quiet tap on my door. "Come in," I called.

I saw her first in the mirror, a pale girl of twelve or thirteen with long, flaxen hair and large eyes whose blueness was extraordinary, cool yet brilliant.

Turning toward her, I smiled. "You must be Thalia."

She nodded silently. There was no shyness in her direct gaze, yet I sensed an attitude of uncertainty, perhaps wariness. Tante Emma had called her strange. Strangely beautiful would have been a better description, a translucent fairness that made me think of a dryad or sylph.

"Tante Emma thought you might have brought some flowers that were here when I came, Thalia," I said. "Thank you."

"No," she answered, the faintly pink lips hardly moving. "I did not."

"Have you come to guide me to the dining room?" I asked. Again she nodded but did not speak. "That's thoughtful of you."

"Tante Emma sent me, Miss Dumont. I did not think of it." Her denial of any thoughtfulness for me was not unfriendly. She was merely stating a fact. Yet the reply, along with her continued inspection of me, was irritating.

"Thank you, anyway," I said curtly. "Shall we go?"

She stepped aside to let me pass, then followed. In the corridor Thalia said, "You did not lock your door."

"Should I? Do you think the burglar is still in the house?"

"I don't know."

The passages and stairwell were faintly illuminated by gas jets adapted for electricity, and the inlaid panels and carved doors were thrown into deeper relief by shadows. The château, now that I could see it in a semblance of light, was a museum of Canadian wood and wood sculpture. Every closed door we passed testified to the richness of Québec's vast forests.

Thalia paused on the landing between the first and second floors, and the boards creaked as they had when Tante Emma halted in the same place earlier. "That arch leads to the gallery," she said.

"Where your stepfather's paintings are hung?" I asked.

"No. There are pictures on the walls, but it is not that kind of gallery. It was for minstrels. The ballroom is below. Would you like to see the gallery, Miss Dumont?"

"Not just now, thanks."

"Are you afraid?" The question was expressionless.

"Yes," I told her. "I'm very much afraid of missing dinner."

We continued down the stairs, Thalia gliding beside me, moving as smoothly as a dancer. She was tall for her age, and the straight lines of her forest-green skirt and matching blouse accented her height and slenderness.

Crossing the entrance hall, we left the east wing of the house and I found myself in another world. This was where the family lived their daily lives. Lofty ceilings had been lowered, huge rooms divided, so the study and sitting room we passed through were cheerful places, comfortable with rustic furniture and gaily patterned draperies. Life at River Rising became more comprehensible to me.

There was another short hall leading to the dining-room entrance, which was flanked by cherry-wood colonnades. As we came into this hall I heard voices raised in sharp disagreement.

"Regina will never consent to it. Never!" The unseen woman's tone was high-pitched and angry.

A man replied with equal vehemence, "She'll have to face facts someday. She's not getting any younger. Or any richer!"

The argument was cut off abruptly by our entrance, and the opponents, a man and a woman seated at opposite sides of a refectory table, turned their heads toward us, startled, then both rose at once.

"Dear Cousin Rochelle!" The woman hurried to greet me, a plump cloud of rose chiffon. She was elderly, with a great beehive of gray curls, yet the rouged cheeks, the fluttering gestures betrayed a determination to cling to the airs and appearance of youth.

"Welcome to River Rising." Cool lips brushed my face and I caught the scent of lavender sachet. Taking both my hands in hers, she stepped back to inspect me. "I'm Eunice Armitage, your Cousin William's widow. So that makes me your cousin too, although I'm almost old enough to be your aunt."

Eunice's round face beamed at me. The gold-rimmed spectacles, cameo brooch and the color of her hair, if not its styling, were grandmotherly, a complete contradiction of her coquettish pose. The yards of chiffon fluttered as she turned to introduce me to her dinner companion, who only a moment before had been her opponent in a bitter quarrel.

"Rochelle, this is our old friend Howard Palmer."

"Good evening, Mr. Palmer," I said, taking his extended hand.

"Not Mr. Palmer. Please call me Howard, as your mother did, my dear," he said solemnly. "We were very dear friends. She was a remarkable person."

"Did you also know my father?" I asked.

He chose his words too carefully. "We were acquaintances. I had no opportunity to know him well. But your mother— Charlotte was like a younger sister to me."

I had no reason to doubt this, but I did. Howard Palmer, with his correct country tweeds and military mustache, appeared the essence of conservative respectability. Although the sandy hair was beginning to thin, he looked solid and even athletic. Yet there were small cracks in this façade, the faintest trace of cockney in his speech, fingernails that needed trimming and a puffiness around his eyes that suggested too much whiskey.

Still, he proved to be a good storyteller, a man whose wanderlust had led him to every corner of the world. During dinner he spoke of famous and romantic hotels in Cairo and Singapore, had anecdotes of Tangier and Istanbul.

Monopolizing the conversation, he gave me no chance to ask the countless questions I wanted answered. Talk never turned to River Rising, the Armitage family, or even the burglary that had happened only this morning.

The meal was served by Angélique, an awkward but willing girl who seemed freshly arrived from some remote farm. Eunice watched her sharply, correcting her in an undertone. "*Non.* Serve from the left . . . *Non,* leave the service plate." Eunice, I realized, was paying no attention to Howard Palmer's tales of faraway places. Despite a fixed smile, her eyes wandered, she fiddled with her wineglass and brushed imaginary crumbs from the linen tablecloth.

Thalia sat even more removed than Eunice. The storm had abated, but Thalia appeared to listen only to the dying wind, lost in her own world.

As we were finishing a dessert soufflé which Tante Emma's

heavy hands had somehow made light as foam, the note of a bell stroke penetrated the walls. Palmer ceased speaking in midsentence and Eunice looked up suddenly, as though prompted.

"I forgot a message, Rochelle. From your Aunt Theresa. She hopes you'll call on her and she'll send a note as soon as she can."

"Aunt Theresa?" I asked.

"Well, she's actually your mother's cousin, but Charlotte always called her Aunt Theresa. Surely she spoke of Dame Theresa Armitage."

Dame? A relative with a title? "I never heard of her," I said. "My mother never spoke of the family."

Eunice stared unbelievingly while Palmer ran a thoughtful finger over his mustache, then said, "Charlotte certainly made a clean break."

"Perhaps she had good reasons," I remarked, and turned to Eunice. "It might help if you'd give me a list of my unknown relatives. I'd appear less rude when I meet them."

"A short list, I'm afraid. The family has dwindled. There's Aunt Regina, of course, and I'm your cousin by marriage. Morgan is a distant cousin, but Regina's brother, Andrew, adopted him when Morgan was a small boy. That's all of us." She added an afterthought. "And Theresa, whom your mother called 'Auntie.' "

"Tell me about Dame Theresa," I said. "Is it a British title?"

Howard Palmer answered. "No. Theresa is a Benedictine nun, and they use the title 'Dame.' I met Theresa briefly when she was a young woman, before she went into the cloister at Clarendon Abbey. I haven't seen her since then. More than twenty years."

"Is Clarendon Abbey the huge building I saw from the village?"

"Yes," said Eunice. "The nuns' property adjoins ours at one point. The Lady Abbess, she's the mother superior of Clarendon, is dying. The nuns are keeping vigils or whatever they do at such a time, so your Aunt Theresa can't see you just now." She raised a disapproving eyebrow. "Theresa is the only Armitage who's a Roman Catholic, a convert. Her entering the monastery was a dreadful shock to the family, a bitter time for all of us."

"Still, I'm glad my aunt followed her convictions," I said,

suddenly realizing that Dame Theresa and my mother must
have had a good deal in common. Charlotte Armitage was
also a woman no one could deter or dominate. Would I ever
have such strength? I was very curious about my newly discovered aunt. "Is she a teacher? Or a nurse?"

"Not at all," replied Eunice harshly. "She does nothing.
Theresa has simply buried herself alive, along with a hundred other such women who must be equally mad."

"It's not quite fair to put it that way, Eunice." Howard
Palmer's tone carried a condescending tolerance. "After all,
nuns of her order devote themselves to prayer."

"A lot of good it does! The Lord helps those who help
themselves."

"He must also help people who *can't* help themselves,"
said Thalia quietly. Until now she had not spoken during the
entire meal and the gentle words were startling.

"And who might such people be?" Eunice demanded.

"People like ourselves," replied Thalia, then lowered her
grave eyes and said no more.

Howard Palmer rose from the table. "Well, Eunice, isn't
it time for coffee and brandy in the living room?"

The living room at the front of the house was so skillfully
decorated and furnished that I was hardly conscious of its
baronial size. I admired the lovely japanned cabinet, the two
teardrop chandeliers. Then I saw the harpsichord.

It stood a little apart at the far end of the room on elegantly slender legs; brass candleholders gleamed at either side
of an Orphian lyre that served as a music rack. The ancient
instrument was so beautiful that I moved toward it with a
sense of reverence and rested my fingers lightly on the mellow ivory of the keyboard.

"Do you play, Rochelle?" Eunice asked.

"Yes. May I?" Perhaps the harpsichord was too old, too
fragile to be used.

"Please do, my dear." Eunice's grandmotherly smile had
returned; the harder self displayed moments before in the
dining room was utterly submerged.

I sat at the small stool, hesitated, then my fingers themselves made the selection. The living room rang with the
flashing notes of Mozart's *Turkish March*, not loudly, for the
harpsichord's power lies not in volume but in brilliance and
clarity. I played only for myself and for the instrument, hard-

ly aware that there were listeners, and the plucked strings sang with the glitter of sunlight on silver scimitars.

After the last chord ended, there was silence in the room, a long silence broken at last by Thalia's speaking a name. "Lady Judith. Lady Judith Crenshaw."

Rising, I turned to the others. Eunice sat stiffly, her face blanched beneath its rouge and coats of powder. Howard Palmer stared at me, then shook his head. "It's uncanny," he murmured. "Why didn't I notice before? Of course, it's the pose with the harpsichord."

"Not a pose," said Thalia slowly. "Lady Judith. I knew when I first saw her."

Eunice, recovered from some shock, suddenly applauded. "You play superbly, Rochelle! I had no idea you were a professional musician."

"Thank you, but I'm not. Thalia, what did you mean about Lady Judith?"

Howard Palmer, not Thalia, answered. "Forgive my saying this, my dear, but you're a throwback to one of your ancestors. If the word 'throwback' offends you, let me assure you that Lady Judith was a remarkably beautiful woman."

"She was also a murderess." There was no condemnation in Thalia's remark; once again she was merely giving information.

Color rushed to Eunice's cheeks. "Really! Pay no attention, Rochelle. Thalia is trying to attract attention by shocking you."

"I'm not shocked, I'm fascinated. Tante Emma mentioned Lady Judith earlier. Tell me about her."

Eunice closed her lips firmly, but Palmer was happy to oblige with yet another story. "It's just a legend, of course, but part of it may be true. Captain Malachi Armitage founded the family fortune here, even though he was English and this part of the province was supposed to be reserved for the French. As a fur trader he earned enough to buy the Rising from the Sulpician missionary priests who built the first walls here. Soon his fortune multiplied because of some —well, we might call them lucky accidents. Lucky for him, at least."

"Shipwrecks," murmured Thalia. "He moved warning lights inland and lured ships to the rocks."

"At any rate, that's the legend," said Howard Palmer. "To put it kindly, he was in the salvage business."

"Absolutely untrue." Eunice was more than annoyed; she was angry again.

"True or not," Palmer continued, "one ship that foundered on the rocks at Wind-Whistle Cove was the *Duchess of Glenway*. She'd sailed from Boston bound for western Québec with a hundred souls aboard, most of them Tories fleeing the American Revolution. Fleeing with a great deal of money and not a few jewels."

Thalia interrupted, her eyes wide and distracted. "Lord and Lady Crenshaw were aboard with their little son. Lady Judith was the only survivor."

"You might add that Captain Malachi saved her," Eunice said severely. "He rescued her at great cost to himself. His leg was crushed by the rocks and timbers. He lived out his life a cripple, as you can see in his portrait in the gallery here."

Palmer nodded. "Yes, he lost his right leg rescuing her, and she must have been grateful, for they were married a year later. Captain Malachi ordered that harpsichord from London as a gift for his bride."

The fire on the grate sputtered and the wind whispered faintly in the chimney, but otherwise the room was still. Howard Palmer seemed unwilling to finish his story. "Surely that's not all," I said. "The legend can't end with a rescue and a wedding."

He shook his head. "It's said that eventually she learned about his murderous business, his part in causing the wreck. Then she took revenge."

"More nonsense," Eunice exclaimed. "Captain Malachi fell from the north cliff by accident. Why not? He was crippled, wasn't he?"

"It might have been an accident." Palmer spoke quietly, too quietly, I thought.

Thalia leaned forward, her cool, masklike face animated. "Then why does Captain Malachi still walk at night? Why does Lady Judith weep for her lost child? I've heard them. We all have."

"You mean River Rising is haunted?" I tried to smile as I spoke, but somehow the smile did not quite come.

"Idiocy!" Eunice turned furious eyes toward the girl. "A superstitious servant hears a shutter bang and suddenly the château is full of ghosts. I, for one, haven't heard anything."

"I think you will," Thalia replied quietly.

The prediction was delivered with such calm certainty that I hardly managed to suppress a gasp. Thalia, the strange child, had suddenly changed the legend from a fascinating story into what, for a moment, seemed a present reality. I believed Thalia, believed she sensed something unfathomable and menacing. Then the feeling, and the chillness it brought, passed from me and I was in the solid everyday world again. "What do you think, Mr. Palmer? Do you agree with Thalia?"

I expected him to dismiss the notion with a chuckle. Instead, he hesitated, turning slightly away. For the first time I saw his face in profile, and its features were not so ordinary as I had thought. The sharpness of his chin, the thin arch of the nose conveyed a coldness I had not suspected.

"Years ago I would have agreed with Eunice," he answered slowly. "But I've knocked about the world and lived in some peculiar places. I've seen things that—" He broke off with a shrug. "Let's just say I'm not sure any more, I don't jump to conclusions. The idea of ghosts used to be laughable to educated people. Science is beginning to change some of that. We know about ESP, of course. Investigators have turned up some other peculiar things. Who knows the whole truth?"

Eunice smiled derisively, but I thought her hand trembled as she lifted a glass to finish her brandy.

Howard Palmer checked his watch. "It's late and the rain's stopped. Bedtime for me. I have to work in the morning."

Despite my intense curiosity about River Rising and the Armitage family, I was relieved that this conversation was ending. "What work, Mr. Palmer?" I said. "I thought you were a professional wanderer of the globe."

"Howard is an artist," said Eunice. "A painter, like Morgan."

"Not quite like the famous Morgan," he remarked, chuckling. "But I make a living. There's a sample of my work on the wall behind you."

I turned to a group of four portraits, none of them large, and I thought no two were by the same artist, although they had identical frames. The first was a charming picture of Eunice as a much younger woman, not beautiful but endowed with a soft prettiness that almost passed for beauty.

"I painted the one on the far right," said Palmer.

I took a step and found myself looking at the rugged features of Captain Lachance. Howard Palmer had caught the physical aspects well enough: the straight, arrogant nose, the strength of the jaw, the slash of dark eyebrows above eyes that smoldered in equal darkness. Yet it was a bad likeness, lacking the force and energy of the man I remembered, the full lips were too soft, the attempt to give him a gentle smile ridiculous. If Howard Palmer really made his living as a painter, the public taste was worse than I thought.

"Regina commissioned it," said Eunice. "The young man is a neighbor of ours, Pierre Lachance."

"A difficult job," Palmer added. "He wouldn't sit for me. Told me it was nonsense and I could work from a couple of snapshots."

"Aunt Regina must have been very pleased." It was the kindest remark I could make without stretching truth past the breaking point.

We moved toward the entrance hall, Palmer linking his arm in mine in a gesture of affection that I did not appreciate. "I'm living at Chimney House," he said. "That's the Rising's guest cottage. Only a few hundred yards away, so you've no excuse for not dropping in. The daughter of a dear friend is always welcome. Especially such a beautiful daughter."

He held my arm too fondly and I withdrew it on the excuse of offering a handshake. "Thank you, Mr. Palmer. Goodnight."

Glancing back, he saw that Eunice had lingered to turn off the living-room lights, and Thalia had apparently left us. He leaned toward me and said in a rapid whisper, "My dear, this can be an unpleasant place. If you ever want to leave suddenly, I have a car at your disposal, no matter what the hour."

Before I could reply or even understand this odd offer, Eunice had joined us to say goodnight and express another welcome, then repeating it yet again after Howard Palmer had gone.

"Don't worry about corridor and stair lights. Tante Emma or Madame Sud, the housekeeper, makes a final round to check everything." She explained about breakfast, assured me of Regina's early return, then fluttered away to another part of the château.

I started up the stairway, moving carefully in the dim light. It had been a peculiar evening, forced and artificial, the conversation skillfully steered away from such subjects as my father and no mention of my mother's estrangement from her family. Nor any questions about my own life. Aunt Regina, I suspected, had given orders, told them to say nothing until she herself talked with me.

The only honest emotion had been Thalia's. She spoke what she thought and fully believed that the souls of the murderous captain and his vengeful wife prowled the passageways of River Rising, believed it so strongly that I myself had become momentarily convinced.

Nonsense, I told myself. But just as that word formed itself in my mind, I reached the shadowy landing and the floorboards creaked beneath my step.

The arch of the gallery breathed its chill breath, an icy draft that made me shiver under my warm dress. I could see nothing beyond the entrance, not the shapes of frames or furniture, not doors or walls, only utter blackness. I knew the portrait of Lady Judith hung there, as did that of Malachi Armitage. Were they side by side, the murderer and murderess unseparated even in death?

Then, from the gallery's depths, I heard a sigh, a strange and prolonged sigh that seemed neither human nor natural. "The wind," I whispered, not believing my own words.

I mounted the next flight of stairs quickly, yet I did not permit myself to run ahead as my pounding heart commanded. I would not admit fear by yielding to panic; still, it became a struggle to control the speed of my steps.

Reaching the upper corridor, I paused to catch my breath. The château lay shrouded in silence now, even the wind was stilled. The unnatural sighing in the gallery had ceased with the wind, I told myself, because the wind had caused it. I stood chiding myself for letting my fancy run wild, when I heard another sound, this one unmistakable. Although distant and hardly audible, the tones of a harpsichord rose from the stairwell.

For a moment I again blamed my imagination, the notes were so faint. But listening intently I discerned a melody, only a phrase, yet enough for me to recognize a minuet. Did it emanate from the antique instrument in the living room, the real harpsichord? Or did the hollow tones echo from the gallery? A mad and eerie picture flashed through my mind, the portrait of Lady Judith coming alive in the darkness, painted fingers touching painted keys, sending forth thin music from a phantom instrument to vibrate in the hollow stairwell. Now the notes seemed to have a timbre resembling the tinkle of Deirdre Cameron's music box, sharp and reedy.

The unknown musician stopped, breaking off without finishing the melody, and once again River Rising lapsed into the stillness of a tomb.

I made my way quickly to the door of the Captain's Country, stepped into its bright, cheerful reality. Safely inside the lighted room, I recovered my good sense. The sigh had been the wind in the gallery, the music had been played by someone in the living room. Perhaps Tante Emma making her midnight rounds, although I could not quite imagine her thick fingers playing a Bach minuet. Yet the tune was simple. Had there been harmony or only melody? I could not remember.

"No more foolishness, Rochelle," I said aloud, deliberately using my mother's special emphasis on that familiar command.

I prepared for the night, keeping my imagination and emotions in tight rein, mentally reviewing questions I would ask Regina Armitage tomorrow. I switched off all the lamps except the one on the nightstand, smiling to notice that Tante Emma or the housemaid had removed the top quilt and turned back the bed so it was ready to welcome me after a long day.

Then my smile faded as I saw something else, a small thing, but I remembered the warning it carried. Standing in its original place, as though never removed, was a vase of monkshood, the pale flowers silently repeating Tante Emma's words: "An enemy is near."

4

I slept badly that night, but thankfully, I slept late, not awakening until well after nine when Angélique, the maid, tapped on my door, coming to deliver a huge Québecois breakfast.

"Tante Emma said you are to be served in bed this morning, mademoiselle." She smiled shyly, but with a trace of mischief. "She also said you can fend for yourself in the dining room after today."

"Merci, Angélique." Her French sounded as strange to me as mine must have seemed to her, yet we understood each other with only a little repetition. "Has the family returned from the hospital yet?"

"More than an hour ago. They must have left at dawn. Your aunt would like to meet you in her rooms when you are ready. She asked me to give you her most special greeting."

Angélique removed the cover from the muffin warmer, seemed uncertain about where to put it and at last decided on a lower shelf of the nightstand. She reached for the thermos pitcher of coffee, then hesitated, not sure which of us should pour. I nodded encouragement, and she filled the cup with a steaming jet-black liquid.

"Have you worked here long?" I asked.

"Non, mademoiselle. No one stays long at the château," she said innocently, then realized her tactlessness. "I mean . . ."

"Why did you accept the job if no one stays?"

"I was lonely on my father's farm, and I wanted to see a city like Ste. Marie du Lac. A cousin said I might not mind it here. She said I had no imagination, and that would help."

Her seriousness made me suppress a smile. "And have you no imagination?"

Angélique blushed. "How can I tell? I am not sure what the word means. I am a dull girl, mademoiselle. Everyone says so. Will that be all?"

"Yes, thank you." As she reached the door, I stopped her. "No, I want a special favor. Do you know if this plant grows near the château?" I indicated the monkshood beside my bed.

"Yes. It is not common, but I know where it is found."

"Good. It's my favorite flower. Please gather some for me today. I want a large vase of it on my dresser."

"But monkshood is—"

"I know all about it. Please do as I ask, and I won't forget your kindness."

"A votre service, mademoiselle." She nodded politely, then left.

The idea of flaunting a bouquet of monkshood gave me pleasure. This was a scornful reply to the person who played these unfunny jokes. Despite the restless night, I felt strong this morning, strong and eager to be under way.

I did full justice to Tante Emma's delicious cooking, bathed and dressed, then opened the draperies of the Captain's Country.

The great river, agleam with pale sunlight, astonished me once more, and I exclaimed at the sheer magnificence of it. A sleek three-decked liner moved majestically a mile or two offshore, dwarfing the fishing skiffs, which seemed like bobbing chips.

Looking down, I felt slight giddiness, for this wing of the house stood not far from one edge of the cliffs.

When I opened the window, air with the freshness of both the river and the distant set flowed into the room, rustling the canopy and the drawn-back side curtains of the tester bed. This was a good day, a day whose wholesomeness banished the imaginary specters of the night.

I descended the stairs, hardly glancing at the gallery entrance. Later I would explore it, would lay to rest forever any fears of its darkness. Last night the squeaking board on the landing had seemed a signal to warn the gallery's phantoms of human intrusion. Now it became only a piece of flooring in need of repair.

Angélique, dusting in the entrance hall, looked at me in surprise. I appeared very different than I had at dinner the previous night, having deliberately chosen to dress in a fashion typical of the islands, a plain blouse of white cotton and a very full, flared skirt ablaze with hand-blocked floral designs. A coral necklace and thong sandals gave further Caribbean accents. The outfit, unlike anything I had actually worn on Antigua, was selected to speak defiance, to announce that I was from another world and proud of it.

"Where are my aunt's rooms, Angélique?"

"I will show you, mademoiselle."

As we crossed the living room I noticed something that had escaped me the night before. Above the mantel was a large rectangular space lighter than the rest of the wall, and near the top a hook had been embedded. The place where the stolen painting had hung, I realized. The theft was another topic Eunice and Howard Palmer had avoided.

We passed through a short hallway, then Angélique pointed to a closed door. "Your aunt's rooms are there."

"Don't leave, please. When the door is opened, you are to announce me. You must say Mademoiselle Rochelle Dumont, and say it very clearly. Do you understand?"

Angélique nodded uncertainly and tapped on the panel. A voice called, "Come!"

The maid opened the door and I held back until my name was clearly given. There were to be no misunderstandings, my name was Dumont, not Armitage.

The sitting room was flooded with morning light, dazzling as it reflected from walls and carpets of white and gold. Regina Armitage sat erect in a Sheraton chair, her right hand resting on the head of a Malacca cane. She rose slowly to greet me; her movements seemed painful, but the pain was almost concealed by a taut control that reminded me instantly of my mother.

"Rochelle," she said quietly.

"Yes . . . Aunt Regina."

For a moment we stood unmoving, the length of the room between us, silently examining each other. She wore a long lavender gown which, except for full sleeves, was almost Grecian in simplicity. The left arm was supported by a sling made from a scarf, silk as pure white as her curled, puffed hair. She was much smaller than I had supposed, no taller than five feet, but at a glance one felt her regal air, saw the elegance of fine bones and arched aristocratic eyebrows. Her lips were full, and when she smiled the pale, unlined face had an incandescent quality, a startling brilliance.

Moving toward me, she appeared taller and younger. Although over seventy, she had the carriage of a poised, graceful woman half her age.

"Rochelle," she repeated. "I must kiss you because you are Charlotte's daughter."

I lowered my cheek, and the touch of her lips was warm and dry.

"It has been a lifetime, it seems." Again the captivating smile. "I would take your arm, but I have my hands full. As you see, one in a sling, the other glued to a cane. Come, we'll sit near the window. It's too early for lilacs to bloom, but I thought I caught their perfume only a few minutes ago. It is your being here. I have an illusion of summer."

"On the contrary, I seem to have brought bad luck," I said. "A burglary and injury. I hope you're feeling better."

She tossed her head, dismissing what had happened. "I am quite myself again. The hospital visit was needless, but Morgan chose to smarm over me. However, Dorothy, Morgan's wife, really did need medical attention. Her condition is always uncertain, and this stupid affair upset her. For me, the only serious consequence was that I could not be here to greet you."

She paused, her eyes radiating warmth and welcome. If she suspected that my islands costume was a gesture of defiance, nothing in her manner revealed it.

"Charlotte was a beautiful girl, but you surpass her, my dear." She nodded thoughtfully. "Yes, I think you have brought real summer, not just its illusion."

She spoke so simply that her remarks gave no impression of flattery. Everything about Regina Armitage confused me, overwhelmed me, and I did not know what to make of her. I rallied my defenses, determined not to be taken in by her graciousness and almost magical charm.

"I suppose the stolen painting was very valuable," I said, shifting the conversation onto a less personal level.

"People seem to think that all Morgan's works are valuable. I am not an enthusiastic fan, but this painting, which I own, has great sentimental worth."

"Indeed?"

"It is a portrait of your mother as a child, done from memory, of course, and Morgan's memory is not very accurate. Still, it represented Charlotte, so I loved it. Most of his work is too abstract for my taste. This was not; critics call it a transitional piece."

We sat facing each other on matching settees, gilt with white upholstery, Regina Armitage's official colors. The room resembled a stage set created for a great star, and its occupant measured up to that role, commanding attention with the least flick of an eyebrow.

"I am lost," she said lightly. "I have waited long for this moment, and now I can think of nothing to say. How do we get to know each other, to become friends?" Then she added, with a wry chuckle, "There's also the chance we may discover only mutual dislike. It's a risk one takes."

When I did not reply, she continued, "Tell me about your life, about Charlotte's."

I gave a brief, impersonal account, touching only on outer facts. She proved an intent listener, and her slight changes of expression convinced me that she inferred much from the little I told.

"Not an easy life," she remarked when I had finished. "Yet no terrible hardship. I suppose the most difficult part for you was that you didn't much like Charlotte."

I bridled at this. "I was devoted to my mother!"

Her pale eyes regarded me gravely. "No doubt. Still, there is a difference between liking and loving. You are Charlotte's daughter, so it will be natural for me to love you. But I may find I don't like you at all."

"This paradox is beyond me."

Her laughter tinkled like crystal. "Loving and liking need not be connected. I loved your mother with all my heart, yet often I disliked her intensely. She exasperated me all too often. Doubtless she felt the same toward me."

"I wouldn't know. She never mentioned you," I replied, and against my will regretted her wince of pain. "I never heard your name until your first letter arrived. I told you that when I answered."

She considered this. "Yes, you said you didn't know me, but I took that to mean I was a shadowy character. Now I learn that Charlotte banished me utterly. That was cruel, cruel and undeserved."

I rose instantly to my mother's defense. "She must have had reasons for banishing all her family."

"You know only her side of the story."

"I've heard no side at all. Nothing! And I think it's time I did."

The keen gaze studied me closely. "You mean you know nothing of your father and the . . ." She groped for a word, then said, "Tragedy."

I shook my head. "I want to know. I need to."

"My dear, I did not expect this." Her poise, which I had thought unshakable, deserted her, leaving behind a bewildered, disturbed woman. Then she steeled herself; the perfect control returned. "Very well. Charlotte has cast me as the messenger of ill-tidings and I must do my best. I do not wish to hurt or upset you, but it is better that I tell the exact truth."

"The truth is what I want."

She regarded me doubtfully. "No, my dear. The last thing you want is the truth. Still, it is necessary for you to know."

Regina rose, moving toward the fireplace, then back to her chair, searching for a way to begin.

"Your mother's parents and Theresa Armitage's parents died when Charlotte was a baby and Theresa a very young girl. The two couples were traveling together and were lost in the same plane crash. The task of rearing the girls fell upon me, and I did not welcome the responsibility. I was occupied with my own career, the demands were heavy."

"Your career?"

"I was a gambler," she said with a glint. "Not at cards or dice, but with money. I had little to start with, River Rising was heavily mortgaged and I shared the estate with four brothers. Not one of my brothers had a sense of business and three of them died fairly young, which is why I have the Rising today.

"I gambled first in small things like marketing village crafts, handmade clothing and folk art. Then I moved on to larger risks, cargos and wheat futures. But that is another story.

"At any rate, I had the care of your mother and Theresa. My one surviving brother, Andrew, was of no help. He was a widower; he had to manage his difficult son, Philip François, and later, Morgan. Morgan is not my nephew by blood, but I think of him as such."

"Eunice said he's another cousin," I told her.

"A rather distant one. He was born to relatives of ours who died in the bombing of London. As a child he was sent to Canada for safety. Later Andrew adopted him and we looked upon him as Philip François's younger brother. Morgan has brought great fame to the family."

I caught a note of reserve in her praise of Morgan. Was this another case of loving without liking?

"I was occupied with business, with paying the debts against River Rising, yet I considered myself a good foster mother to Theresa and Charlotte. To this day I do not know how I failed!" The tip of her cane tapped the carpet, and the white cheeks became tinged with crimson. "What went wrong? I lost Theresa to the Benedictines, but resigned myself. I believe she is happy. Still, it was like a daughter taken from me. Then losing Charlotte to Jean-Paul Dumont was really too much to bear."

She uttered my father's name with bitterness that shocked me.

"Do I surprise you? I detest the lies of diplomacy, and will not disguise my opinion of Jean-Paul."

"Such a disguise would be transparent," I retorted. "Your hostility is too obvious."

Tilting her head, she glanced at me sharply. "Spoken like your mother's daughter. Jean-Paul was an architect, but his ambition, if one can grant him ambition at all, was to be an artist. One summer he came to Ste. Marie du Lac with several students who worked with Henri Berthelot, a well-known painter who still lives here. Also, he came because he had met Charlotte at the university. The first time she brought him to dinner I saw that he was a dangerous, objectionable young man."

"You are speaking to that man's daughter," I reminded her, hardly keeping my anger in check. "Do you think I'll listen to much more?"

"You'll listen." Now her smile was not brilliant, but thinly cynical. "You may become furious, but you'll hear me out because it concerns you."

She moved about the room, seeming unable to stand still or stay seated. Her gestures, the dramatic rise and fall of her voice gave powerful emphasis to the words.

"Jean-Paul had animal attractiveness—nothing wrong with that. I chose not to marry, but I am not inexperienced. I understood Charlotte's being fascinated. Still, a brief affair should have ended it. She knew he drank too much, knew he was violent. Yes, savagely violent. Three times he was locked in jail here as a tavern brawler.

"Had he possessed a shred of talent, I might have felt he was driven by some powerful emotion. But Jean-Paul was merely a draftsman. Greeting-card art! Cheap and sentimental. Charlotte knew that."

"No doubt you told her," I said tartly.

Regina's small, jeweled hand protruding from the sling clenched and unclenched. "Of course I warned her. I loved her! My opposition made no difference. I forget who said 'It is not given to men to love and to be wise,' but it is an eternal truth. Charlotte loved him beyond wisdom and, worse, beyond insight.

"Since he could hardly be considered serious as a painter and he avoided all other forms of labor, I suspected Jean-Paul was a fortune hunter. Well, I disabused him of any illusions about Charlotte's money." She frowned, then added grudgingly, "There, I misjudged him. He answered me with the rudeness I deserved, and at that moment I almost admired him."

"Bravo for my father!" I exclaimed. "At least one good quality. Or perhaps merely the absence of another bad one."

She turned to me, eyes flashing. "You think I misjudged the man, that I was possessive and jealous of Charlotte's love? Quite right! I was guilty of the last two faults. I berated Charlotte, I pleaded, I nagged without realizing I could hold her only with open hands.

"She married Jean-Paul at the end of the summer. My young, lovely impulsive niece! They lived awhile in Montréal, then returned to this village, renting a house that was little more than a shanty. They went hungry at times."

I could no longer remain silent. "You permitted this poverty? And now you claim you loved my mother!"

"Rochelle, now you are guilty of misjudgment." Her voice lost its anger. "Jean-Paul would accept nothing from me, and I must grant him his pride. I had insulted him, and he repaid me in full." Her smile changed again, now to an expression of cunning and triumph. "Several times I fooled him. I gave friends money to buy his worthless paintings. Eventually he discovered this and came here shouting drunken threats to me. Physical threats! Well, he chose the wrong woman. I had a pistol, and he knew I could use it."

"And I was born into this atmosphere of hate," I said. "How much better not to have known."

"No, Rochelle, no." She moved quickly to my side. "Never think that. Your birth changed matters, reconciled us. I learned to respect what was good in Jean-Paul and to ignore the rest. I held my terrible tongue and he held his terrible temper. You were a blessing to us."

She sat beside me, taking my hand. "My brother Andrew died, and his son, Philip François, turned idealistic and impractical. I detest idealists, they justify anything in the name of righteousness. It was a difficult time. Morgan had just reached manhood and became rebellious. Meanwhile, Philip François grew worse every month. He dropped the Philip from his name and demanded we call him François because he wished to be French; he announced his engagement to a penniless village girl and took on the task of educating a wild ragamuffin boy. Thank heaven you and Charlotte were here. You held us together."

"And my father?"

"Your birth steadied him for a time," she said carefully. "He took a position with an architectural firm in Québec City and visited here on weekends." She sighed, a despairing sound that I knew was prelude to the end of her story. "And then we were destroyed. One Saturday night in August our world collapsed.

"Several of the art students were drinking in the local tavern and a quarrel erupted, an idiotic political quarrel between your father and François. Jean-Paul lost his head completely—he tried to attack François; he shouted threats against his life. The tavern owner ordered them out. If only that had ended the evening! Instead, four of them, including your father, came to the Rising. They continued drinking on the porch of the studio built for Morgan, and the argument broke out again, this time with dreadful consequences." She closed her eyes, reluctant to go on, then forced herself. "The night ended in murder."

"Murder?" My shoulders stiffened, my blood seemed to pound. "My father was murdered? I thought he died in an accident! My mother said—"

"No, Rochelle." She slipped a delicate arm around my waist. "Jean-Paul killed François Armitage, my nephew. A pointless crime committed in a drunken rage."

"I don't believe it!" I cried, but even as I spoke, Madame

Jeanette's words screamed themselves in my brain: *"The murderer's daughter has returned."*

We sat in silence, Regina Armitage's face unreadable, set in ice, then she said quietly, "I do not ask you to believe it. If it helps you to think otherwise, you must hold fast to that faith."

"Where is my father now?" I asked numbly. "In prison? Or was he . . ." I could not finish the sentence, and Regina came to my aid.

"He died that same night. Either by accident or by his own intention when he realized what he had done. Jean-Paul plunged from the porch of the studio. He was not the first those cliffs and the river have claimed."

"Was there proof of all this?" I asked desperately. Perhaps at least some doubt of my father's guilt remained.

"There was proof. Many people heard the earlier quarrel and threats. The weapon was an artist's framing hammer, with the expected fingerprints. Two witnesses were so close they were almost able to prevent the tragedy. And a third witness—Pierre Lachance—saw Jean-Paul fall."

I did not want to hear the details, yet knew I must. "Were these witnesses from the village?"

"No. You have already met one of them, Howard Palmer. The other was Morgan." Regina read my reaction instantly. "You are telling yourself there is a chance that Howard and Morgan are actually guilty. Believe me, the police entertained this suspicion too, but it came to nothing. You are free to arouse dead suspicions—I hope you will not."

Regina's animation had faded; she seemed drained as she continued in an impersonal monotone.

"Charlotte blamed us all. She accused me of causing Jean-Paul to drink because we had exchanged angry words that day. She blamed Morgan for allowing the party to continue, although Morgan could hardly be expected to control a man as violent as Jean-Paul. She left River Rising a week later, taking you with her, telling us she was going to Australia to begin a new life and we would not hear from her again."

"Did you ever try to find her?" I asked, my voice trembling.

"Not at first, because I believed she would return. It seemed unlike her to continue holding her family responsible."

"Yet she did," I said.

"I finally realized that. I hired detectives—Australian detectives. I tried to find her myself. Wherever I traveled, I found myself searching telephone directories, inquiring at embassies. Once in Paris I saw her name over the door of an antique shop. I rushed in, almost weeping, and learned that this Charlotte Dumont was a woman in her seventies, as old as I am now." She shook her head slowly, recalling the years of futile search. "At last a friend vacationing in the West Indies sent me a newspaper clipping. A death notice." She looked away from me. "The first news and the final irony."

Her story left me dazed and helpless, unable to think clearly. "Why did you ask me to come here?" I asked. "Better to have left me in ignorance. This house can mean only unhappiness for me."

"That is what Morgan advised, that is what everyone advised." She squared her shoulders, lifted her chin, recovering the steel of her character. "Quite wrong! True, I did not know you were utterly ignorant of the past. But what's done is done, and all of it long ago. Why shouldn't Charlotte's daughter come home? Once Charlotte was happy at River Rising, why not Rochelle?"

"The villagers, for one thing. They——"

"No! If there was one quality both your parents had, it was pride. You are their daughter, you will hold up your head anywhere." Her fierceness vanished as she touched my hand, almost timidly. "You are my flesh and blood. I need you. Please give us both a chance."

I hesitated, moved by the unexpected appeal, yet unsure of her. Still, I believed the words. In the last hour she had aged, and the plea in her face was unmistakable. "I will stay awhile," I said. "I don't know how long, I am making no promises."

"I am asking none."

As I rose to leave, she said, "One last thing. I meant my harsh words about your father; that was my opinion and it remains so today. Yet I admit he and Charlotte were completely devoted. The years they had together were unhappy for me, but not for her. Hardship did not matter, disgrace did not matter. I cannot deny their love. It was total."

"Thank you. I needed to know that."

"And, Rochelle, my name is Aunt Regina."

I managed to smile. "Yes, Aunt Regina."

If I had character, as Regina believed, then the next hour was its heaviest test. Alone in my room, I paced the floor, avoiding the window with its view of river and cliffs. She had dealt me blows in the form of blunt truth, or at least the truth as she saw it.

"Don't believe them! Don't trust them." My mother's warning seemed futile. Against my will, against my instincts, I was forced to accept Aunt Regina's story. My father might not have been the scoundrel she described, but murder was a matter of fact, not opinion. Now I understood my mother's lifelong silence. Witnesses might lie, but the telling argument for my father's guilt was that Charlotte herself must have believed it.

I could also understand Charlotte's choice of a lover in later years. True, Jean-Paul Dumont and Paul LaFarge had both been artists, but there all resemblance ceased. Charlotte had sought all the qualities absent in my father, and in Paul she found gentleness, kindliness and peace, a man who never raised his voice in anger and whose patience would have been an example to Job. Her two lovers were opposites in yet another way. My father had apparently been a dabbler who lacked the ambition to persevere in his work. In Paul LaFarge, my mother had known the opposite extreme. To him, painting had been life itself, and his devotion, however unsuccessful, was all-consuming.

Tragic as my mother's life had been, I took comfort that two very different men had loved her deeply and she had returned their love.

I heard a light tap at the door and Angélique entered carrying a small basket heaped with monkshood.

"Tante Emma saw me bringing this," she said. "I am to tell you she thinks you are crazy. Also, Monsieur Morgan asks if you will take lunch with him on the sun porch in an hour."

"I'll be happy to join him," I said falsely. I wanted only to be alone, to think, to quiet my emotions. Yet I must not stay here pacing, with my mind going in a circle.

I changed my West Indies costume for a more characteristic jersey skirt and tailored blouse. Dressing up for my meeting with Regina now struck me as childish and trivial. Her story had altered my perspectives, swept aside the monkshood as a stupid practical joke, reduced the ghostly Captain Malachi and Lady Judith to the ancient legends they were.

On my way downstairs I felt the chill draft from the gallery which seemed not to change day or night. Deciding to look at Lady Judith's portrait, I walked calmly through the archway, with no worries about spectral sighs or music.

Yet I could not help admitting that this was an eerie corridor. Flicking the electric switch brought no result, and I was forced to move more slowly. Faint illumination seeped in through a lattice screening the gallery from the enormous ballroom below, and peering through the openwork, I looked down at a floor that generations ago must have been thronged with hoop-skirted ladies and gentlemen with powdered hair. I could see little, for the ballroom draperies were closed and sunlight entered only through the small panes of a lantern dome high above me. A huge chandelier of bronze and brass hung suspended from the center of the dome, its burned-down candles forlorn reminders of a way of life existing no more.

Moving on, I passed several family portraits of various eras, neglected and forgotten, their gilt frames gathering dust. This was a minstrels' gallery, not intended for the display of pictures, but perhaps the word "gallery" had caused it to be put to this unfortunate use. My departed ancestors had been relegated to silence and solitude.

Then I saw Lady Judith, the portrait hanging in the lightest section of the wall where a single ray of reflected sunshine gave it dramatic and vital emphasis, making it emerge from the paneling to dominate the canvases on either side.

Although not quite life-size, the painting was large and executed with skill and feeling. Posed at the harpsichord, Judith Crenshaw appeared to have just looked up from her music to smile at a welcome visitor. Now I understood the surprise I had caused last night, for at first glance this might have been mistaken for a portrait of myself. The eyes, like mine, were green; her hair was similar to mine but a deeper chestnut; and we had the same high cheekbones.

Staring at the portrait, fascinated yet repelled, I told myself that the similarities were superficial and misleading. Her eyes, the tone of dark emeralds, were not the same as mine and her chin was sharper, more delicate. I hoped my smile did not resemble Lady Judith's, for the upturned lips had a cruel aspect, a tinge of hurtful mockery. Had the artist failed with the mouth as so many portrait painters do, or had he caught a facet of character that others had not yet discerned? Legend said she was a murderess. Had the painter predicted this future?

Murderess. For an instant, perhaps by a trick of light, Lady Judith's smile seemed not a fixed, painted expression set for the centuries. I felt she smiled for me alone, smiled to taunt me, and in a moment the full red lips would speak, would form words. "The murderer's daughter . . ."

Turning quickly, I hurried from the gallery, forcing myself not to look back. And I wondered if in time I would forget what my father had done, if it would become unimportant to me. Or if I would live with this terrible knowledge forever.

5

The sun porch, where I was to lunch with Morgan Armitage, lay at the rear of the house, a long veranda with French windows open to catch the brief warmth of midday. Below, the rather unkempt garden gave way to a meadow dotted with wildflowers. Half a dozen tables surrounded by cane chairs were scattered the length of the porch, giving the impression of a resort hotel whose summer guests had not yet arrived.

At the farthest table Morgan Armitage, a tall and powerfully built man, rose to greet me.

After seeing *Indian Summer,* I had formed a vague mental picture of the artist, imagining a gaunt man, pale and unworldly. Now I found myself in the presence of a broad-shouldered athlete who had to be over forty yet looked ten years younger. The light-brown hair was close-cropped and the sunlight gave it the same flecks of gold which seemed to reflect in his eyes. I could appreciate Deirdre Cameron's schoolgirl crush. Morgan Armitage, not exactly handsome, conveyed magnetism, a sense of strength and determination.

"Welcome to the Rising," he said, and for a second the intensity of those eyes held me, a probing gaze that belied the warmth of his smile, a look too piercing to be comfortable.

The table was laid for two, and he drew back a chair for me. "We'll sit in the sunshine. In Québec every hour of sun is too precious to waste."

"You don't appear to have wasted any," I said. "Your suntan reminds me of Antigua. How did you manage in the Canadian spring?"

"Hardy, clean outdoor living." Then he chuckled. "Plus six weeks in Acapulco. I'm restless in winter, I want to follow the sun."

"You travel a great deal?"

"Dorothy, my wife, hasn't been well for three years. That's limited my wanderlust." The shadow of a frown crossed his face. "It's been difficult with Dorothy's illness and then Thalia's troubles. You met my stepdaughter last night. I hope she didn't annoy you."

"Annoy me? I only thought she was a shy child and much too silent."

"Silent, yes. But until yesterday I never knew her to do anything sinister."

"I don't understand."

"Really, Rochelle!" He made a small gesture of impatience. "Tante Emma has told me about her putting monkshood in your room."

"That's hardly sinister. Just some superstition about enemies. Thalia probably didn't know the meaning. And she denies doing it."

"She knew," he said grimly. "Besides, monkshood is poisonous. A concoction from a bouquet of it could wipe out the household. I don't find the episode amusing; I'll speak to Thalia this afternoon."

Despite his controlled voice, there was no mistaking Morgan's anger. "Please be gentle with her," I said. "Thalia's only a child. Even if she did it, she meant no harm."

He said nothing, but the look he gave me was cool, accusing me of a foolish softness. The hard stare vanished almost as quickly as it had come, yet it had given me a disconcerting glimpse of Morgan Armitage's character. Here was an implacable man, one who despised any sign of weakness. I felt sympathy for Thalia. Morgan would not be an easy stepfather.

Looking past me, he smiled again. "Madame Sud is here with our lunch. *Bonjour, madame.*"

A short, stout woman had entered carrying a tray. *"Bonjour, m'sieur. Bienvenue, ma'm'selle."* Her slurred speech had a guttural thickness.

The housekeeper's swarthy face was expressionless, and thick-lidded, almost oriental eyes regarded me incuriously.

Her dark dress with its white cuffs and collar was not a uniform, yet suggested one.

"It was good of you to interrupt your holiday, madame," said Morgan. "You really should not have returned."

"Naturally I returned. When I heard the household had been disturbed, I came at once. I know my responsibilities, m'sieur."

She served us silently and efficiently, acknowledging my praise of the coquille St. Jacques with the briefest nod of her dark head. Murmuring she would bring fruit and coffee later, Madame Sud glided from the sun porch, the chunky figure surprisingly lithe, her thick-soled shoes soundless.

"Formidable, isn't she?" Morgan remarked, and I agreed. "I think her mother was an Iroquois. Charlotte nicknamed her Madame Defarge and I once did a sketch of her knitting beside the guillotine. She never liked Charlotte or Theresa, but I was a boy and her favorite, unhappily."

"Why unhappily?"

"She used to tell me the most bloodcurdling stories, folk tales. There was one about a flying head that's supposed to ride the storm wind. I could still have nightmares about that head."

Somehow I could not imagine Morgan having nightmares about anything, he seemed much too solid and secure.

"We're lucky to have Madame Sud. And Tante Emma, of course. River Rising needs an army of servants, quite a problem when almost no one from the village will work here."

"Why not?"

"They believe the Rising is haunted," he answered easily. "Well, I can't deny the place is unlucky. We've had more than our share of trouble."

For a moment neither of us spoke, there was no need to discuss what "trouble" meant. Then he asked me about my mother's later life.

I told about our lives in Antigua, but despite his probing questions, I created a picture far short of the whole truth, less than I had given Regina. Pride and a sense of privacy made me describe Charlotte as a happier woman than she had been, and I did not mention her lover. That would remain my secret. When I finished, he studied me keenly, doubtfully.

"Strange that Charlotte never married again," he said. "I supposed she had."

"She never ceased to love the memory of my father," I answered, trying not to sound defensive. "Maybe that's hard to believe. I suppose you agree with Aunt Regina and think my father was worthless, dangerous and violent."

"Dangerous and violent? He certainly was. I never met a man as wild as Jean-Paul. The devil was in him." Morgan spoke with assurance, making no effort to spare my feelings.

"Maybe your bluntness is brutality." I did not permit my voice to tremble, but could not control the reddening of my cheeks. "Aunt Regina at least tempered her honesty with a little tact."

"I never claim to be tactful."

"Why should you? It would be a preposterous pose."

He pushed his plate away. "I'm sorry for offending you with the plain truth. Remember, I *saw* what happened that night. And other nights as well."

Yes, I thought, and Regina's words came back to me: *"Two witnesses were so close they were almost able to prevent the tragedy."* Morgan was one of those witnesses, his friend Howard Palmer the other. Why should I believe the story they had told the police those years ago? Regina had warned me against arousing what she called dead suspicions, but I could not help myself. What if my father had not been a murderer, but a second victim? Victim of the man who now sat across the table from me, speaking with such compelling sincerity.

"I want your friendship and confidence," he was saying. "I hardly know you, but I loved your mother deeply. For her sake, I want to help you."

Listening to his voice, I believed him, not for any logical reason but because I so needed someone to rely upon in the strange, confusing world I had entered at River Rising.

"Help me?" I asked. "How?"

"I've just talked with Regina. Her idea of keeping you here at the Rising is madness. She's trying to pay a debt she owes your mother. Naturally, she's never considered the consequences or dangers to you."

"Dangers?" I was taken aback more by his manner than his words. "You exaggerate."

"I'm no more given to exaggeration than to tact. I only returned a few hours ago, and already I know about your meeting with Madame Jeanette."

"A madwoman," I protested.

"She isn't the only one who is mad where Jean-Paul is concerned. Half the village will feel the same way. You've had a sample of how you'll be treated here. Regina can ignore all this. She's the grand lady of the château, but it's a dream world. She doesn't realize that Charlotte left because she had to go. Did Regina want her to stay and be stoned in the streets?"

"You can't mean that!"

Again he leaned forward, speaking impatiently. "You and Regina won't grasp that Jean-Paul did not commit an ordinary crime. François, the victim, was a man many loved. The villagers wouldn't forgive Jean-Paul's wife, and they won't forgive his daughter."

"Monkshood. An enemy is near," I said. "An appropriate greeting, wasn't it?"

"Leave here, Rochelle. Leave quickly." It was almost a command. "Go to Québec City or Montréal. You'll be near your family. But it's senseless to stay in this village and suffer for what isn't your fault."

His concern aroused an unfamiliar emotion, a feeling that someone actually cared about my welfare. Morgan Armitage, whom I had met only half an hour before, appeared honestly troubled and worried.

"Québec City would be ideal," he continued. "All of us visit there regularly. Regina has an apartment there for the winter, and so do I. Now that you've returned home, I don't intend to lose you again."

I avoided the intensity of his eyes, not sure what he meant. The tone conveyed something deeper than keeping in touch with an unknown and distant family member.

Suddenly I realized that this newly felt emotion had, in only seconds, taken a dangerous turn. Morgan had been devoted to my mother, he said. Now I was mistaking that devotion for an affection toward me. It would be easy to delude myself. Any woman would enjoy believing that Morgan Armitage had discovered a special concern for her on first meeting.

I banished this illusion, telling myself that Morgan was married and his worry was not for Rochelle Dumont, but for Charlotte's daughter.

"Thank you. I need time to think. So much has happened—"

"Yes, and I'm afraid much more will." He rested his hand

gently on mine. "You must not let Regina's possessiveness cloud your good sense."

His closeness confused me and I drew back, afraid that my emotions were all too apparent. A retreat into practicality seemed the best course. "There's the problem of money. I don't know how I'd live in Québec City."

He smiled. "From what I've heard about your talent for music, that's no problem. Also, you'll have quite a large amount of money whenever you want to claim it."

"Manna from heaven?" I asked.

"No, the furnishings of the Captain's Country. Maybe they don't impress you, but they'll overwhelm antique dealers I know. Two rooms crammed with museum pieces. That means money and freedom to go where you choose. It's not a fortune, it wouldn't last forever. Still, the money's yours when you want it."

I considered all he had said, wondering if local hatred for my father could really be so powerful and abiding. I had no fear for my physical safety, yet I could not ignore my encounters with Captain Lachance, Gilles and, above all, Madame Jeanette.

Still, I had a promise to Regina. Although what Morgan said was probably wise, no quick departure seemed possible. I was about to explain this when I realized that Madame Sud, silent as a cat, stood at my side.

I looked up quickly, startled by the notion that she had materialized from the air. Caught off guard, the inscrutable face could for a moment be read, and I saw a glare of malevolence. Her features composed themselves immediately but not before I had glimpsed the truth behind the mask.

"Café au lait, ma'm'selle?" she inquired stiffly.

"Oui, merci."

As she cleared the table and placed the cups, Morgan told me again about the praise for my music he had heard. "I'm surprised," he said. "Musical talent has never been an Armitage trait."

"Perhaps it's a Dumont trait. After all . . ."

Madame Sud, pouring my coffee, seemed to stumble. I saw the stream of scalding dark liquid and jerked back so quickly that it only grazed my fingers.

"Zut! I am clumsy today. Fortunately you were not burned."

"Most fortunately," I snapped. My fingertips stung enough

for me to imagine what the pain would have been if the steaming coffee had struck my whole hand, as I fully believed Madame Sud intended.

"What happened, madame? Did you turn your ankle?" Morgan asked. No one could have missed the suspicion in his voice.

"*Non, m'sieur.* Merely an accident. I must remove the cloth before the stain sets. Please seat yourselves elsewhere and I will bring more coffee in a moment."

Imperturbable, she offered no further explanation or apology. If there was a trace of regret in her expression, I felt certain it came from her failure to scald me thoroughly enough.

"No coffee," I told her, rising abruptly. "I find the service too dangerous."

Madame Sud remained unfazed. "Pastry then? Or fruit?"

"Don't trouble."

Morgan had also risen, seeming to expect a stormy scene from me, but I had decided that this would not happen. My thoughts and feelings, muddled a moment ago, were suddenly clear, as though Madame Sud's small act of malice had crystallized a decision in my mind.

I would have no battle with Madame Sud because she had become utterly unimportant to me. The housekeeper had shown that all Morgan had warned me about was true. No happiness would be permitted me at River Rising or in Ste. Marie du Lac, and it did not matter that so far the hostility had shown itself only in small vindictive acts and scenes.

Looking directly at Morgan, but speaking French so Madame Sud could not fail to understand, I said, "Thank you for your advice. I am heeding it, and will stay here only two or three days more. Before leaving, I want to call on Dame Theresa at the Abbey. Once I've done that, I'll be happily on my way."

I expected some gleam of victory to flash in Madame Sud's eyes, but she did not deign to glance at me.

Morgan hesitated before nodding in agreement, an odd hesitation since I was doing exactly what he had urged. "I'll try to make arrangements for you to see her soon." He started to say more, but Madame Sud's listening presence constrained him, and he only lifted his hands in a gesture that seemed to say, "This is best, this is wise. And I am sorry."

That afternoon I strolled the broad grounds of the Rising, content with my decision. I felt no sense of defeat, although I recognized that I was being driven away by pettiness and spite. If there had been anything to keep me at River Rising, pride alone would have made me battle to stay. I hoped I had too much character to yield an easy victory to Madame Sud and the others who hated me because I was my father's daughter.

But why struggle when I had nothing to win? Certainly I would go to Ste. Marie du Lac and walk the length of its main street with my head held high. In the few days remaining to me here, I intended to show that the murderer's daughter was in no way ashamed of herself or her parentage. If Madame Jeanette chose to have a second encounter with me, she would not meet an unprepared opponent!

Only once did my feelings waver. Lingering near the cliffside, gazing at the great avenue that was the river, I sensed once more that this landscape was strangely ingrained in me, that somehow I belonged to these rocks and the white-churned cove. Had my father long ago held me in his arms at this spot and could that moment be indelibly imprinted on my memory even though it lay beyond my conscious recall? I believed it, I wanted to believe it.

"The river also flows past Québec City," I told myself, although I had not really accepted Morgan's plan for my future. I could not yet think about what lay ahead, and even less did I want to dwell on the past.

But the past was inescapable. I wandered beyond the west wing of the Rising, following a flagstone walkway, and there I discovered an odd building standing at the brink of the precipice. Its construction, planed logs and a steeply pitched roof of asbestos shingles, was not unusual, and a huge window set high on the north slope of the roof showed clearly that this was a painter's studio. Approaching nearer, I noticed that all the lower windows were fitted with solid metal shutters. Rust on their hinges gave an impression that no window had been opened for years.

I mounted three steps to a wooden porch which jutted out over the cliff, and there I was struck by another oddity—a chain-link fence almost shoulder height to guard against a fall from the porch to the rocks and eddies below.

Certainly one would expect a guardrail, for the porch could be a dangerous place and a false step would mean certain death. A rail, yes. But hardly this tall, ugly barrier. Then I understood, as Regina's words about my father's death came back with terribly clarity: "Jean-Paul plunged from the porch of the studio. He was not the first those cliffs and the river have claimed."

Unthinkingly I reached out and touched the steel wire of the fence, and the shudder that passed through me did not come from the coldness of the metal. I had come upon the place where, as Regina put it, we had been destroyed those years ago. The fence had been erected afterwards—when it was too late.

I knew I should turn away, should leave the porch and banish all thoughts of it from my mind, but I felt rooted here, compelled to lean against the chain links and try to look down to see the shallows, the rocks. Far below, the crosscurrents waged perpetual war against each other and against the jagged stones that confined them. The seething of their turmoil was plainly audible even at the cliff top, a whirlpool to crush the timbers of a ship, to sweep the body of a man seaward to the Atlantic to that gulf of perpetual mists and hidden shoals.

Giddy and light-headed, I felt a terror that the fence would give way, that I would feel the surge of air against me as I plunged downward—so far, so very far. Yet I could not draw back; a compelling fascination paralyzed me and held me there.

I hardly heard the creak of a plank, a soft footfall behind me, and just as I realized someone was approaching, a heavy hand gripped my shoulder. Whirling in alarm, I found myself facing Tante Emma.

She spoke softly. "You should not have come here, *poupée*. This is not a place for you."

What was she doing here? Had she followed me? Last night I had trusted her, believed her show of affection was real. Now, after all that Morgan had said, I believed in no one.

When she took my arm, her touch was gentle. "Come back to the house and think of other things. Tante Emma was in the kitchen garden gathering sorrel for tonight's soup and saw you coming this way. Why come here? It can only make you sad, and if Monsieur Morgan knew, he would be angry."

"Angry? Why should he be?"

Smiling, she continued in a lighter tone, "That is his studio where he paints those strange pictures that cost so much money. He allows no one to visit the studio, and you must not go there again."

"I don't want to," I told her. "Tante Emma, that is the place where . . . where . . ."

Squeezing my hand, she nodded. "It happened there. Jean-Paul killed François Armitage on the porch."

"How?" I asked, dreading any answer, yet knowing I must hear from someone besides Regina.

"A blow on the temple with a wicked little hammer painters use. Then, they say, he crashed through the old railing and fell. Tante Emma has never believed it was an accident. I think Jean-Paul realized what he had done. He threw himself against the railing, and I would swear this by Saint Anne herself."

We had reached the entrance of the house, and I felt forced to ask one more question. "Why do you think that, Tante Emma?"

"He was a man with a tortured conscience, always knowing he was doing wrong but never able to control himself." Her voice thickened, the small, sharp eyes became misty. "He was not born for happiness. Now I can pity him, but at the time I felt no pity. Only rage! Sometimes I feel it still."

We parted in the entrance hall, and as I climbed the stairs to my own rooms, I told myself again how wise was my decision to leave the Rising quickly, that it was morbid and futile to torment myself with events of a distant past I could never undo. I had learned that at River Rising the past would confront me on every side.

Entering the Captain's Country, I noticed at once that my defiant bouquet of monkshood had been removed. Morgan's orders, I supposed, and felt relieved that the poisonous stuff was gone. How pleasant life could be if all the poisons at River Rising vanished as easily.

Late that afternoon when sunset made the casements glow and the river seemed shot with pale fire, there came a tap at the door. Before I could answer, Madame Sud slipped quietly into the room carrying a large paper bag.

"A message for you, ma'm'selle," she said tonelessly. "The Lady Abbess at the monastery seems to be enjoying a miraculous recovery. If all continues well, you may visit Dame Theresa day after tomorrow."

"Thank you." So my departure was to be speeded by an apparent miracle. Perhaps it was a good sign.

"Also, this came for you." Madame Sud handed me the paper bag, clearly intending to linger until I opened it. Very well, I certainly had nothing to hide and no doubt she had already inspected the contents.

One glance told me that the yellow shawl I had allowed Deirdre Cameron to wear had been returned. Then I touched the garment and felt dampness, drew it from the bag and gasped. The beautiful shawl was so ripped that nothing but tatters remained, tatters spotted with ugly black marks that looked like grease. How dared Deirdre send it back in such condition?

I searched to find a note of apology or explanation, but the bag was empty. "Did Miss Cameron send no message with this?" I asked, hardly able to contain my anger.

"Miss Cameron?" Madame Sud's thick brows lifted in question, yet conveyed an impression of total indifference. "I do not know of such a person. A village boy brought it. The driver of a truck coming from downriver said he was to deliver it to you here."

She stood silently, lips compressed, determined that if I wanted information, I would be forced to pry it from her.

"Surely there was some message!"

"Quite so, ma'm'selle." She matched my anger with her stolidity. "It was delivered with the compliments of Captain Pierre Lachance."

She left me then, closing the door carefully behind her. I stood looking down at the remains of the shawl, slowly realizing that these rips came from no ordinary tearing. The cloth had been hacked and slashed, shredded with brutal force. Attacked, I thought. Attacked.

6

———◆———

I delayed speaking to Aunt Regina about the shawl and about my decision to leave River Rising. Madame Sud was aware of both matters and I felt sure the housekeeper would lose no time in informing her mistress that through my negligence, Regina's lovely gift had been destroyed and, far worse, that I was about to depart as treacherously as my mother had done before me.

It seemed best to wait, to let Madame Sud report and then endure whatever scene Regina chose to have. Madame Sud's telling tales would be further evidence of the impossibility of my remaining here.

This plan failed entirely. Either Madame Sud kept silent or Aunt Regina chose to play a waiting game, for the next day and the evening following it were an interlude of calm.

To my surprise, I discovered I had inherited some of my mother's single-minded ability to concentrate only on the present. I contained my worry about the strange reappearance of the shawl and its destruction because there could be no explanation until Captain Lachance returned in a day or two. I banished the past, put questions aside and forced myself to pretend I was the temporary house guest of gracious hosts.

On the surface that was true. Regina, although not fully recovered from the shock of the burglary, performed the role of *grande dame* with elegance and wit. The mincing affectations of Eunice now appeared more amusing than ridiculous, causing Aunt Regina and me to exchange twinkles of understanding when at table Eunice flirtly coyly with Morgan. He responded with gallantry and banter that surpassed duty.

Morgan's wife, Dorothy, confined to her bed, sent me an effusive apology for failing to greet me. The postponement of our meeting, I later learned, was the delay of an unpleasant experience.

Thalia paid me the compliment of slipping into the living room when I was alone, and listened silently for half an hour while I played Bach preludes and Mozart's *Eine kleine Nachtmusik*.

There came no news of the stolen painting nor did the expected ransom note from the thief arrive, which troubled Regina but left Morgan unmoved.

"You insured it for well over fifteen thousand, didn't you?" he asked, and when she agreed, he gave a gesture of dismissal. "Then you're money ahead. It isn't worth that much."

Regina's eyes became the points of twin stilettos. "For a man of little critical ability, you have great artistic talent, Morgan my dear." The words, lightly spoken, carried a measured combination of honey and vitriol.

"I yield to superior judgment," he answered blandly.

She was not content to end the matter. "Any perceptive collector would force you to yield. *Wistful Child* is a great masterpiece. And do not accuse me of letting sentiment warp my perception."

Morgan smiled. "That is the last thing on earth I'd ever accuse you of, Aunt Regina."

They understood each other perfectly, I thought, and felt mutual respect, yet remained almost constant opponents. Was it merely a game of words they enjoyed, or something deeper? I could not guess.

Knowing little about the value of works of art, the price of *Wistful Child* awed me. So much money! One of my last memories of Paul LaFarge was the evening when he said happily, "The check for those three paintings arrived. Almost five hundred dollars!" I had childishly supposed that that was quite wonderful.

On the morning for my visit to Clarendon Abbey, I found Regina in the entrance hall angrily shaking the telephone.

"Useless! The service is off again. I've tried for twenty minutes to reach either Louis Gagnon's garage or the one living taxi driver in Ste. Marie du Lac."

"Is it an emergency?"

"I want to make sure you get to the Abbey. Of course, Morgan could drive you, but he's in his studio and it's worth our lives to disturb him."

"Why don't I drive myself? I'm sure I can find the way."

She shook her head. "My car is at the village garage, and Morgan's priceless automobile may be touched by no hand but Morgan's. It's another of his idols, that colossal machine, the height of extravagance and vulgar design."

Morgan, it seemed, was out of favor this morning. "Can't I walk?" I asked. "I'd enjoy it."

"Exhausting. Oh, it's easy enough to get there, downhill most of the way. But the climb back . . ." She hesitated as an idea occurred to her. "I've solved it. Walk to the Abbey, then go to the village and retrieve my car from Gagnon's garage. Louis Gagnon has the keys; just tell him who you are and that I sent you."

She did not see me flinch at her suggestion. For all my planned defiance, I was not quite prepared to enter Ste. Marie du Lac and announce my name. Yet I knew nothing was gained by delay. I was going to face the village in a day or two and now was as good a time as any. "Louis Gagnon's garage?"

"Yes, a little repair shop with a gasoline pump in front." She smiled at solving the problem, oblivious to any qualms I might have about the village. Glancing at a tiny jeweled watch pinned to her dress, she said, "You'd better start, it's quite a long way. Take the path through the garden, then follow the firebreak. You're usually within sight of the Abbey. But don't wander onto any of the side trails."

"Where do they lead?"

"Nowhere," she answered. "Into wilderness." Moving forward impulsively, she took both my hands in hers. "I know you'll like Theresa. Please tell her I love her deeply and she is often in my thoughts." The message, I felt, contained more than love, it was somehow a plea, an apology.

A few minutes later I had crossed the garden separating River Rising from the forest and soon found the path to the firebreak, a swath of cleared and often plowed land running down the hillside like an unpaved highway. Now and again I heard gulls in the distance, but for the first time since my arrival here I felt unaware of the great river. The forest was another country, deep-shadowed and alien.

Every step away from the Rising lightened my spirits. A bobolink, concealed by tangled foliage, seemed to accompany me, whistling a friendly greeting, and once a lark flashed past on golden wings. Where the firebreak was newly ploughed, I saw imprints of small, sharp hooves and knew that deer had bounded across this open space to vanish in the thickets.

As Regina had said, it was a long walk and there were many meandering side trails, yet I seldom lost sight of the towers of Clarendon Abbey for more than a few minutes. They rose against the northern sky, forbidding stone turrets no more welcoming than the grim façade of River Rising.

More than an hour later, when I reached the spot where a short path connected the firebreak with the Abbey's long driveway, I wondered how any young woman could bear to go behind the gray walls in front of me, knowing that a lifetime of imprisonment lay ahead. Yet that was what Theresa Armitage had done, and I knew from Regina that she had not set foot outside the monastery for a quarter of a century.

The enclosing walls were windowless, and as I approached the doors, nail-studded and set in a Gothic arch, I felt reluctant to pull the bell chain, unwilling to leave the sunlight even for an hour.

Unexpectedly, the bell had a merry peal, and when a small door cut into the great one opened, a beaming woman wished me good day.

She wore a simple black habit almost concealed by a voluminous apron, faded blue. "You must be Rochelle Dumont," she said, her accent in English bookish but clear. "Dame Theresa Armitage is expecting you. Do come in!" Honest eyes set in her motherly face studied me with frank but friendly curiosity. Her cheeks and chin were a wreath of dimples.

Inside, I discovered that the somber walls were a mask. Clarendon Abbey was set in several acres of parks and gardens where daffodils and tulips in full bud lined the flagstone paths we followed, and the dungeon-gray buildings were softened by thick ivy. Two young girls, novices, played a strenuous game of tennis on a clay court, while a third girl, also wearing a dark gown, short veil and blue apron, applauded loudly.

The corridor we entered had a stone ceiling, vaulted and ribbed, but the tinted windows warmed the walls with pale-pink light. An elderly nun in a habit more elaborate than the one my guide wore passed us.

"*Benedicite,*" she murmured.

"*Benedicite,* Dame," came the soft reply.

I was ushered into a parlor, sparsely furnished with pleasant Victorian chairs, a plain room made extraordinary by the iron grille dividing it in half, impassable bars reaching from the floor to the low ceiling. This was the barrier beyond which I, an outsider, might not pass.

"Dame Theresa has been attending the Lady Abbess," said my guide. "She will be with you soon. Would you care for tea? Perhaps coffee?"

"Coffee, thank you."

Alone in the parlor, I examined the curious grille. A narrow shelf was set into it and there was a drawer which apparently opened to both sides so objects—gifts, perhaps?—could be passed through. The bars were straight vertical shafts of black metal; no attempt had been made to disguise or decorate them.

The sister returned with coffee and a small slice of cake, set the tray beside me, then departed quietly. During the next few minutes I had the illusion of being Alice in *Through the Looking Glass,* for the half of the room beyond the grille was almost the mirror image of the part I occupied—identical upholstered straight chairs and marble table, an identical crucifix. Then, when a door opened and Dame Theresa entered, the mirror illusion was shattered, the room became utterly and irrevocably divided by the strong bars.

She moved in a rustle of sleeves and scapular, rapidly but giving no impression of haste. "Good morning, dear Rochelle. God bless you."

Dame Theresa was tall and regally slender, the flowing lines of the black habit emphasizing an imperial quality that reminded me of Regina, but not of my mother. The cowl and wimple framed the thin, classic features of a patrician face.

Our first few minutes were awkward as we spoke of the weather and my first impressions of Québec. Then she smiled, cool eyes warmed by wry amusement. "You aren't sure how to address me, are you? Let's forget the title Dame and I'll be Aunt Theresa. I was eleven years older than your mother, I thought of her as my niece. Will that be all right?"

"Yes, Aunt Theresa."

"Also, you're bothered by the grille, aren't you? You've never spoken to anyone behind bars before."

Reddening, I admitted this was true.

"The grille separates us, but its bars are a reminder. In the world, Rochelle, each person has a private grille keeping him apart from all others. Here the bars are visible, surprisingly. Yet this is not so different from the invisible ones you've spoken through all your life."

She spoke lightly, dismissing the matter, but the point had been made and the bars became less forbidding.

"Aunt Regina asked me to give you her love," I said. "She thinks of you often."

"Oh? Charitable thoughts, I hope. I have always been certain of her love, less sure of the charity." Dame Theresa had a knack for irony. The years as a contemplative nun had not turned her blood to sugar water. I suspected she could be as tart as Regina and not a whit less frank.

When I talked of my mother's life and my own, I realized her ears were sharp to catch any omission. Twice she glanced at me with skepticism.

"I'm thankful Charlotte had such a happy life," she commented drily when I had finished. "I would not have expected it." She rested her long, fine hands on the iron shelf. "Rochelle, something is troubling you. Would it help to talk to me?"

"I'm not sure," I answered, yet I sensed I had found a woman wise and compassionate. "I've promised Aunt Regina that I would stay at River Rising. Now I intend to break my promise. I have to leave, but I feel incomplete. As though I had failed."

"Failed at what?"

"I wanted to find my father, a man I can't remember. I ask questions, and all the answers seem wrong. Maybe I can't bear to face the truth about him."

"Who knows the truth about another person?" She frowned thoughtfully, then spoke my father's name.

"Did you know him, Aunt Theresa? What sort of man was he?"

"I never really knew Jean-Paul very well, yet he affected my life. I had come here as a postulant about a year before Charlotte married him. As you know, my vocation caused resentment. No member of my family except Charlotte visited me until Jean-Paul Dumont arrived on the scene."

"How did he change things?"

Dame Theresa smiled ruefully. "Charlotte and Regina and even Eunice all decided to use me, each thinking I had influence on the other. They visited me separately and constantly, pouring out complaints. Their conversations became a heavy cross. Then, praise heaven, they learned I had no influence and stopped coming."

"What did you think of my father?"

"I knew him so slightly I had no opinion. Your parents brought you here once as a baby, but my attention was really on you; babies claim any scene, Jean-Paul seemed pleasant." She hesitated, then added, "I saw him a second time, only for a moment, and we did not speak."

She seemed to have nothing more to tell me on that subject. Our conversation turned to her life as a religious and to the Abbey itself, but her manner had changed. I had a sense she was concealing something, skillfully evading me.

"You've never wanted to leave?" I asked, thinking of so many years behind the same walls.

"Never," she replied firmly, then smiled. "I have told you a lie. How quickly one forgets! At one time I not only wanted to leave, but actually did. I ran away and was gone almost three hours. A grievous breach of obedience, and quite unnecessary. There was no need for me to have stolen away like a midnight fugitive when I had only to walk out the front door." Again I had the odd feeling that something was withheld. Her eyes did not meet mine.

When I left my new-found aunt, I felt a combination of pleasure and disappointment, pleased that I had discovered a member of my family I could love, yet regretful that her greater love lay elsewhere and our lives could only touch, never blend.

The road to Ste. Marie du Lac wound through pasture land, but behind the rocky pastures a wall of forest marked the edge of the wilderness. The little farms seemed a temporary intrusion, pitiful attempts by men to assert ownership of this vast, untamed country.

At the outskirts of Ste. Marie du Lac, I steeled myself for any possible confrontation, determined that no taunts about "the murderer's daughter" would hurt me. Anger, I could show. Anger and contempt, but nothing else.

The first passer-by was a middle-aged woman struggling

with a stubborn porker tied by the leg with a length of clothesline.

"*Trudeau!*" she snarled at it. "*Allons!*"

The pig squealed and moved an unwilling step ahead.

"*Bonjour, madame,*" I said.

"*Bonjour.*" She hardly glanced at me. "*Trudeau! Quelle honte! Marchez!*" Trudeau uttered a final grunt of despair, then trotted beside her like a dog.

I felt relief that the woman had taken no notice of me, as though I had passed a first obstacle.

An old man mowing a lawn returned my greeting politely, yet his eyes narrowed watchfully. Was there hostility in the lift of his grizzled chin? I reproached myself as overly sensitive. It would be so easy to imagine enmity where none existed.

Gagnon's auto-repair shop proved to be a converted barn not far from the center of the village. Monsieur Gagnon, wizened and grease-covered, received me with elaborate courtesy, but explained he was "desolated." There had been delays, the car was not ready, and would I have the graciousness to return in, perhaps, an hour?

I walked to the main street, resolved that this would be my complete test of the villagers' feelings, however uncomfortable I might find it. In an hour I could stroll down every street in Ste. Marie du Lac.

I paid little attention to a young man in a light-gray business suit who was coming toward me, obviously not a villager and therefore no concern of mine. But I could not fail to notice the sharp, inquiring look he gave me. We passed, then he turned back quickly.

"Roxanne?" he asked. "It's Roxanne Dumont, isn't it?"

Halting, I faced him. He was of medium height, had sandy hair, and his pleasant face was dominated by horn-rimmed spectacles.

"I'm Rochelle Dumont," I said, puzzled.

"Rochelle, of course!" He snapped his fingers at the mistake and his smiled broadened to a grin. "Sorry, my memory slipped. But then, I certainly didn't expect to see you here, of all places. I mean, just to meet you walking down the street."

"Yes, it's an out-of-the-way spot," I said, sparring for time. I seemed to have a vague memory of his face, but it was such an ordinary face that I could connect no name to it.

"It's a wonder I recognized you at all," he continued. "You looked so different the last time I saw you."

"Forgive me, but when was that? I don't remember—"

"You couldn't possibly remember. I was just another member of the audience. You and two other girls were playing a concert in the chapel at Eastfield Hall. The music was eighteenth-century and so were you. Only the powdered wig was missing. Afterwards we were introduced, but there was a big crowd."

I could not help returning his infectious smile, but still no name came to me.

"You've forgotten me," he said, the grin changing to an expression of mock tragedy. "I'm used to that, being a very forgettable character. The name that escapes you is Brad Copeland."

He paused, awaiting recognition, but I saw no use in pretending. "I have a wretched memory."

"I forgive you," he said cheerfully. "My sister is Gloria Copeland. She graduated from Eastfield two years ago."

"Oh, yes." A dim recollection stirred, a plump but pretty girl, winsome and freckled, like her brother. I had hardly known her. The family, as I remembered, was supposed to be fantastically rich.

"When she was in college I used to come down from Boston to prey on the young girls. I dated several. There was Elspeth Hurley, for instance, and Deirdre Cameron. You were on my list but escaped in time."

Elspeth had been the campus beauty queen, and naturally I knew Deirdre Cameron. Knew her much too well, I thought.

"Do you speak French?" he asked abruptly, and when I nodded, he seemed so delighted, I felt he might applaud. "My life is saved! Would you explain to my landlady that I want to leave very early in the morning and need to borrow an alarm clock? I left mine behind and you can't buy one in the village."

"I'll be happy to," I said. This would take only a moment, then I would resume my tour of Ste. Marie du Lac.

Around the next corner stood Auberge du Lac, a village house converted into a tiny inn. Three tables with umbrellas stood on a patch of lawn and a chalked sign advertised lunch.

If the stout, robust landlady recognized me, she gave no

sign, but turned deeply mistrustful when I asked her to lend a clock to an overnight lodger.

"I am already busy in the kitchen by five o'clock every morning," she said. "I will call the gentleman."

When I translated, Brad Copeland agreed that five was early enough. "Surely she doesn't think I'd steal her alarm clock!"

"It has happened before," said the woman in clear English. "No disrespect, but two alarm clocks have walked themselves away."

We chuckled, and as I turned to leave, Brad lightly took my arm. "Lunch is on me," he said. "I have to pay for that needless translation work."

I hesitated only a second. My long walk that morning had whetted my appetite. Besides, a sidewalk café was an ideal vantage point for seeing the villagers' reactions to my presence.

"Meeting you was a lucky coincidence," Brad said when we were seated. "What are you doing out in this wilderness?"

"Visiting my family. And you?"

"A short vacation wandering in Québec. I work in New York now, and it's good to see open country."

The landlady did not bother to take an order. "You will have brook trout," she told us. "My husband caught them this morning. To start, I give you a tiny omelette with bits of smoked meat. *Formidable!*" She bustled away, intent on creating a masterpiece.

Brad Copeland, whom I still could not recall from college days, was a few years older than I had thought at first, perhaps thirty. The boyish face and the forelock he kept brushing away from the rims of his glasses gave him a rather naïve look. He was far from handsome, yet his genial manner and attractive smile must have appealed to many of my classmates, although I suspected girls like Deirdre Cameron would have pronounced him too square, too conventional.

"I miss those weekends at Eastfield," he said thoughtfully. "I'm in another life now, yet I wish I'd kept in touch with Elspeth. And especially with Deirdre. She's a fascinating girl."

"Yes, she was very popular."

"That was a cautious comment, Rochelle. Weren't you and Deirdre friends?"

"Not really. We happened to be fellow Canadians."

He snapped his fingers again, a habit of his when he wanted

to reproach his memory. "I'd forgotten that. Does she live near here?"

"No, she's from Ontario."

My answers seemed too curt, but conversation about Deirdre made me uncomfortable. I tried to put the memory of the tattered shawl out of my mind.

Then he asked the direct question, the one I had almost expected. "You haven't seen her recently, have you?"

A girl, I supposed the landlady's daughter, brought glasses and a bottle of white wine at that moment, and the distraction gave me a chance to think before answering. Brad Copeland was disarming and plausible, but our apparently accidental meeting now followed by these questions seemed to stretch coincidence rather far. Deirdre had been emphatic about keeping her whereabouts secret. Why should I give any information to a complete stranger?

"I don't know where she is," I answered truthfully, wondering if he noticed the evasion.

"Well, that's how it goes with college friendships. You separate and don't see each other for years."

"In this case there was no real friendship."

Touching the wine bottle, he frowned. "Warm. If we're going to enjoy a *formidable* omelette and a *formidable* trout, we need chilled wine. Excuse me, Rochelle, I'll see what I can do in the kitchen."

He vanished into the inn and was gone a long time. The landlady brought puffy little omelettes, glowering at the empty chair. "They will not keep," she warned me. "Your friend should learn to wait for his dinner, it will not wait for him."

Brad returned a moment later, bottle in hand. "I haven't improved things much. This place isn't rustic, it's downright primitive. But it's the only hotel in town, if you can call it a hotel."

I was happy to change the subject. "Strange, isn't it? Ste. Marie is perfect for tourists, yet it's still undiscovered."

"The Auberge is hardly an attraction. Flat bedsprings." He took another bite of his omelette. "I admit the landlady can cook. Delicious!"

"Have you been here long?"

"No. I arrived this morning. I've been moving around—Montréal, Québec City, Gaspé. Now here."

"That's a lot of driving."

"I'm flying. The company I'm with has a small plane. I borrowed it."

The omelette disappeared and the trout arrived, crisp and golden. He did not pursue the matter of Deirdre, and I decided that either my evasion had been successful or his interest in her was slight.

Yet I felt an almost imperceptible change in his manner, a watchfulness in the blue eyes, a stiffness behind the affable smile. Although he talked easily of his travels, at moments he appeared distracted, as though something more serious occupied his mind.

The warning that things were not as they seemed came when the landlady's daughter served our coffee. He glanced at the table absent-mindedly, then said, *"Veuillez m'apporter du sucre, s'il vous plaît."*

"Remarkably good for a person who speaks no French," I said. My shoulders had stiffened the instant I realized his fluency and clear accent.

The boyish grin was turned on instantly. "You've just heard one of my five phrases. Should I show off the other four?"

"Not good enough," I said.

Who was this man, what was he attempting? I remembered the strangely long time he had been gone with the wine bottle, and realized I should have been suspicious then. Did the wine taste odd, bitter? Could he have put some drug in it?

"I'm cornered, you've caught me." He gave a mournful sigh. "I confess to four years in a Swiss prep school. But how else was I going to lure a pretty girl to lunch?"

I did not believe a word of this, and glanced uneasily toward the entrance to the inn. Neither the landlady nor her daughter was in sight, yet they must be within calling distance. At least I hoped they were.

This supposedly chance meeting had been no accident, I was now certain. And the questions about Deirdre had not been so casual as they seemed. What lay behind Copeland's pleasant manner?

Not thinking, I touched the wineglass, then pushed it away.

"I hope I'm forgiven?" he said lightly.

As I was about to answer I caught sight of a jeep slowly approaching in the street, a familiar and unwelcome figure at the wheel. The vehicle halted in front of the inn only a few yards from us, and Brad Copeland exclaimed, "This is my lucky day for meeting old acquaintances. Hello, Captain Lachance."

What game was being played? I felt uneasy, almost fearful, yet at the same time angry at having been tricked, although I did not know to what purpose.

The captain acknowledged Copeland's greeting with a lazy salute, strode through the gate and came to our table, towering over me, the customary and annoying ironic smile on his full lips.

"Rochelle, may I present Captain Pierre Lachance?" Copeland's voice was smooth with false innocence.

The captain bowed. "I have already had that pleasure."

"And I have not been spared it," I retorted.

"Join us for coffee, Captain." The invitation was superfluous. Lachance was already seating himself and the girl had automatically appeared with a glass of nut-colored wine.

His severely tailored uniform had been exchanged for a blue-striped sailor's shirt and dungarees, yet his buckskin moccasins suggested the woods as well as the river. Casual dress did not lessen Pierre Lachance's air of authority. The tilt of his strong jaw, the square set of his shoulders announced that the captain remained very much the captain.

He might look like a gypsy, with his curling blue-black hair and the jet eyes that flashed when the sun struck them, but his least gesture made it clear that he was accustomed to taking charge of matters whatever they were.

He said to Copeland, "Forgive my being delayed. I was not expecting your telephone call."

"Telephone call?" I asked, then realized why so much time had been spent in the kitchen, supposedly. "You know, Mr. Copeland, you are not very clever at arranging accidental meetings. Why bother with the excuse about cold wine? You had only to say you had a call to make."

When he did not deny this, my impulse was simply to leave. Whatever game the two men were playing infuriated me and I resented being put in this position. If Brad Copeland and Lachance wanted to talk with me, they could easily do so at the Rising and without pretense. On the other hand, I was not going to be put to flight.

"I already know who the captain is. A river pirate, I believe," and as I said this it struck me that Lachance *did* look rather like a pirate. "But you, Mr. Copeland, or whatever your real name is, are a complete stranger, as I suspected from the start."

"My name is Copeland and everything I said was true." The winsome charm had turned to grimness. "But I neglected to tell you that I am Deirdre Cameron's fiancé."

"Then I wish you good luck. I wonder why you didn't say so, instead of acting out this pointless charade."

"Not so pointless." He leaned forward, intent. "You were with her when she disappeared. I've checked on you, and what I learned makes me uneasy."

"Checked on me!" I shot a look at Captain Lachance, who was quietly lighting his pipe. "I can imagine how."

"You're wrong," said Copeland. "The captain gave me some facts but no opinion at all."

"How kind of him!"

"Kindness is one of my many virtues." Lachance grinned, the strong teeth a white contrast to his dark complexion.

"I'm pleased to hear it," I said. "Also, astonished."

"When I arrived here in Ste. Marie du Lac, I learned more," Copeland said.

"Charming village gossip!" Indignation made my cheeks blaze. "What did you conclude?"

"That I ought to find out more."

I started to rise, to leave, then changed my mind. This was something I would see to the end, and they would learn that I was quite capable of holding my own.

"Do tell me how you went about gathering information, Mr. Copeland. And please tell me to my face what you heard here in the village."

"What he heard here is of no importance, Miss Dumont," said the captain. "You have shown your defiance, now let us hear what Mr. Copeland did."

"Well, I remembered you were at Eastfield." He seemed relieved at having avoided the confrontation. "I telephoned a friend of mine who works in the registrar's office."

"To discover what? That I barely passed algebra?"

"You had a scholarship in music. Even with that help you couldn't afford to finish school. But you seem to have money to take an expensive voyage on the St. Lawrence. Who paid for that trip, Miss Dumont? Dierdre? What was the plan?"

His questions were so preposterous that I felt my anger changing to scorn. Brad Copeland, who had seemed so fully in control, was a desperate man grasping at anything. Before I could answer, Captain Lachance spoke quietly.

"You will stop now, Mr. Copeland. When you called and asked me to join you here, I did not suspect an interrogation." He turned to me, the hard face almost gentle. "I assure you I did not share any plan of Mr. Copeland's. His pretense was unnecessary and, I think, rather contemptible."

"Now listen here, Captain!" Copeland was halfway to his feet. "After what I heard in the village I——"

"Sit down, Mr. Copeland." Lachance's tone, although not loud, would have echoed across a quarter-deck and sent a whole crew scurrying. Copeland sat.

"I am glad you are both calm again," said the captain, who was the only calm one at the table. "Mr. Copeland, for almost five days and nights you have been racing across this province. You are distressed and nervous, your thinking no longer has logic. Miss Dumont has perhaps been under strain also. *Non?*"

I tossed my head and did not reply. Lachance hesitated, then went on. "We will be reasonable now. When Miss Cameron left my ship—I will not say she disappeared—Miss Dumont concerned herself greatly. She took her friend's departure with more seriousness than I myself did. She is now willing to answer your questions if they are courteously asked."

"Don't take that for granted, Captain," I said. "Any questions might be better asked in a police station."

"Police stations!" Copeland's voice was bitter. "I've talked to the police in three cities. They write down Deirdre's name and then forget it. Another runaway girl! Even her father won't help. He says he's sorry for me but won't take this seriously because it's happened before." He sighed, shrugging his shoulders wearily, and when he spoke to me his hurt and frustration were painfully apparent. "I apologize, Miss Dumont. It's worry, I'm not myself. Really, I didn't plan to trick you, I was going to call on you at River Rising. Then, when I saw you on the street, I thought I'd be clever. I decided to play detective. The whole thing was stupid and I'm sorry."

"We'd better try to forget it and start over again," I said, deciding that Deirdre was more important than my anger at her fiancé.

"So we will talk this through," said Lachance. "But not

here. Madame Houard, the concierge, is almost falling out the window trying to hear us. *Madame, l'addition, si'l vous plaît?*"

I reached for my purse, intending to accept nothing from Brad Copeland, but Pierre Lachance stopped me with a withering look that changed to the mocking half-smile. "Must you be so difficult? You resemble your Aunt Regina. She, too, has the temper of Catherine the Great."

"Why shouldn't I resemble her? She's my aunt."

"That, mademoiselle, is quite obvious."

Captain Lachance drove us to a small park at the shore of the lake. Its benches were deserted; no swimmers lingered on the sandy stretch of beach. Brad Copeland began talking at once.

"There's not much to tell. I met Deirdre when she was in college. We had several dates but it was nothing serious. I thought she was too wild, I suppose she thought I was too dull. Six months ago we met at a party in New York. She had changed, grown quieter, more settled. We fell in love, or at least I did, and planned to be married last Friday. Just a legal ceremony at City Hall."

The notion of the legal ceremony seemed to depress him. "My parents wanted a church wedding in Boston and Deirdre's family wanted one in Toronto. I wouldn't have minded." He swallowed hard. "It would have been rather pretty. Something to remember. But there was no changing Deirdre's mind. On Friday I went to the hotel where she lived, and they told me she'd checked out early that morning. No message, no address. Nothing."

"Did she not return your engagement ring?" Lachance asked.

"There wasn't one. She said it would remind her of the ring in a cow's nose. Oh, I saw her point," he added quickly and defensively. "I'm a little old-fashioned, but I understood her feelings."

Poor Brad Copeland, I thought. As conservative as the flannels he wore, he would be the least likely man on earth to understand Deirdre. Love her, yes. Understand her, never.

Tracing her had been simple for a man with Copeland's money. She was a girl who attracted attention, and an airline clerk was almost certain he had sold her a ticket to Montréal. Deirdre had often talked of her favorite restaurant,

Le Coq d'Or, and in Montréal that was the first place where Copeland inquired. The doorman had seen Deirdre board the *Etoile Filante*.

"So I flew to Gaspé to meet the ship."

After talking with Captain Lachance, he tried Québec City without success, and it was there he first went to the police. "Then Montréal again and two more police stations. Absolute zero. I was desperate, so I came to see you, Rochelle." He spoke my name tentatively, as though worried that we were not now on a friendly footing. I nodded encouragement.

"That's the whole story," he concluded.

"Doubtless it is not my affair," said Lachance gently, "but I wonder why you follow this young woman. She left of her own will, with no message for you. Her intention seems clear enough."

Taking off his glasses, Brad Copeland rubbed a hand across his eyes. "I don't know why. At first it was anger; I wanted to make her tell me face to face that she was walking out on her promises. Now it's something else. I'm frightened, worried that she's had an accident or . . . I don't know. I'm just afraid." He avoided the captain's gaze. "I must seem a fool to you, chasing after a girl who doesn't care, who . . ."

Pierre Lachance did not answer. Instead he rested his hand gently on Copeland's shoulder and his expression conveyed a depth of understanding and sympathy I would never have believed him capable of feeling in such a situation. Then he turned to me. "Now it is your turn. Tell us everything about your time with Miss Cameron."

I had not finished two sentences before he interrupted impatiently. *"Non, Mademoiselle Dumont, non!* It is details we want. Go slowly, omit nothing at all. Tell not just what you did, but what you thought and felt."

It was slow going indeed! Pierre Lachance, a frown never leaving his rugged face, cross-examined everything I said until my memory seemed to ache. Small incidents that really had nothing to do with Deirdre came back to me. I recalled the empty envelope delivered to me in the airport, a matter that had slipped my mind.

When I spoke of the speeding truck, Brad uttered an exclamation, but Lachance merely nodded, then asked more sharp questions.

The interrogation ended only after the last wisp of information had been plucked from me.

We were silent then until Brad said, "I can't believe it. You sound as though some character from Deirdre's past saw her and deliberately tried to kill her."

"You find that incredible?" the captain asked.

"Yes, I do. Deirdre poured out the story of her life in Montréal to me—I was a father confessor. The people were weird, all right, but no violent types. All that was settled long ago. They had no reason to harm her, nothing to avenge."

"But I'm sure she was frightened," I protested.

"Wouldn't you be if a truck nearly killed you?" Brad inquired, and I had to agree.

"I can't tell you more," I said, "but maybe Captain Lachance will explain about my shawl that Deirdre was wearing. It came back in damp shreds."

"A small mystery. A crewman noticed it while we were at anchor in Gaspé. It was fouled in the propeller blade of our emergency engine and had traveled all the way downriver. But do not leap to a conclusion. Miss Cameron was seen on deck talking with a young man, perhaps a student. She had draped the shawl over the rail. A girl not too careful of her friend's property, I think. It might easily have fallen overboard."

"You could have sent a note, an explanation, with the shawl."

He smiled faintly, undisturbed by my annoyance. "You forget the nature of our parting. I did not think our relationship encouraged the sending of notes."

As we rode back to the village, I realized I had developed a respect for Pierre Lachance. His fairness had brought him immediately to my aid against Brad's outrageous suspicions, and I admired the firm way he took charge of a difficult situation. That same firmness, I remembered very well, could make him seem domineering and insolent, but at times like this afternoon it was an invaluable strength. In any emergency I would want Pierre Lachance on my side. But was he ever on anyone's side except his own? His face, too young to be so weathered, remained unreadable.

"I'm going back to Québec City," said Copeland. "I have

another lead now. I'll look for a Hungarian named Paul who claims to be a poet."

Copeland left us at Auberge du Lac, repeating his apologies and promising to telephone any news about Deirdre.

"I can walk from here," I told Lachance. "The repair shop is only a block away."

But he started the jeep before I could open the door on my side. "This is your first trip to Canada, *non?*" he asked, and I nodded. "Before this trip you knew no one, had no acquaintances here at all?"

"Not a soul."

My replies seemed to deepen his gloom. Then another abrupt question. "You are planning to leave soon?"

"You needn't sound so hopeful, Captain Lachance," I said, smiling. "I promise to avoid you carefully."

His hand slapped the steering wheel. "Do not play games! What kind of answer is that?"

My stubbornness arose. "I have made no plans."

"No plans? *Sacrebleu!* Can you not grasp that someone else may have made plans for you, Rochelle Dumont?"

He stopped the jeep in front of Gagnon's shop, then turned slowly in his seat to study me for a moment, an unfamiliar expression in his dark, deeply set eyes. Sympathy? Pity? I could not tell, and it was oddly disturbing.

"Today you told an alarming story. *Non, mademoiselle,* I do not tell you what I think—you would not believe me. You are very sure of yourself and must find your own conclusions. Besides, I have only suspicions, not facts."

I started to leave, then changed my mind. "I'm curious about something, Captain Lachance. From the first moment we met you disliked me. I knew this before we exchanged a word. Will you tell me why?"

He hesitated, then chose his words carefully. "You were a reminder of the past, and the past should stay buried. Regina made a mistake in resurrecting it, a mistake that may prove dangerous."

"I assure you I'm neither dangerous nor in danger. Also, your feelings on the ship showed a personal dislike and I know it. It doesn't matter, I was merely curious."

"You want my reasons?" He gave a Gallic shrug of indifference. "*Tant mieux!* We will clear the air. I asked myself what sort of young woman would accept this foolish invitation, would come to a place where the past is bitter and memories are long? Probably one seeking a fortune from an elderly relative."

"Of all the—"

"Do not protest, you asked for this. There was also the company you chose. I did not recognize Miss Cameron the first night out of Montréal, her disguise fooled me in the lantern light. But I knew a girl you were traveling with behaved in a way to shock other passengers at the dance. I stopped this, but it seems I did not offend her." Again the shrug of indifference. "A few minutes later she approached me on deck. I do not mind if an attractive girl tries to seduce me, I have even cooperated in such affairs. But not in public when the girl is drunk and I am in command of a ship."

I stared at him in surprise, wondering what sort of scene had taken place between him and Deirdre. "Thank you for making things clear," I said, getting out of the jeep.

"A moment," he said. "Late this morning I talked with Regina. Now I realize you did not know the circumstances when you came here. You must forgive my first opinion." The faint half-smile returned. "I still do not like your choice of traveling companions."

"How gracious of you to relent a little," I answered. "And, Captain, I suspect you are a prude."

His look shifted to an expression of extreme gravity. "A prude? You are at liberty to test that suspicion at a time of your choosing."

As I slammed the door of the jeep, he saluted me. *"A votre service, mademoiselle."*

Late that night, alone in the darkness of the Captain's Country, I listened to the old clock chime midnight, then turned on the lamp for the second time.

Sleep was impossible. Earlier I had spent nearly two hours at the harpsichord in the living room, trying to lose myself in music, trying to seal off the world, as I had done so often in childhood. But that serene, uninhabited plane of unreality seemed to reject me and offered no escape from facing questions I must answer.

Now the room was chilly, yet not cold enough for me to light a fire. I put on a warm robe, fluffy slippers, and lit another lamp for cheer. Pacing between the bed and the window, I forced my thoughts into some sort of order.

Because of meeting Brad Copeland, memories of Deirdre dominated my mind and I had to compel myself not to think of her. My concern had to be for Rochelle Dumont, and Deirdre, whatever had become of her, had little to do with me.

Morgan, a man whose judgment I should trust, had urged me to leave River Rising as quickly as possible. Pierre Lachance even indicated that I was in physical danger here, an exaggeration, I thought, but it was disconcerting that the idea should cross his mind.

Yesterday I myself had decided that leaving was the wisest course, not in fear but because for me this house offered no happiness. I would be forever uneasy, forever questioning. And I would be lonely, as I was lonely tonight.

Deirdre came to my mind again, but in a different context. I envied her because of Brad Copeland. To me he was not an especially attractive man, not one who could arouse any emotion I could in my imagination identify with love. Yet, although Deirdre had hurt him deeply, he was searching the breadth of Québec for her. How fortunate to have anyone who cared so much, who cared in spite of faults, in spite of fecklessness.

I pushed this thought away and tried to think about tomorrow, tomorrow when I should tell Aunt Regina that I was leaving.

To go where?

To become what?

All my life I had drifted. Not as a person who is aimless drifts, but drifted the way a fallen branch caught by the current or the tide moves without choice, without alternatives. I had been moved from school to school when my mother was alive, had tried after her death to move into her place because I could imagine no other life within possibility. I sold her house and business when necessity demanded it. And now, despite telling myself there were other reasons, I suspected I had come to River Rising because no other door was open to me. This, too, was part of the helpless drifting.

To go where?

To become what?

Québec City had caught my imagination with its mellow antiquity. I could go there. Morgan said I would have money from the sale of the antiques I had inherited.

My eyes moved over the sea chest, the japanned cabinet, and I hated the thought of parting with them. But they meant the money to finish college, perhaps at the university in Québec City. Then I could teach music.

A suppressed memory of Antigua suddenly engulfed me, the picture of a dreary clapboard house with a cardboard sign in the window: "Miss Ethel Pruitt, Teacher of Piano." Inside, the eternal metronome ticking away the years of Miss Pruitt's suffocated life while she herself counted the drab seconds. "One, two, three, four . . . Mind the rests, dear . . . A rest is music, too . . . One, two, three, four . . ." Never, I thought. Never!

I gestured unthinkingly, my hand brushing across the top of the dresser and striking Deirdre's music box. It fell to the braided rug, where it tinkled thinly:

Alouette, gentille alouette,
Alouette, je t'y plumerai . . .

I stood gazing at it, waiting for the mindless tune to cease, but it played on and on, starting over again, until I knelt and picked it up, returning it to its place on the dresser.

Thoughts of my own future were overwhelmed by the sensation that I was again on shipboard, lying in my cabin in the grip of the nightmare of another human presence there, footsteps so soft I could hardly hear them, the muffled sound of things being moved, packed.

The sounds had not come from my cabin, but from Deirdre's. What if it had not been Deirdre, but someone else quietly packing her long cotton skirts, her peasant blouses and macramé belt? The intruder could work unseen, aided by a flashlight in the dark cabin. Cloth and leather make no sound, do not cry out. The music box was different; lifted, it would play. Play on and on loudly unless one knew the secret of turning it upside down. The music box would sound its alarm, the alarm I had heard, and had been left behind because someone did not know how to silence its voice . . .

I opened the draperies, the window and let cool night air flow over my face and arms, hoping that the river breeze would banish the memory, that its cold reality would make me see that what I now thought was an illusion.

But the night offered no comfort or security. Below my window the branches stirred restlessly and far away toward the lake a night flying bird taunted me with its laughter.

There was the sound of a heavy footfall in the corridor, a creaking board, and I turned quickly from the window as a muffled voice called, "Rochelle?"

"Yes, who is it?"

"Morgan."

I rushed to open the door, wondering what emergency could have brought him here at so late an hour.

"Has something happened?" I asked.

Morgan smiled. "No. I was just checking to make sure the house was secure. I saw a light under your door and thought you might be awake."

"I am. I've felt restless."

In his dark trousers and turtleneck sweater he seemed to blend with the shadows of the corridor, but his light-brown hair and oddly gold-flecked eyes stood out dramatically in the darkness.

"Howard and I both felt uneasy after the burglary. We're going to do a bit of patrolling for a night or two. Just long enough for word to get back to the village that we're alert here."

"That's probably wise."

"Howard has the harder job, he's outside. Look." Moving past me, Morgan crossed to the window and I followed. Below, where Morgan pointed, I made out the still figure of a man leaning against the trunk of a pine. My eyes must have passed over him earlier without noticing.

There was a metallic reflection in the moonlight. "Is he carrying a gun?" I asked. "A rifle?"

"He's armed to the teeth," said Morgan lightly. "Howard sets great store by his collection of guns. He's rather given to violence, I'm afraid."

Howard Palmer violent? I had dismissed him as drab and harmless. Now the moon again touched the rifle barrel, and I revised my opinion.

Palmer moved silently to another tree, then another, patrolling, of course, yet he seemed to stalk some invisible quarry. Once he raised the rifle, took careful aim, then lowered it.

Morgan chuckled. "He must be pretending that a bear just crossed the lawn."

"Probably," I said. Whatever Palmer's fantasies were, the notion of his prowling the darkness ready to shoot made me uneasy. Did he actually hope an intruder would appear? I suddenly thought so. "Does Mr. Palmer visit here every summer?" I asked.

"No, but he comes often. I've known him since I was a boy. We share memories."

I thought, *The three witnesses*. Howard Palmer, Morgan and Pierre Lachance. Not all the memories they shared were pleasant ones.

"I don't want to talk about Howard," Morgan said, turning to me. "I want to talk about Rochelle Dumont. Have you decided where you'll go when you leave the Rising?"

"I was thinking about that tonight. I've considered Québec City."

He nodded thoughtfully. "It's beautiful. Of course, Montréal is more international. You should look at both before deciding. I know those cities well, I'd enjoy showing them to you."

"Thank you," I answered, suddenly uncertain of myself.

His face seemed half smiling, half sad. "It's right for you to leave River Rising, best for your happiness. But remember that the change won't make any difference with"—he hesitated, then continued—"with your family. You're one of us now. Wherever you go, we'll see each other often."

At the doorway he took my hand, wishing me goodnight. It was a brief, casual gesture. Yet after he was gone I felt troubled by the feeling that his touch had not been that of a friend, but a lover.

7

_____

"An envelope with a maple leaf and tassels? It sounds dime-store," said Regina. "I certainly didn't send such a thing."

I had joined Regina for breakfast on the sun porch, a room which seemed misnamed today. Thin rain mingled with mist obscured the tall windows like a gauze veil.

"I can't think of anyone who would send such an envelope or have you paged," she continued. "A mistake, perhaps. Dumont is a common enough name and there must be thousands of Rochelles."

"I'm sure that's the explanation," I said, not believing it at all.

Eunice entered wearing a pink chenille robe and slippers with floppy rosebuds. "Pierre Lachance called. He's coming to dinner tonight."

"Is his wife coming with him?" I asked, a new thought crossing my mind.

"I certainly hope not," said Regina tartly. "She died about fifteen years ago."

"So long? He must have married young."

"Far too young. He was an inexperienced boy."

Eunice giggled. "You'd hardly call him inexperienced now. I'd say he's made up for lost time."

"You are on the verge of repeating gossip, Eunice." Regina's look was a warning which Eunice ignored.

"Oh, I didn't mean anything sordid. I was thinking of that

television actress, and then that English girl. Didn't she have a title? Lady Something-or-other?"

"Pierre's passing amusements are none of our business." The subject seemed firmly closed, but Regina, being human, had to add her own opinion. "I can't think what he sees in those plastic beauties who call everybody darling in a high-heeled voice. Glitter, I suppose. At least he has the good sense to change models twice a year." Dismissing the matter, she glanced out the window. "What a sloppy day!"

"I don't mind," I told her, although in truth the weather suddenly seemed oppressive. "Half an hour ago the whole river seemed bridged by a rainbow."

"Did you wish on it? What did you wish for?" Eunice asked.

"I forgot to wish."

"Well, one of my wishes came true this morning," Regina said, holding up a letter. "An answer to my advertisement in the *Star*. A husband and wife who want domestic work. Since they don't speak a word of French, they can't be corrupted by local nonsense about the Rising."

Eunice excused herself to dress for the day. When she had gone, Regina said, "Madama Sud tells me Dorothy is feeling better today." After a long hesitation, she added, "I took the liberty of sending word that you'd call on Dorothy this morning. I hope that's agreeable."

"Of course. It seems odd living in the same house with Morgan's wife and not meeting her."

"In the future, if she is able to stay here, I suggest you visit her from time to time. But please don't feel you need see Dorothy frequently. She is difficult and it could become a burden."

"Difficult in what way?"

"In every way," Regina said. "She is an irritating woman. Don't think I'm being uncharitable about an invalid, she was no less self-centered five years ago when she had her health."

"How unfortunate for Morgan."

"Don't waste sympathy. This was merely a marriage of convenience. Dorothy wanted to be the wife of a famous man, and Morgan is famous."

"And what did Morgan want?"

"Oh, she was attractive, had social connections, and I think Morgan was under the illusion that she was very rich."

As usual, her candor startled me. "Surely Morgan didn't need to marry for money. As a painter, he must earn a great deal."

"His income has been high for many years. Almost as high as his outgo." She brushed away an imaginary crumb. "He inherited quite a sum from my brother, but most of that was frittered away before Morgan got his hands on it."

"Doesn't River Rising belong partly to Morgan?"

"Morgan inherited a huge tract of useless land down the slope. River Rising belongs entirely to me." She permitted herself a wry smile. "And when I die I intend to take it with me."

The tiny Sèvres clock on Dorothy Armitage's dressing table showed eleven-fifteen. I had been in this stuffy room less than ten minutes and it seemed that an hour had passed.

Dorothy sat in bed, propped by a mountain of pillows, the vivid embroidery of her oriental bed jacket underlining the pallor of her face, the haggard features that a few years ago must have had a rather feline prettiness. The large, slanted eyes which Thalia had inherited could be called beautiful, I thought, but somehow they emphasized the small nose and sharp chin.

We had discussed the weather, the isolation of the village, the décor of the room, all strained and meaningless small talk in which neither of us had the least interest.

The unexpected presence of Madame Sud multiplied my discomfort. The housekeeper, seated apart from us in a window alcove, carefully brushed the golden tresses of a wig. The wig block stood on a small table, its back toward me, giving the disconcerting impression that Madame Sud was ministering to a severed head, an effect that struck me first as grimly humorous and later as merely grim.

The thick yellow locks being so painstakingly groomed made a pathetic contrast to Dorothy's thinning hair, straw-colored and lusterless.

"I suppose the remoteness of River Rising is good for my husband's work," Dorothy was saying, and I nodded mutely. Then, tilting her head, she at last expressed a genuine feeling. "Also, being here probably keeps him out of mischief. Morgan is terribly attractive to women, as you've no doubt noticed."

I decided not to ignore the barb. "Who could fail to

notice? He's very handsome—for a middle-aged man." I hoped this would allay any suspicions she might have about me, but my remark was, of course, ridiculous. Morgan radiated youthful vitality.

"Middle-aged?" The tilt of her chin sharpened.

"I should think Morgan is only three or four years younger than my father, if my father had lived."

"Perhaps," she agreed doubtfully, then resumed the offensive. "Age hasn't hindered a good many young girls from making fools of themselves over Morgan. Poor things! Artists are notoriously callous, as you know."

"I'll take your word, I have no experience."

Her challenging look warned me against acquiring any. Then a puzzled expression came over her face, as though she had forgotten the subject of conversation.

"I'm much stronger than I was in the sanatorium," she went on. "If the weather clears, I'll walk in the garden today."

"I hope you can."

For a moment she studied me, then asked abruptly, "Do you believe in the pack?"

"I beg your pardon?"

"The tarot pack. The cards."

"You mean fortune-telling?"

"I'm learning how to read the tarot from an amazing old woman in the village. She comes here at least twice a week and we lay out the cards. We've made remarkable forecasts." Her languor vanished; she became intent. "The cards foretold your coming here, for instance. I'll show you. Madame Sud, please bring the pack and my bed table."

"Isn't this a strain for you?" I asked uncertainly. The color that flushed her pale cheeks seemed unnatural, and her breath came too rapidly.

Madame Sud placed a low table with a thin deck of cards on the bed. Dorothy made several gestures, passes, above the cards, then said, "Cut the pack four times. Lay the cards in the shape of a cross."

Reluctantly I humored her, wishing that Madame Sud would return to her alcove and not stand so close to me.

Dorothy turned the cards, exposing their faces one by one. Her hands, thin and waxen, fumbled in their eagerness, then she stared vacantly at the pattern. "The drowned man is near you," she murmured. "The drowned man separates

you from the hanged man. But are they one? The identity
card is touching both."

The unsubtle reference to my father's death did not escape
me, but I gave no sign I noticed.

"See how the Deniers, the golden circles, have swarmed
near you! Gold circles, yellow circles like the sun." Her
murmur was rising to a chant, a throbbing singsong punc-
tuated by quick gasps of breath. "But it is not gold coming
to you, not even sunlight. Yellow is the color of danger for
you, the color of death."

"This is enough," I said, rising. "You are too excited, under too much strain."

Dorothy Armitage did not hear me. "The old man is hidden from you, the philosopher, the wise King of Cups. He
holds the answer but you cannot find him. Go away. Safety
is far from you. Go away . . ."

The fortune-telling seemed over, yet she stared at the
cards, entranced.

"Who is teaching you this?" I asked. "Who is the woman
from the village?"

"She is called Madame Jeanette," said Dorothy, her voice
toneless and vacant. "She knows the special reading, too.
The one that can be done only on Friday and only at midnight. She sees a long life for me. She sees . . . everything."

Suddenly Dorothy lay back on the pillows, her eyelids
fluttered, then closed. Madame Sud put her finger to her
own lips, enjoining silence, and nodded toward the door.

I had never been happier to leave a room. During the
card reading, Dorothy's mind had wandered, yet the fortune
she told was clearly based on the promptings of Madame
Jeanette and Madame Sud. Yellow meant the golden shawl,
no doubt of it. But who was the philosopher who held the
answer?

Go away. That was the climax of her message—it was
everyone's message to me.

The morning shower had moved southeast, crossing the
river. From the living-room window I saw Howard Palmer,
wearing a slicker and a Montmartre beret, amble across the
lawn. I had still not determined his place in the household.
Supposedly he was Morgan's friend, yet Morgan ignored him.

Sitting at the harpsichord, I began to play softly. "Jesu,
Joy of Man's Desiring" brought back the garden of Clarendon Abbey and the serene features of Aunt Theresa. "My

Heart Ever Faithful" was the smiling nun, the motherly door-keeper. Then I unconsciously shifted to an improvisation of chords and counterpoint, playing badly, a confusion of themes reflecting my own emotions.

I paused, sensing rather than hearing that someone was near, and found Thalia standing close to me, her hands tight-ly clenched and two great tears in her eyes.

"I didn't mean to make you stop," she whispered. "You were playing a dream, weren't you, Rochelle?"

"Something like that." I saw her glance at the keyboard, almost hungrily, then look away.

"Do you play, Thalia?"

"I once did, just a little on the piano. Long ago."

Long ago. How long would that be for a twelve-year-old girl?

"You should play," I told her. "You're named for one of the muses. Thalia is a lovely name."

"I like the name Rochelle better. Ro-chelle," she said, breaking the syllables. Again she studied the keyboard. "I used to practice for hours. Sometimes . . . my father . . ." It seemed hard for her to say the word "father." "He some-times made me stop. He thought that it might harm my eyes, yet he liked to hear me. Maybe that's why I can't play any more."

She forced back tears which would have been better re-leased, bit back her grief. The bench was narrow, but I drew her to my side, my arm around her.

"I lost my father, too," I said. "Maybe music gives him back to me, at least a little."

"No. Nothing could do that."

"Thalia, the rain is gone and it's becoming a beautiful day. Should we take a walk? Along the firebreak are bobolinks and larks. I saw a silver squirrel and I think there was a doe in a thicket."

"No!" She drew away, frightened. "I hate the forest. I never go past the kitchen garden. Captain Pierre has tried to take me to a waterfall he knows; he planned a picnic for me and some boys and girls from the village. I ran away. The forest, I'm afraid of it, I . . ."

Sinking to the floor, Thalia buried her face in my lap and wept, the suppressed pain pouring out with every sob. When no more tears would come, she began to speak, her voice choked and muffled. She told the story of her father's death, forcing it out bit by bit, shifting backward and forward in time, yet I understood what had happened and shared at least a measure of what she had felt.

After her parents' divorce and her mother's marriage to Morgan, Thalia lived with her father. A year ago last October he had taken her on a weekend vacation, first stopping at River Rising to visit Dorothy, then going to a rustic lodge twenty miles away.

"To see the colors of the leaves. The oaks are scarlet, chestnuts yellow . . . maples are the sign of Canada . . . tamaracks weep because their wood was the Cross . . ." Departing from her story, she mumbled the lesson her father had taught her.

They were not far from the lodge when the blizzard struck, and foolishly they took shelter in the hollow of a lightning-struck tree, thinking the snowstorm would end quickly. But the swirling white became deeper, impenetrable, while the scream of the wind rose to an unbearable shriek.

"The wind screamed until we couldn't stand it. I covered my ears, but I couldn't shut it out. We had to run from it."

Clinging together, they stumbled through a raging world where all landmarks were obliterated, all directions erased. Then the snow seemed to blaze, dazzling them with blinding white as though a thousand lights pierced their eyes. Thalia's father, sightless then, collapsed in a drift.

They shouted against the wind, and when their voices began to fail they tried to sing, hoping someone would hear. Her father's song became weaker, seemed like a lullaby, and Thalia fell asleep.

"When I awoke, Captain Pierre was holding me. He led the woodsmen who found us. I didn't know him then, and I was afraid. But he kept saying rhymes in my ear and telling me magic words until I went to sleep again."

Thalia looked up at me, dry-eyed now. "That was long ago. I don't remember any more."

"Long ago," I agreed, still holding her.

"Tante Emma told me that if I said exactly one thousand Aves on Christmas Eve, any wish I made would come true. Last Christmas, I counted the Aves, counted so carefully. But my father didn't come back. Of course, I know he's dead. I've forgotten, but I still can't play any music and I'm afraid to go into the woods."

Turning to the keyboard, I began to play tunes from

childhood, little practice pieces I had not thought of in years. "Now you play," I said firmly.

Thalia blanched. "I can't, Rochelle."

Putting her hands on the keyboard, I waited, hoping desperately, knowing there was no more I could do.

Then, hesitantly, she began. Her fingers were awkward from lack of practice and she did not understand the action of a harpsichord, but I recognized the familiar air of "Country Gardens" and at that moment no symphony could have been so beautiful.

When she finished, I said, "We'll practice together, Thalia. We'll learn a duet and surprise everybody."

"Oh, I couldn't."

"But you will!"

"Well, maybe if you help me, Rochelle."

A little later I found Tante Emma in the kitchen, sleeves rolled up, her face beet-red as she peered into a steaming kettle of ragout.

"Tante Emma, you told me monkshood grows near here. Exactly where is it found?"

"Tiens! You are not bringing more of that bane into the house?"

"No. Does it grow near the garden?"

"What an idea! A plant or two might slip into the garden like a weed, but monkshood is a devil of the woods."

It was as I suspected. Thalia never ventured into the forest, so whoever had placed the monkshood in my room, it could not be the child.

I next called on Regina. Since hearing Thalia's story, listening to her painful but heartwarming attempt to play music once again, new feelings had suddenly swept through me. I could not yet tell what those feelings were, could not define my emotions, but one of them was certainly determination.

"Aunt Regina, I'd like to go to the village. May I use your car?"

She looked up from her crocheting. "Kindly call it *our* car or at least *the* car until you have one of your own. The keys are in the Wedgwood bowl in the hall."

Regina followed me, caught up at the front door. "I don't mean to burden you with kitchen errands, but Henri Berthe-

lot telephoned a short time ago. He has some endive for us
from his conservatory."

"Henri Berthelot?" The name seemed familiar. "Does he
have a shop?"

"No, dear." She chuckled. "Henri is an artist. He was
Morgan's teacher, and your father's. His house is on the
main street; you'll see the name on the gate."

I looked forward to meeting anyone who had known my
father, but my call at Henri Berthelot's would have to be
delayed. My first task was the one I had left unfinished yesterday, the testing of the village of Ste. Marie du Lac.

The tiny town, from the first, had struck me as medieval,
a relic of a past world. What I now saw on the church lawn
surpassed any imagining.

A score of men and women had gathered there, brilliant
figures in fancy dress. Hose and doublets, buckled shoes and
plumed headgear startled me with a royal panoply of New
France in the days of the *ancienne noblesse*. There was
music, instruments usually known only as pictures in books,
the *cor anglais, dolcian* and flageolet.

As I halted the car, a small boy dressed as a page skipped
past. "What's going on?" I asked.

"Rehearsal for the pageant," he called breathlessly. "The
Feast of St. John the Baptist."

I lingered near the sidelines of the rehearsal for a moment, but the participants were too busy to give me more
than cursory glances. Then I walked on, passing a man in
everyday coveralls, who nodded to me, reserved but polite.
When two young girls stared at me with open curiosity, I
felt myself tense. They were looking at "the murderer's
daughter," of course, and without meaning to, I glanced
away. Then, when they were beyond me, I heard one say.
"Her dress is *tres chic*. From Paris, do you think?"

I almost laughed aloud at my foolish apprehensions, and I
did smile at the girl's mistaking an off-the-peg fawn jersey
for the work of a Parisian couturier. The bit of flattery firmed
my step for a harder test, entering the general store.

The dim room was deserted except for the proprietress,
who seemed anchored behind the counter in her stiff white
apron.

"I am looking for the home of Monsieur Henri Berthelot,"
I said, gazing at her coolly.

"Across the street, second block on the corner." The tone was polite, her expression bland.

Before leaving, I decided to push matters further. "Madame, as you know, I am newly arrived here. Were you acquainted with my parents?"

"Forgive me, mademoiselle, I did not know them. I, too, am a newcomer here. Only seven years." Her neutrality seemed complete, but then she added, "I hope you were not too upset by what happened here a few days ago. You must realize that Madame Jeanette is a little mad."

"More than a little."

"I am told she was not always so. It was the tragedy of her daughter."

"What of her daughter?"

She lowered her eyes. "I do not know the details. If you visit Monsieur Berthelot, ask him. He was here when the girl killed herself; I was not."

"Killed herself? Tell me, madame!"

"I was not here then," she repeated, and dismissed me with a shake of her head.

In front of his house Henri Berthelot had placed not a fence, but a grape arbor. The season was too early for grapes, but I could see that the vines had been trained so clusters of fruit would hang on the public, not the private, side of the stakes. A discreet sign said: "Take what you need. But leave some for others." I suddenly liked Henri Berthelot.

The stone cottage resembled twenty others in Ste. Marie du Lac, but on the north side a clapboard studio with high windows had been added. The studio needed paint as badly as the flower beds needed weeding.

An old man whose balding crown gave the impression of a tonsured monk answered my knock, peering at me through thick lenses shaded by a tortoise-shell band. The strange spectacles combined with a bristling goatee gave him the appearance of a mad scientist.

"Bonjour, monsieur, je—"

He interrupted in English. "Rochelle Dumont! Such a pleasure. Regina telephoned just now to say you were calling. Do come in. My eyes are so old and uncertain that I cannot see you clearly, but Regina tells me you are beautiful and I am sure you are. As beautiful as your mother and father were."

He spoke of my father without hesitation, and I was touched to hear Jean-Paul Dumont called "beautiful."

Inside, the front of the house was a single, lofty room that served for both cooking and dining. The walls were hung almost solidly with paintings, drawings and etchings.

"Take this chair, my dear," he said, leading me to a round table one would expect in a farmhouse kitchen. "When you tire of my conversation, your eyes will rest on the south wall. My best paintings are there. Probably they are not as fresh as they were thirty and forty years ago, but I hope some remain at least charming."

His work was delightful and heartfelt, the daily life of Ste. Marie du Lac glowing on the canvases—a girl milking a cow, a patriarch enjoying his mug of ale—homely subjects his strong brushstrokes had saved from sentimentality.

After pouring homemade wine into two water glasses, he sat down to savor his pipe. Conversation came easily, and I learned that Regina had informed him about my past and my mother's.

"Is Howard Palmer again at River Rising this summer?"

"Yes."

He nodded. "I thought I saw him pass my house. My vision is fickle, but sometimes fairly clear." The old painter sighed deeply. "So he still returns. I suppose he still tries to paint Ste. Marie du Lac."

"He talks mostly about hunting and his travels, but I did see him with a sketch pad this morning."

"*Pathétique!* He is middle-aged now, he should realize what a maladroit hand he has. And the eye! None at all!"

"I suppose he keeps hoping."

"Yes, hope." He shook his head slowly. "How many great hopes and dreams have been expressed at this table. When I recall my students, I try to think of their hopes, not their failures. It is best to remember the dreams."

"Was my father a dreamer?"

He hesitated before answering. "Yes, because some dreams are nightmares. Jean-Paul was a copyist, he imitated me. He hated himself for this, but could not break the mold. Jean-Paul handled paint like St. Luke himself, but had nothing to say or found no way of saying it. Forgive my harshness. Your father died young, he had little opportunity."

"Of course, your most famous pupil is Morgan."

"I do not claim him, I taught him little enough. Nor can I

comment on his work, since I have never seen it except as a blur. But I am not surprised that he is famous."

"He showed great talent early?"

Henri Berthelot looked grim. "He showed great determination. Morgan was going to be famous one way or another at any price. Forgive me, but the Armitage family frightens me. There is a fierceness in their blood. I have known almost four generations of Armitage tigers and tigresses. Some, like Regina, I enjoy and admire. Yet I would not choose to be in the same cage with them."

"I hope you don't include me."

He smiled. "You are still a kitten. But who can tell?"

One painting on the south wall kept catching my eye, a portrait, different from the others. "Who is that beautiful girl?" I asked. "The one in the white dress?"

"You like her? What a model she was! But I never caught the sheen of that black hair, and her skin was not quite the olive I painted. There was a glow about her; she was translucent. It was one of my last works. Perhaps because my eyes were failing I showed her only as a dreamer. Actually, the dream was unbridled ambition and the girl was a wildcat. But a beautiful wildcat."

"But who is she?"

"It is a portrait of Madame Lachance."

"The wife of Pierre Lachance?" I asked slowly. The beauty of the painting suddenly seemed both hurtful and tragic.

"Yes, painted before she married him. She was sixteen then. And to think that only a few years later she hanged herself."

"Hanged herself?" I gasped. Then I remembered the remark of the woman in the store about another suicide. Madame Jeanette's daughter. "Who was she? Did she come from the village?"

"Yes, from the poorest of the poor. Her mother was a widow who scratched out a living for the two of them by selling potions and herbs. Quite a repulsive woman."

"Madame Jeanette?"

"Why, yes. Jeanette Massine. Her daughter was Giselle."

I stared at the portrait. "You are telling me that a creature like Madame Jeanette could have produced a daughter as lovely as . . ." I could not finish. The connection between Madame Jeanette and Pierre Lachance astonished me, left me unbelieving.

"Jeanette Massine was not always what you see now," he said, gently reproving. "I remember her as an attractive woman, strange and unstable, but by no means mad."

I was forced, unwillingly, to accept this. "Why did the daughter kill herself? What happened?"

"Thwarted ambition, I suppose. Giselle was engaged to marry François Armitage. It was a local sensation—a girl they said was brought up in a sty marrying a grand gentleman from the château. How tongues wagged, Madame Jeanette's among them. Giselle was going to be rich, going to be known as the greatest beauty in Canada. But the dream did not come true. François died before the brilliant marriage took place."

"Yes," I said, "François died." And now I understood Madame Jeanette's hatred of me. My father's act of violence had destroyed Giselle's future of wealth and what to Madame Jeanette must have seemed little short of nobility. For years Madame Jeanette had nursed her hatred and malice. Before, I had detested her, now I felt something closer to fear.

"A little later Giselle married Pierre Lachance, a boy, really. No one thought he had much future, but he was handsome, the village athlete. It was not enough for Giselle. She left him at least once, something about trying to succeed in films or television. I have forgotten the details. In the end, she died by her own hand."

Monsieur Berthelot glanced at my empty glass. "More wine? I am sorry I have upset you with this tale of an old tragedy."

"You have not upset me. I'm grateful. It's important that I understand why people here behave as they do. But no wine, I must go now."

"Wait! I have two small gifts for you." From the sideboard he brought a basket of crisp endive. "Grown in the tiny greenhouse I keep in my fumbling way." Then he handed me a rectangular parcel clumsily wrapped in newspaper and tied with kitchen thread.

"A drawing?" I asked, feeling a frame through the paper. "Really, monsieur, you are too kind."

"Not a drawing, a small painting done by one of my students and left here long ago. No, do not open it here. It is for you alone."

Leading me to the door, he said, "Return soon. Then we

will talk of pleasant things and the wine will have a brighter taste." He hesitated, peering at me again through the thick, distorting lenses. "A bit of needless advice, my dear. I have said the people at River Rising are tigers, and I was not making a joke. Remember tigers have claws, even when their paws look soft."

But on the way back to River Rising, I did not consider Henri Berthelot's advice and its possible implications. I thought only of the story of Madame Jeanette's daughter, Giselle Massine. Pierre Lachance had been in love with the girl François Armitage intended to marry. And Pierre had also been present on the scene at the time of François' murder and my father's death. I saw the captain's dislike of me in a new light, and yet I could not be sure of what I felt.

But another matter was certain. Madame Jeanette was indeed my implacable enemy, and that enemy came and went freely within the walls of River Rising, the invited guest of Dorothy Armitage. I thought of monkshood . . .

In the Captain's Country, I locked the door behind me before unwrapping the little painting that was "for you alone." I thought I knew, hoped I knew, what the gift would prove to be. Monsieur Berthelot, I felt almost sure, had kept some work done by my father when he was a student in Ste. Marie du Lac. A landscape, I supposed, or some scene of village life. Deliberately prolonging the suspense, I undid the paper so the back of the picture was toward me.

My eyes fell on a neatly typed label glued to the frame, and my heart seemed to leap when I read it: "No. 183. *Self-Portrait by Jean-Paul Dumont.*"

I closed my eyes, afraid to turn it over, knowing I would see for the first time the face of the stranger who was my father. Would I have some vague memory of him? Would I, and I hoped desperately, *like* him?

Then I looked and gasped.

Smiling at me across the years was the dearly familiar face of Paul LaFarge, my mother's lover.

He had cheated death that night, had not been crushed on the rocks below River Rising! The words seemed to shout themselves, to shake the silent room where I stood holding the portrait with trembling hands.

"Paul," I whispered, "Paul."

Time would have to pass before I could understand all the implications of my discovery, yet even then I knew that the landscape of my childhood was utterly changed, my view of my whole life had just been swept away as by a hurricane. Nothing would be the same, I would not be the same.

I wanted to race through the corridors, run from room to room crying out the news. Charlotte Dumont did not leave here because she was ashamed or frightened, she left to join her husband, to share with him the remaining years of his life.

Suddenly I loved my mother with a fullness I had never imagined. I had thought her cold and ungiving, yet she had given everything, chosen a life of exile where her love had to be concealed.

My blaming her for not marrying Paul—I could not think of him as Jean-Paul Dumont, my father, yet—seemed cruel injustice. How could they have lived together as man and wife? He was believed dead; the police had closed the case. Yet Charlotte, widow of a murderer, remained a marked woman. Someone from the past might have appeared at any time.

The danger of being recognized must have followed Paul like an accusing shadow every day of his life. My mother would never have allowed him to double that risk by living openly with him.

They were right to keep their secret from me. As a child, I could have blurted out everything. In the years after Paul's death, my mother must have tried to spare me the burden of the past, or perhaps secrecy was so ingrained in her that it became impossible to break her silence. Now I realized that at the end she had tried to tell me, had meant to share everything, but then it was too late.

"The murderer's daughter," I said aloud, and the words had no sting. How could I be ashamed of being Paul's child? No man could have been kinder, more gentle.

Ever since coming to River Rising, I had harbored suspicions that someone else might be guilty of the death of François Armitage. Although saying nothing, I had secretly wondered about Morgan, about Howard Palmer. Today I had found a motive pointing to the possible guilt of Pierre Lachance.

These suspicions vanished now. Paul's fleeing Canada, his living in isolation under an assumed name, showed his legal guilt. Yet I had known Paul, and if he had committed such a crime, he must have been driven to it. Regina was wrong, Morgan was wrong, everyone who had described my father to me was mistaken or deceived. Or they were lying.

The firm features and clear gaze of Jean-Paul Dumont's portrait gave me new resolution. The true story of that night had not yet been told, but it would be. And I would be the one to tell it.

8

—◆—

"Rochelle, you look radiant tonight. Our Québec air agrees with you," said Regina.

We had gathered in the living room for the after-dinner ritual of cognac or port. The family was present except for Dorothy and there were two visitors, although Howard Palmer seemed a full-time boarder. He spoke often of cooking for himself in Chimney House, but usually managed to be on hand in the dining room at mealtimes. Our other guest was Captain Lachance, who joked easily with Regina, smiled at Thalia and ignored everyone else.

"Yes, radiant," she continued. "But too silent. You didn't say ten words at dinner."

Startled, I realized she was right. Preoccupation with my discovery of the afternoon, a subject I could not mention, had driven all other thoughts from my mind. In the future I must learn to be less obvious.

"Silence can be a lovely quality in a woman," Morgan remarked.

"Indeed it is," agreed Eunice, who had been chattering for the last half-hour. "My mother said that silence lends a woman an air of mystery. I've found that true." Everyone looked at her in disbelief except Captain Lachance, who was contemplating the empty spot above the fireplace where the stolen painting had once hung.

"I have an announcement to make." Regina lifted her head rather grandly. "An announcement sure to please everyone. We are going to celebrate Midsummer's Eve and St.

John's Eve at the Rising, as we used to. The ball at River Rising was a charming tradition more than a century old. I should never have allowed it to die. Now we will revive the celebration."

Regina, who had expected delight, caused consternation instead. Her listeners sat dumbfounded, then came a chorus of objections.

"An enormous undertaking! Where would we find servants?" Eunice looked utterly lost.

"Would there be a lot of people here?" Thalia asked doubtfully.

Morgan scowled. "This will cost you a fortune."

"I *have* a fortune." Regina's eyes flashed. "And I intend to busy myself spending it. Here is my beautiful niece, a stranger in her own country. Rochelle must meet people, hopefully a few of them her own age, and not merely villagers. I expect many friends from Québec City to accept the invitation."

"A debut," said Captain Lachance with his irritating half-smile. "Regina, is not the debutante to be consulted? Perhaps Miss Dumont would not enjoy such a launching."

"Oh, stop calling her Miss Dumont!" Regina controlled her temper with difficulty. "Pierre, this is Rochelle. You have now been introduced and will end this annoying formality." When she turned to me, her chin was still high but her tone no longer imperious. "Of course, I should have consulted you, my dear. But I regarded this as a delightful surprise for everyone. Have I been thoughtless?"

"On the contrary, you're being very kind," I assured her. "But you see, Aunt Regina, it isn't . . ." I groped for words, wanting to explain that a lavish party was unnecessary, yet not wishing to diminish the pleasure she had felt when she made her announcement.

Pierre Lachance interrupted me. "I think Miss Dumont—forgive me, I mean Rochelle—is trying to say that St. John's Day is a few weeks in the future. She may not intend to remain here so long."

Regina's expression showed hurt and astonishment. I felt like a traitor for having assured both the captain and Morgan that I was leaving at once without speaking to Regina about it. I had not expected my plans, now completely changed, to be revealed to Regina so bluntly.

"Please don't put words in my mouth, Captain Lachance," I said.

"Not Captain Lachance," he corrected me politely.
"Pierre."

Ignoring this, I went quickly to Regina and kissed her
cheek. "Of course I'll be here. I haven't the least intention
of leaving, but you must not go to extra expense or trouble
for me."

Facing Regina, I could not see the expressions of others in
the room, yet I sensed a sudden tension, even shock.

She took my hand lightly but warmly. "Thank you. My
motives are not as unselfish as you think. I myself intend to
have a wonderful time. The Rising will be filled with music
and celebration. The notion pleases me."

As I returned to my place on the couch I realized I had
been right—the atmosphere of the room was changed. Eunice began talking gaily of brilliant parties held at the Rising
in the past, and Thalia smiled at me shyly, but hers was the
only smile. Never had Pierre Lachance's dark face seemed
more like granite, the strong jaw outthrust, the deep eyes
narrowed. Morgan also gazed at me, a questioning look that
conveyed disapproval.

My change of plan annoyed both men, but what did it
matter? I had made no promises about leaving and had
every right to stay as long as Regina wished.

When Eunice paused for breath, Lachance spoke. "I am
happy you are eager to have guests here, Regina." He managed the ghost of a smile. "Now it is easier for me to bring
up my own invitation."

"Of course I expect you. You know you're invited."

His smile broadened slightly. "I do not mean the party. I
want another favor, the same one you granted two summers
ago. Some vacationers wish to rent my house for a good deal
of money. Alas, they do not care to rent me at the same
time. I am left homeless."

"You will come to the Rising at once, Pierre," Regina told
him, "but I warn you, I may never permit you to leave."

"A pleasant captivity," he answered. "We will arrive tomorrow. Both of us are grateful."

"Both?" Regina hesitated, then laughed. "So you're bringing Viking! Your tenants won't put up with him."

"You are as astute as ever."

"Viking is your police dog, isn't he?" Eunice sounded faintly panicky.

"Viking is a German shepherd dog," he explained. "They

are a breed sometimes used for police work, but they are also gentle enough to be guide dogs for the blind."

Howard Palmer leaned forward and took a quick puff of his pipe. "Tell me, is he a good gun dog? I've been looking for a dog, or even two."

"Viking is a superb hunter, in his own way. Unfortunately, he works only for me." Lachance paused, glanced again at the blank place above the mantel. "He may be useful. You suffered a burglary here."

"The burglar won't return," said Morgan flatly. "Art thieves never do. It isn't their pattern."

"True, but events at River Rising seldom follow usual patterns. For instance, I believe art thieves often send ransom notes. Oddly, that has not happened." He stood up and bade us a rather formal goodnight. "Until tomorrow."

Later, in my room, I resisted a temptation to look once more at my father's portrait, which I had hidden in the sea chest, feeling it was too precious to be displayed. Tonight I must not arouse more emotions, more memories.

Nor did I wish to think what the presence of Pierre Lachance in the house might mean to me. He was a disconcerting man, who made me feel awkward and ill-at-ease. Certain persons, I supposed, were born antagonists, and this seemed to be the case with Pierre Lachance and me. It was unexplainable that my anger rose so close to the surface when he was near.

The story of his youthful, tragic marriage did not explain the man to me, nor did the gossip about his frequently changing love affairs. It was nothing to me, I told myself. Nothing.

Dismissing such speculation as useless, I took pen and paper and wrote a note to a storage company in St. John asking them to ship a trunk I had left there, a trunk containing the few possessions I had not brought with me. Sealing the envelope seemed an act of finality, a commitment to remain at River Rising much longer than I had ever expected. Then I changed to my robe and was brushing my hair when a thin, frightened voice called my name in the corridor. "Ro-chelle, Ro-chelle!" Thalia's way of saying my name.

I had hardly opened the door when she rushed in and threw her arms around me. "Oh, Rochelle, you're safe! Nothing has happened to you!"

"Happened to me? Of course not, Thalia. Why, you're trembling. What happened?"

Her face was blanched. "I went to my mother's room to say goodnight, as I'm supposed to do. But I didn't go in because . . . because . . ."

I knelt beside her. "Yes, Thalia?"

"The witch was there. I heard her voice before I knocked, so I stayed outside. I listened. She was telling a fortune."

"There aren't any real witches, Thalia. Do you mean Madame Jeanette from the village?"

She nodded vigorously. "It was your fortune she was telling. She said terrible things about the cards meaning danger, and death being near you and getting closer. I was frightened, then I ran here to make sure nothing dreadful had happened."

"You must not believe such stupid things, Thalia. I'm glad you came to me. Nothing has happened to me and nothing will."

Her enormous eyes regarded me gravely. "Are you sure of that, Rochelle?"

Pierre Lachance arrived as expected the next morning I watched him approach from a vantage point I had just explored, the Captain's Walk.

After an early breakfast I had climbed the steep stairs that led from the old nursery adjoining my room to the roof. At the stairwell top a small door opened to an outside walkway made of oaken planks, the Captain's Walk, where a retired mariner might pace and gaze at the vast sweep of the river and its passing ships. The walk, fronted by a low parapet, was not visible from below, and behind it rose the great chimneys and gables of the uppermost attics like the crests of a storm-driven sea. There was one attic window above me; otherwise, I had found the highest, most commanding point at River Rising.

Looking down from the rather dizzying height, I saw the captain leave his parked jeep, a black-and-copper dog at his heels. A bulging duffle bag was balanced on Lachance's left shoulder and he carried a leather grip in his right hand. A long visit here, I thought, to judge from his luggage.

He and his canine companion vanished under the porte cochère. A moment later Morgan emerged from the house and, to my disappointment, walked in the direction of his studio, ending any chance of my returning this morning to the place where my father had supposedly plunged to his death. The cliffs, so frightening only a few days ago, now held no terror for me, but I wanted to see the place again, to learn how Jean-Paul Dumont had made his miraculous escape.

I lingered a moment, held by the vista of the eternally moving water, the dark outline of the south shore. Had my father ever painted this scene?

The self-portrait evoked no memories of other pictures. The man I knew as "Paul LaFarge" worked on his ramshackle boat or in what he described as his grass-shack studio on a nearby island. I had never visited this place, and now realized its exact location had been deliberately kept from me. I did recall delightful sketches he had drawn for me when I was a child. There was a purple pelican and a dancing flamingo.

Then the memory of pink-striped Sandy-Panda came back to me with a rush of sentiment. Somehow I had lost my favorite doll, left it on the beach and the tide had come in. Now I vividly recalled the strong, warm hands that comforted me. *"Tiens, I will make you a new one, ma petite."*

I had not believed a big man like Paul could possible make a doll, but that day I watched him create Sandy-Panda. I sat on the floor, wide-eyed, as he stitched with a sail-mending needle, then painted the gay stripes and the smiling bearlike face.

"He is yours forever," he said, presenting the doll to me solemnly. "And he loves you almost as much as I do."

Sandy-Panda slept at my side for at least two years, then became a beloved daytime pillow ornament. Sandy-Panda, always dear to me, now had a special value as my father's gift.

Shaking away my reverie, I started toward my room, careful to check the spring lock of the door to the roof behind me. I had just passed through the nursery when I heard an authoritative knock.

"Come in."

Pierre Lachance strode into the room, the black-and-copper dog moving, it seemed, in step with him.

"Bonjour. I want you to meet your new friend, Viking. And, Viking, I present you to Rochelle, a lady we must never call Mademoiselle Dumont. We are under orders."

The dog's eyes, almond-shaped and deep amber, studied me. He sat smartly at his master's side, pointed ears alert, an animal of power and pride. Even so, I had to force myself not to think of a wolf.

"Does he shake hands?" I asked uncertainly.

Lachance looked pained and offended. "Certainly not. It would be unnatural for him. After all, do you bark?"

"I have been known to," I said, making a very tentative move forward.

"Non!" He shook his head impatiently. "I see I must teach you everything. Approach him confidently, but not too fast. Extend your right hand, but only a little and with the palm down."

"Aye, aye, Captain." I obeyed with deep misgivings, then felt relief when Viking, instead of baring his white fangs, gently sniffed my knuckles. Still, I was far from being at ease and not sure which made me more uncomfortable, the nearness of Viking or his master.

"Now pet him," came the command. "No, do not be so gentle, he will not break. *Alors,* where is all that confidence you showed on shipboard?"

"I'm a fake," I confessed, "confident only when I'm angry."

"Luckily for you, that is most of the time."

I started to reply, then saw he was smiling.

Pierre took a brown envelope from his pocket. "These lozenges are Viking's favorites. You will present him with one now and keep the rest. He is to be given one each time he calls on you."

"Calls on me?" I asked, astonished. "Do you think that likely?"

"Pourquoi pas? That is what friends do. They call on each other."

I shook a dark lozenge from the envelope into my palm. "It looks like dried-up liver," I said.

"It tastes like it, too. No, no, I do not usually eat them. But one winter I was in the woods and there was no other food. I had some of these in my pocket and hunger greatly changes the flavor. I had not eaten for two days."

Viking, a gentleman, took the lozenge carefully from my hand, pulverized it with one crunch of his jaws, then looked at me hopefully. I decided we might become friends after all. At least I was grateful we were not enemies.

"A good beginning," Lachance said, glancing at the watch strapped to his wrist by a thick leather band. "Now you must change clothes. Your skirt is very pretty but will not do for a picnic, which, if we are lucky, will end in the woods."

"What?" I exclaimed.

"Sacrebleu! Control your panic. The child Thalia is frightened of the forest, and that is a terrible thing. She has confidence in you and, I think, in me. We are going to help her conquer her fear, and a very uneventful picnic will be the beginning. So change into slacks or pants or whatever women call them and meet us in the garden."

"So you have planned my day?" I said, my chin lifting. "Not everyone is a member of your crew, Captain Lachance."

"It is forbidden to call me anything but Pierre. Not my command, your aunt's. And why this protest? The day is beautiful, and you know you will enjoy yourself."

He turned to leave, and when Viking followed, he made a quick gesture with his hand. The dog promptly sat and Lachance left, closing the door firmly behind him.

"Of all the arrogant—!" I sat on the edge of the bed, planting myself as firmly as the dog had done, determined not to budge. But after a moment I could not help smiling. He was quite right, I wanted to go.

I put on a pair of comfortable jeans and tied my hair with a crimson bandanna. Viking, still sitting near the door, gave me a sympathetic look. But Viking, I thought as I knotted the bandanna, was more used to taking orders than I would ever be, and Pierre Lachance would discover this fact quickly.

At noon we turned onto the abandoned trail leading to the ghost town, Castaways, Viking frisking a little ahead of us.

"We are not going too far for you, *enfant?*" Pierre asked Thalia. "Remember, we still must walk back."

"Oh no. I love hiking, I'm not a bit tired."

It was a brisk day, the sky a shimmering translucent blue. The swiftness of the Québec spring astonished me. Only three days ago I had noticed the whites and pale yellows of early wildflowers blooming along the firebreak. Now buds had opened in a profusion of pinks, reds and purples. I saw a flame-colored bush half hidden in the alders.

"Let's pick some to take home," I said to Thalia, but she shook her head and would not leave the open trail.

Now, on the rutted corduroy road to Castaways, Pierre said, "This settlement was called Castaways because its people were survivors of ships that foundered in the river. They stayed, even though it was against the law in those days."

"Against the law?"

"Englishmen were not supposed to settle among the French, but to go farther upriver. The castaways stayed here anyway. They had seen enough of ships and death. Their village lasted almost two centuries."

"But the Armitages were English," I said, "and they had the biggest house on the river."

"Oh, they claim to be more English than the Queen. But most Armitage wives have been French."

I glanced at a metal sign, a warning to passers-by to be careful with fires and matches.

"Thalia," said Pierre, "you will soon see a very ugly but interesting place. We will call it the Sawdust Desert. Does the name please you?"

"I don't know. I've never seen a desert."

But now she saw one. We emerged from forest into open space, barren ground, some of it a peculiar greenish blue, scarred by potholes and small craters. It was sterile land where not even the warmth and showers of spring had been able to coax forth life.

"You are looking at sawdust," said Pierre. "Miles of it, left by sawmills that once were here."

"May I step on it?"

"Surely. It has become as firm as earth." His eyes, hard and dark, scanned the wasteland. "This was once beautiful forest. A crime. Such things are better controlled now."

"My stepfather owns this, doesn't he?" asked Thalia. "I heard him talk about his fortune in sawdust."

"Ah, so small rabbits have long ears!" Pierre chuckled. "*Oui.* He owns much of this and most of Castaways."

"Morgan inherited all this?"

Pierre's smile was ironic. "Not inherited. It was bought for him with his own money, purchased by his guardian, François, before Morgan had control of things." He glanced ahead. "And here is our city of specters."

A forlorn collection of tumbledown shacks lay before us. Time and weather had sent roofs crashing down on rotted floors, marauders had carried away doors and window frames, leaving openings in the few remaining walls that gaped like wounds.

"No one lives here?" Thalia whispered, as though the ghosts of Castaways would resent disturbance.

"Only a watchman, a man named Gilles who has worked for Morgan for many years."

"And has a horse named Horse," I said grimly.

"Yes, that is Gilles."

We crossed a weed-grown open space that was once a village square and saw the single building that remained intact. Intact but unfinished, for the stone structure was solid below but had only steel girders showing the plan for a second floor.

"That was to have been François Armitage's headquarters and publishing center. Here he intended to print his magazine for an independent Québec."

"Here in the middle of wilderness? He must have been mad," I remarked.

"Eccentric, yes. He enjoyed the irony of building in a village that hard times had forced the English to abandon. The idea amused him."

"Utterly mad," I repeated. "Everything about François Armitage seems insane."

"You will not insult him." Lachance's voice was cool but dangerous. "He did foolish things, but also he bought me clothing when I was a child in rags, he gave me my first skates, my first skis. He paid money so I could go to school." Pierre turned away from me and I could not see his face. "In life I repaid him badly. In death I can at least defend his memory."

"We see the man differently," I answered. "There's no reason for us to speak of him again."

"No reason at all." He whistled for Viking, who trotted to his side. "Now let us enjoy our picnic."

But the day had been spoiled. During lunch and throughout the long walk to the Rising, Pierre Lachance remained withdrawn and sometimes almost hostile. For Thalia's sake, he attempted to conceal this, answering bird calls with uncanny imitations, pointing out game crossings and describing a salt lick. At such moments he assumed the role of the classic Canadian *coureau de bois,* the strong, uncomplicated man of the great woods and rivers.

In most ways the role fitted him, but I knew Pierre Lachance was far from being uncomplicated. My remark about François had struck some deep chord, aroused deep self-reproaches. But as he absently patted Viking, eyes far away, I saw an expression that I understood because it sprang from an emotion we shared. It was a look of loneliness.

I was still thinking of this later that evening in my room as I tried to concentrate on a novel, distracted by my confused feelings.

Firm footfalls sounded in the corridor, then a knock. "Who is it?"

"Le Capitaine Pierre Lachance et ami."

"Come in."

He and Viking were hardly inside the room before he was giving me another curt order. "Lock your door in the future. Anyone could have entered. And no, do not argue with me again."

"This is a most unexpected visit," I said.

"I am not visiting you. Viking is. Sleep well, but behind a locked door, *s'il vous plaît."* Then he left, releasing the catch of the lock and trying the door after he was outside.

Rising from my chair, I stared from the locked door to Viking, who gave me an amber-eyed look of sympathy and friendship. It was after ten o'clock. Could Pierre intend to leave the dog here all night? Viking, who appeared to read my mind, answered by trotting to the foot of the bed and lying on the floor, tail wagging, perfectly at home.

"So you've taken possession," I said.

Thump, thump went the tail.

"Well, I hope you're a quiet sleeper."

Yawning contentedly, he closed his eyes. The long pointed ears lay back softly, an expression of peaceful lassitude. There could be no evicting him even if I wanted to, and although his presence seemed strange and unaccustomed, he conveyed a sense of comfort and companionship I had never expected.

"Why are you here? Are you supposed to be protecting me? You and the locked door?"

He gave a deep sigh that might have been dutiful.

"Well, you're welcome if you behave yourself. But it's quite unnecessary."

When I knelt to pet him, still unsure of myself, he promptly rolled over on his back, became suddenly ungainly and clownish.

"So you want to be scratched!" I exclaimed. "You're just a big baby after all. You may look fierce, but I know better."

"Rrrum," said Viking, squirming with pleasure.

"I don't think you'll be much use to me, but I admit you're lovable, despite all those teeth."

Viking waved a happy paw, seeming to indicate that it was much better to be loved than used, and I agreed.

But when I thought of the uneasy hours I had spent last night, knowing Madame Jeanette was in the house, her dark clothing blending with the darkness of the corridors, I decided that Viking might have his uses after all.

The dog stayed with me the next night and again the third, brought by Pierre rather late and leaving by himself early in the morning, signaling me with a polite scratch at the door. Pierre, for his own reasons, and nothing to the others about Viking's presence in the Captain's Country, nor did I, not wishing to answer the inevitable question, "Why a guard dog?"

The third night I smiled as I prepared for bed, thinking what a bluff Viking really was, a puppy in grown-up disguise. He dozed contentedly, paying no attention although a shutter banged in the rising wind.

Pushing back the draperies to hook the loose shutter, I gazed out at a troubled night. Dark clouds edged in silver moonlight scudded and tumbled before the wind. The radiance of the moon flickered, dimmed in cloud banks, then shone brilliantly again. My eyes traveled from the flashing surface of the river, its waters swirling before the gale, to the cliff edge, then to the lawns of River Rising.

A figure moved along the drive, coming from the gates toward the porte cochère, a hunched woman swathed in black. For a second I had the unlikely thought that one of the nuns had, for some emergency reason, come from the Abbey. With the uncertain moonlight and the height of my window, I could discern no details, only the movement of the dark figure that was somehow familiar to me.

Then I realized I was watching Madame Jeanette, and instinctively drew back from the window, not wanting to be seen, although I could not explain why. After all, she, not I, was the intruder at this late hour. I glanced at my watch, remembering Dorothy's words about a strange and special ritual at midnight. It was not yet twelve, but soon would be, and this was Friday, the night Dorothy called the most favorable.

So she had come again to read the future. Read the future for a woman who hardly had a present, a grim thought, but not as disturbing as the picture of Madame Jeanette lighting candles, chanting incantations and casting spells.

Tomorrow I would have to speak to Regina about this. If she allowed Madame Jeanette to enter freely at all hours, it was not my affair, but at least Regina should know. I looked out the window again, but the figure had vanished.

The day, devoted to another long hike and a picnic, had exhausted me and I soon slept, hardly aware of the heightened anger of the storm, hearing yet not really hearing the long peals of thunder, the slash of rain against the walls. The violence of the night, a natural and expected clamor, did not disturb me, but I sat bolt upright, completely awake, when Viking uttered a loud, menacing growl.

Switching on the bedside lamp, I saw that the dog had moved near the corridor doorway and stood slightly crouched like a poised leopard, ears alert and nostrils quivering.

Any thought of his being a playful puppy vanished as I stared in alarm at the bared fangs, the bristling coat. No intruder could have entered that door and survived the attack sure to follow.

Getting out of my bed, I called, "Who is it? Is someone there?"

No answer came, but I heard a different sound and felt a rush of cold air across my bare feet. From the adjoining nursery there sounded a harsh persistent creak of metal, the loud complaint of unoiled hinges. The door to the Captain's Walk, I realized, must have blown open. Blown open? Or had someone entered the nursery and now lurked in its darkness? But that seemed impossible; no one could climb over the roof or down the sheer wall of the attic.

I shivered, my feet chilled by the icy draft, then quickly put on slippers and a negligee too thin for the cold night but the first garment I could reach.

"Come, Viking," I whispered, and the dog, after a second of hesitation and a suspicious snarl at the corridor, came to my side and moved with me toward the nursery, his growls fainter but none the less threatening.

"Is anyone there?" I called again, and still no answer came, only the roll of thunder and the whine of the wind in the eaves. As I opened the nursery door I almost expected Viking to charge past me in furious attack, but he did not leave my side.

I flicked the wall switch to the right of the door, but the nursery remained dark, the single overhead lamp unresponsive. I did not really need more light, enough spilled through the doorway from my bedroom to give a pale illumination. The ancient figurehead stared at me fixedly, the wood features expressionless, a drowned woman propped up stiffly and grotesquely. Nothing moved in the shadows except the door at the top of the stairs.

I paused, knowing that the door had to be closed and locked, yet reluctant to enter the gloom of the narrow stairwell.

Go lock that door, I ordered myself, and stop these childish jitters.

I moved ahead, but on the first stair riser, encountered a difficulty. Viking would neither lead nor follow, but insisted on remaining at my side, his hard shoulder bone pressing against my thigh, forcing me to the wall.

"Either go ahead or go back!" I said, but the dog ignored me and growled more savagely as, crowded together, we went up step by step.

My hand had just touched the doorknob when I heard the voice, a faint, thin whisper in the darkness outside. "Rochelle, help me! Ro-chelle!"

It seemed both near and distant, only a whisper yet strangely piercing. Holding the door tightly, ready to slam it at the first sign of danger, I listened, every nerve tingling.

But Viking was calmer now, wary, but his growling was stilled.

Again the voice spoke, "Help, Ro-chelle . . . Oh, please, Ro-chelle . . ."

Thalia, I thought, suddenly close to panic. This was her way of saying my name, breaking the syllables. Somehow Thalia had climbed to the roof and was trapped among the steep, slippery gables. Injured, I thought wildly, as my name was whispered faintly again.

"Ro-chelle . . . Ro-chelle . . . Help me . . . Please, Ro-chelle . . ."

I drew courage from Viking's sturdy assurance. If anyone except a friend should be on the Captain's Walk, the dog would have caught the scent. The voice did not alarm him at all.

"Thalia?" I said and stepped outside, Viking still close to me.

The wind caught my loose hair, blowing it across my eyes, and I brushed it back, now aware that the force of the gale was far greater than I had thought.

I took a few cautious steps forward, bracing myself against the parapet. "Thalia? Where are you?"

My voice was lost in the wind, but the whispered reply came at once. "Ro-chelle, help me . . . Ro-chelle . . ."

Viking tensed, seemed uncertain. The moonlight, almost obscured by thunderheads, remained bright enough for me to see the sharp outlines of the roof and to know that the Captain's Walk was deserted.

Then I whirled in alarm at a sharp banging sound behind me and found myself staring at the door I had left open and which was now shut. Rushing toward it, I seized the knob, twisted and pushed with all my weight, but it did not yield. The stairway door was locked; the dog and I were trapped on the exposed Captain's Walk.

"Thalia!" I shouted. "Where are you?"

Fighting the heavy gusts of wind and flinging out an arm as if it could ward off the icy raindrops, I struggled along the Walk toward its far end. The voice seemed to come from that direction, yet how could I be sure? The maddening whisper had no certain source and now, as I heard it once more, it sounded less like Thalia.

"Here, here . . . Oh, Ro-chelle . . ."

It had become inhuman, the bodiless, hollow tone of a specter, such a voice as I had always imagined a phantom would have, and I forced myself not to think of Lady Judith. Yet, as I fought the gale and tried to control my shivering, her image seemed to float in the impenetrable shadows of the garret eaves, Lady Judith's voice luring me on, enticing me toward . . . what? In terror I looked down at the planks of the Captain's Walk, fearing they might abruptly end, that I would step off into nothingness to plunge helplessly through the air to death below.

"Ro-chelle . . ."

I wanted to scream in reply, but now I knew I must not answer, some primal instinct telling me that safety might lie in silence.

Viking's muzzle touched my hand gently, but I was not reassured. What was the matter with the dog? Why should the whispering voice, which provoked such fear in me, leave him calm and unfrightened? Was this a voice that I alone could hear? Or were animals deaf to the whisperings of specters?

I stood still, straining to catch the sound of the voice again, to determine its direction, but I heard only the rush of the storm and far away a frantic ringing of bell buoys that marked the river channel, clanging as the mounting waves tossed and tilted them.

For an instant the roof and landscape were illuminated in the flash of pale lightning, and in that split second I saw the ladder ahead of me.

It leaned against the face of a gable at the point where the parapet turned, the end of the Captain's Walk, and when lightning flashed again, I realized the ladder reached to the sill of a high garret window, the very summit of River Rising. Now I moved more quickly, knowing that the Walk would not end, no concealed hazard lay ahead. It was an ordinary household ladder, aluminum, light but strong, the rungs cold and wet to my tentative touch.

Wind tugged at my thin clothing and another slash of rain swept over the roof, rattling on the slates. My teeth chattered with cold and my shoulders trembled. It would be the folly of a madman to attempt to climb the ladder in the darkness and in the face of the storm, yet it tempted me. The window above had neither bars nor shutters. If closed, I could easily break the glass with my slipper.

An escape from a night of cold imprisonment on the roof, the only hope of avoiding perhaps hours of exposure to the storm. Climbing the ladder began to seem less difficult, less dangerous than I had first thought. Enticed, I rested my hand on a rung, gazing upward longingly. Only ten steps, not so very high.

"Ro-chelle . . ."

Stifling a cry of fear, I drew back, snatching my hand away as though the metal rung had been white-hot. A trap, an enticement, I thought dimly, my senses muddled and numb.

Suddenly Viking, quietly watchful until now, broke into frenzy. Barking wildly, he leaped at the ladder, struggled to climb. Falling back, he threw himself against the wall, nails clawing the sheer sides as though he could scramble to the garret window, where he would slash to pieces whatever was hidden above. Again he fell back, and this time his heavy, hard-muscled body struck the ladder with tremendous force. It lifted upright, teetered, then plunged backward, sliding over the parapet to plummet through the air. Thunder drowned the crash of its striking.

Galvanized by Viking's action, I ran back to the stairway door and beat on the panel. "Help! Help!"

I knew my shouts were useless, that no one could hear, yet I cried out until I was hoarse and at last my voice failed.

Huddling behind the parapet, I sheltered myself as best I could, painful with cold, yet no longer terrified now that Viking had become protective again. Somehow I knew that my name would not be whispered once more, that the unknown voice was now stilled.

Viking's barks changed to long howls of frustration, but I hardly heard him as my senses seemed to fade. An unfamiliar half-sleep of exhaustion and futility settled over me, and I did not feel alarm when twice lightning flashed down the cables from the rooftop rods, bathing the Rising in crackling, unearthly light.

I had left my watch on the bedside table and could not tell, nor did I care, how many hours passed, knowing only that it seemed an eternity. The rain pelted me and the wind struck like a whip.

Then a sound . . . an opening door? And a flood of light.

"Poupée? Alors, mon enfant!"

Vaguely I realized that Tante Emma, flashlight in hand, stood in the open doorway. The beam struck my face, and I tried to answer, but no sound came.

She stepped toward me, but Viking leaped between us, challenging her, daring her to move an inch closer to me.

I tried to say "Awaken Captain Lachance," not sure that the strangled rasp of my voice was audible. Then I drifted into a pleasant dream, puzzled that my bed was so hard and cold, wondering why the roof leaked so badly. In the midst of the rain, stars of enormous brilliance shone, dazzling me, sometimes appearing in the sky, sometimes only behind my eyelids. Had Tante Emma actually spoken to me a moment ago? I was not sure, but it did not matter. Nothing mattered.

Then Pierre Lachance was beside me, speaking my name, lifting me in his arms. Tante Emma shouted something. What was it? "I will carry her. Let me take her."

"Non."

I felt the warmth and softness of my own bed, I felt protection, but I wished the people in the room would go away. Their angry voices confused me, their words were jumbled, but a man, I thought Pierre, spoke clearly.

"A devil has done this."

As darkness enveloped me it seemed that Lady Judith stood beside the bed, mocking me with her painted smile.

Fever dreams, fantastic and meaningless, assailed me. People came and went from my room, I was given an injection by a doctor, a young man with a dark beard, who said, "Exposure and shock." He asked me something, and perhaps I answered.

Daylight faded and returned again, and I knew that Pierre, Thalia, Eunice and Regina often sat near my bed, but they were ghosts of themselves, as unreal as the haunting voice that forever called me. "Ro-chelle . . . Ro-chelle . . ."

During one interval of darkness I thought Deirdre visited me. She stood near the wardrobe, trying on my dresses, rejecting them one by one, tossing them carelessly on the floor.

"Stop it, Deirdre," I said, and she vanished, laughing.

Then I slept deeply, and awoke with sudden and complete clarity. I saw Regina sitting in the rocker, her tapering fingers moving rapidly as she crocheted with yellow wool.

"Good morning," I said, my voice hoarse. "Is it morning?"

"Sunday afternoon," she answered. "So you're awake at last." Coming to the bed, she sat on its edge. Her face looked worn and tired, but the fine features were smiling. "How are you, my dear? Better?"

"I'm all right," I answered. "A bit weak."

"Food is what you need now. You have been very stubborn about refusing broth."

"Really? I don't remember."

Regina turned the switch of a small electric kettle on the bedside table. "Hot consommé in a moment. I thought you'd

awake this afternoon. The doctor from the village said the
sedatives would wear off about now."

"How did Tante Emma happen to . . . ?" Speaking was a
struggle, my throat still raw from an hour of shouting on the
roof.

"Happen to find you?" Regina finished my question. "Because of a nightmare. She kept dreaming of a howling dog,
to her a sure sign of death, and awakened herself with fright.
Then she realized the dog was real, and decided to drive the
animal away. Finally she discovered where the sound came
from."

Regina poured the consommé into a cup. "She found you
in the nick of time, too. The doctor said you barely escaped
pneumonia."

The broth tasted delicious and strengthening. Regina re-
filled my cup, then said, "I didn't realize you were such a
dog fancier."

I nodded, but attempted no answer.

"Also, I'm surprised Pierre would let Viking stay with
you. He never lets that dog out of his sight. But then,
Pierre is not quite himself these days."

I gave her an inquiring look.

"He's tense, for one thing. And I suspect he has told me
a lie, which is unusual for him. He cares so little what anyone
thinks, that truth comes out naturally. But I don't believe
his house is rented. That was a pretext to stay at the Rising
for a while." Regina frowned, perplexed. "If it were another
man, I'd know it was an excuse to be near my beautiful niece.
But you're not the type of girl Pierre usually pursues—or
should I say the type who pursues Pierre? Besides, moving in
would be a peculiar way of courting."

Regina rose. "I'll leave you now, Rochelle. We both need
rest. Tante Emma will look in later and you'll have early
supper on a tray." She started to go, then turned back. "Today the telephone was working for a change. Theresa
called from the Abbey. She said you are not to worry about
anything, she has you up her sleeve."

"Her sleeve?"

"In Benedictine jargon that means she had been praying
for you."

"How very kind."

"Theresa has no monopoly on communication with the

Almighty," said Regina, with a slight toss of her silver hair. "I spoke with Him myself soon after we found you."

She left quickly, a slight blush on her cheeks.

I was grateful she had not asked me how I had come to be trapped on the Captain's Walk. I did not yet have the strength to talk about the voice that lured me outside, did not want to think about it. Later, I told myself. Later.

Yet, as sleep returned, one memory of my nightmare hours on the roof stirrred, the blurred image of Pierre's face as he bent over me, lifted me. For a moment his mask of hardness had fallen away, I had glimpsed gentleness. A strange man, I thought. Would he always remain unknowable?

There was nothing gentle about the knock that awakened me a few hours later. Rubbing sleep from my eyes, I called, "Come in," expecting Tante Emma.

Pierre entered, Viking at his side. "I have brought your supper. Tante Emma is furious with me."

He carried a silver tray draped with a frilly cloth and adorned with sprigs of lilac. Pierre Lachance in his heavy boots, rough-woven shirt and leather vest was incongruous as a waiter, and the effeminately decorated tray did not help matters.

When I smiled my chapped lips hurt and I was suddenly aware they were smeared with ointment. So were my cheeks and eyelids. As for my reddened hands, I slipped them quietly under the covers.

"Oui," he said pleasantly. "You look dreadful, but what is one to expect? Besides, I have seen you worse than this— remember, I was on the Captain's Walk."

He set the tray on the table beside me, drew the rocking chair close and sat down uncomfortably, too large for the small piece of furniture. Viking rested his muzzle on the bed, inspecting me sympathetically.

"Eat first. Then tell me exactly why you were so foolish as to be on the Captain's Walk in a storm."

"Foolish? I'm not so stupid as to—" I hated the way my voice croaked, and did not appreciate his chuckle.

"Like a bullfrog," he said. "You may sound better after eating."

Happily, Tante Emma did not believing in starving an invalid. She had prepared a rich coq au vin and tender new peas. At the end of the meal I felt amazingly stronger.

I told the story, beginning from the time when I saw the figure I believed to be Madame Jeanette. Talking was not so difficult if I spoke softly.

When I had finished, he shook his head. "It is wrong. You say that Viking did not bark when you heard this voice. Such a thing is impossible."

"Then the impossible happened," I replied. "I'm not sure how many times the voice called my name, perhaps a dozen. Viking paid no attention."

"The dog always barks," Pierre repeated stubbornly, giving me a doubting glance. "It is not logical. Viking knows Tante Emma well, but in the circumstances of the night, he would not let her approach you."

"Are you suggesting that I imagined the voice?"

He hesitated, then said, "Could it not have been a trick of the wind? A noise caused by the storm?"

"No, I heard every word. Plainly."

He shrugged. *"Alors,* we must accept it."

"You don't believe me," I told him, suddenly weary of thinking and explaining. "I won't try to convince you, but I heard what I heard."

"You are tired," he said softly. "We will talk no more for the present." When he rose to leave, Viking moved promptly to him.

"Thank you for bringing my supper."

"Ah, but I am a poor waiter. I am forgetting the tray." Standing at the bedside table, he suddenly smiled and his dark eyes held a twinkle of mischief. "One last question, Rochelle, than I leave you to rest. Who is this Scotsman you pine for? I did not know you had a lover."

"Scotsman? What do you mean?"

"Perhaps not a Scotsman, but his name is Sandy."

"I don't know anyone—"

"Denials are futile. In your dreams, when you were feverish, his name was often on your lips. You called for him."

"So it is discovered," I said, shifting my head on the pillows. "Sandy slept with me every night for almost two years." I was pleased to see Pierre's surprise and then his frown.

"You are frank. Forgive me, I did not mean to pry."

"Sandy was a rag doll I had when I was a child. His full name was Sandy-Pandy, so he must have been Australian, not Scottish."

Pierre smiled. *"Bien.* You are not so exhausted tonight, you are able to tease me with games." Then he became serious again. "I am going downstairs now. Everyone will be in the dining room, and I intend to tell them all you have said —the voice, the ladder, *tout."*

"They'll think I'm insane."

"That does not matter. Telling everything will halt any further mischief for a time at least. Unfortunately, that is all that can be done now. I think nothing will happen soon, it is unlikely. *Bonne nuit, Rochelle."*

He left, seeming confident that all was well. But when Viking tried to follow, he commanded the dog to stay with me, and I noticed he was careful to test the door from the outside to make sure it had locked behind him.

9

I endured three days of bed rest, more than I thought necessary but the minimum Regina, Tante Emma and the village doctor would allow. Regina tried to limit visitors, and it became apparent she had given orders that no one was to remind me of my experience on the Captain's Walk. In this, she was not universally obeyed.

The first violator was Thalia, who sat gravely at my side a long time before taking my hand and whispering, "Thank you, Rochelle."

"For what, Thalia?"

"Captain Lachance said you thought I was calling you. You went out in the storm because of me. Thank you for answering."

I saw tears form in her eyes, and said quickly, "When you call for help, Thalia, someone always answers."

She shook her head. "No, not always." Then she brushed her lips against my cheek and quickly left the room.

Eunice, who came bearing a stack of old fashion magazines, made no direct reference to what had happened, but kept giving me such doubtful glances that I was compelled to ask her point-blank if she thought I heard imaginary voices.

"Oh, no, my dear!" she replied, flushed and embarrassed. "It was some trick of the wind. Or perhaps crows were nesting in the eaves. Sometimes crows sound very human, don't you agree?"

"Yes. Especially crows that have been trained to talk."

"What a clever explanation," she said, smiling uncertainly. "I'd never considered that possibility."

"Nor have I."

She left then, but not before one final, scrutinizing stare had confirmed her opinion that I was subject to fits of hysteria.

One person, at least, believed everything I had told and was sure of the explanation, although I learned this by accident.

Tante Emma brought lunch to my room on the third day, puffing from having mounted the stairs too rapidly.

"Such a lot of extra work I'm causing you," I said. "If Aunt Regina insists on my being a prisoner, at least the maid should carry the trays. How is Angélique, by the way?"

When Tante Emma grunted disapproval and avoided replying, my suspicions were aroused.

"Is she still working at the Rising?"

"She is an ignorant bumpkin," Tante Emma growled.

"I asked if she is still working here."

"*Zut.* She chipped a Wedgwood plate and I think she stole soap to take home to her family, although her parents are animals who never bathe themselves."

"Tante Emma, tell me the truth. Angélique has gone, hasn't she? I want to know why."

"She thought you heard the voice of Lady Judith," Tante Emma admitted reluctantly. "She was afraid the ghost would harm her, although I explained that no ghost would bother with a person of her class. But the stupid child gave up wages twice as high as anywhere else. *Et alors?* She will be happier at home guarding the pigpen."

Lady Judith. Now, more than ever, she seemed a living and avenging presence at River Rising. Tante Emma could sneer at Angélique, but there was a tremor of uncertainty, even fear in her tone. I, too, might scoff at the possibility of a phantom enticing me onto the Captain's Walk, yet at times my instincts seemed more trustworthy than logic.

For I *had* believed in Lady Judith that night. Easy to deny that truth in daylight, but in darkness I was not so certain.

I could imagine spectral power slamming the stairway door behind me, a spectral summons leading me on. And the whispering voice, human yet not human, coming from everywhere yet nowhere.

The placing of the aluminum ladder, an act I somehow

could not assign to spirits, had been explained by Madame
Sud. The housekeeper had hired an itinerant workman who
sometimes passed through the village to check the roofs in
case slates had been loosened by winter snows. He had forgotten the ladder, she was sure.

Madame Sud, I learned from Tante Emma, denied that
Madame Jeanette had been in the house. She herself had
taken a late stroll and was returning to the Rising wearing
her dark shawl at the very time I claimed to have seen the
village witch.

"A stroll on a stormy night?" I scoffed, but there was no
way to refute her, and it was possible I had been mistaken.
Everyone seemed to think so.

During those days of rest I pondered what had happened on the Captain's Walk, but no explanation, short of
Lady Judith, made sense.

Morgan called that afternoon, and although he was a sympathetic listener, I did not enjoy the ordeal of repeating my
story to still another man who questioned every detail.

"I suppose you think my imagination was running riot," I
said at last. "Pierre Lachance suspects that. He insists that
Viking would have barked at anyone on the roof. In fact," I
added bitterly, "he has a good deal more faith in the dog
than in me."

Frowning, Morgan rose from the chair and moved to the
window. "It's peculiar," he said after a long hesitation. "The
dog is a superbly trained guard. Lachance has won prizes
with him." There was another pause, then Morgan gave a
dry, humorless laugh. "Of course, there is one person Viking
would ignore."

"Who?"

Morgan turned toward me. "Lachance himself, of course."

My eyes widened. Obviously Morgan was right, but this
possibility had never occurred to me. "Are you suggesting that—?"

He interrupted. "I'm not suggesting anything, I'm merely
wondering. You find the idea intolerable?"

I looked away. "Why should I?"

"Because you and Lachance have become close friends in a
remarkably short time." He returned to the bedside chair.
I still avoided his eyes. "Rochelle, what do you really know
about this man?"

"Very little. What can you tell me?"

"I'm not going to be the village gossip," he answered, scowling.

"You brought up the subject," I replied, challenging him. "If there's something I should know, it's only fair to tell me."

I thought he would say no more, then he shrugged his shoulders. "Very well. I suppose you know that Madame Jeanette was his mother-in-law. But do you know where she lives now?"

"No."

"On an abandoned farm near the bottom of the firebreak. It's Lachance's house; it belonged to his family."

"Perhaps he'd find it awkward to evict her," I said.

"I daresay." Morgan's voice was grim. "Still, one can't ignore the connection, especially when Lachance has suddenly become so protective about you." Morgan's palm struck his thigh in anger. "A dog that barks at *everyone?* Not quite! Not at his own master."

Morgan was again on his feet, talking rapidly but quietly. "What's the use? You won't listen. Lachance has a way with women, they'll believe anything he tells them. The romantic, swashbuckling captain!"

"Perhaps you underestimate me," I told him.

"I don't underestimate Pierre Lachance." He paused, lifting his hands in a gesture of helplessness. "I sound like a jealous rival, don't I? Well, perhaps that's the way I feel, Rochelle, and if it weren't for Dorothy . . ."

"But there *is* Dorothy," I said quickly. "Your wife can hardly be forgotten."

Again that wry, rueful smile. "If you were a different type of woman, I'd say Dorothy could be forgotten easily. But you're not. I'm married, I couldn't offer you anything now." He sat on the edge of the bed, close to me, too close. "Yet we both know that Dorothy will not recover, that it's only a matter of a short time. So why shouldn't we talk?"

"I think any talk must wait," I said. "I can't listen to this, not with Dorothy here, ill. It's impossible, ghoulish."

"Not ghoulish. Practical," he said, rising. "But I can wait. Meanwhile, you'll hear no more talk like this from me." His expression and his voice softened. "Whether you feel anything toward me or not, be careful with Pierre Lachance, Rochelle. He fascinates women, but he's ruthless. I always felt sorry for the girls he became involved with." Morgan's eyes met mine, a long, steady gaze. "I'd hate to feel sorry for you, Rochelle."

He left then, but the memory of what he had said, the suspicion he had aroused, haunted me that night as I lay alone in the Captain's Country, listening to the whispering wind, doubts and questions pacing like captives in my mind.

On the morning after my enforced convalescence, I arrived late for breakfast on the sun porch and saw one result of the maid's frightened departure from River Rising. Chafing dishes and warmers stood on the sideboard; we were to serve ourselves. Tante Emma and Madame Sud were busy with other tasks.

Since I was unaccustomed to servants, I looked upon them as a luxury. Now it struck me that a château like River Rising simply could not operate without a staff unless the Armitage way of life changed completely and we all became cleaners, scrubbers and polishers in an inconvenient house. Angélique's loss was no less than a blow.

After breakfast I went to Regina's rooms to say good morning, but halted outside her open door when I heard her voice raised in anger.

". . . And I am telling you, Morgan, that I will brook no argument. Howard Palmer moves out of Chimney House today and the sooner the better."

"Howard has always had use of the place when he wanted it."

"Yes, and he has wanted it much too frequently," she retorted. "There are comfortable rooms in the house. He can use one."

"These servants you're importing from Montréal also have a choice of twenty rooms here. It's unpardonable to push an old friend of the family around this way," said Morgan with considerable heat.

"Not a friend of the family, a friend of *yours*. And please do not repeat again that tale of his heroism in saving your life in Egypt. I am bored with the story, bored with Mr. Palmer, and more to the point, I promised the Carltons a separate house of their own. They are coming to work here on that condition."

Morgan had no intention of yielding easily. "River Rising belongs to you, of course, but I certainly pay my share."

"Yes. And that is not what we are discussing."

I left quickly then, not from lack of curiosity but for fear that Morgan might storm out of the room at any moment and find me eavesdropping.

In the entrance hall I met the subject of the controversy, Palmer himself, whose beaming face revealed he had no hint of his coming eviction.

"You're looking marvelous, Rochelle," he said. "Completely recovered, eh? By the way, do you know if Captain Lachance is here?"

"I haven't seen him this morning."

"I'm buying a brace of hounds from this watchman who works for Morgan."

"Gilles?"

"Yes, that's the fellow. They're supposed to be splendid hunters, but they're dubious-looking brutes with no pedigrees."

"Like dog, like master," I said.

A puzzled expression crossed his rather puffy features, then he said, "I don't want trouble between these hounds and Lechance's dog, so I'll talk with the captain. Of course, I'll keep my dogs down at Chimney House."

No, you won't, I thought, and escaped him to go outside. I found myself in full agreement with Regina that Palmer was a bore whose air of benign affability quickly palled. My eavesdropping had solved one small puzzle. I now knew that Howard Palmer had a claim of gratitude upon Morgan, something about saving his life, and this seemed to explain the man's prolonged visits to the Rising.

It crossed my mind that perhaps a good deal of solitary drinking was taking place at Chimney House. Palmer's face was heavier, becoming jowly; the nose was too red and his military mustache needed trimming. Despite expensive tweeds, he had a seedy air.

Unconsciously I had strolled in the direction of the studio, and now, realizing that Morgan was occupied, decided this was my chance to inspect the porch and cliff again. The scene would no longer frighten me—it was not the place of my father's death but of his survival.

A moment later I mounted the porch, went to the wire barrier and looked down—to find myself gasping. Nothing but sheer, empty space separated the porch from the rock-slashed foam, no projecting rock or stunted tree, nothing to catch a falling man, nothing he could seize to break his fall.

I turned from the appalling drop-off. Something must have changed during the years, or else, concealed from me below the porch floor, there were beams and girders a man might cling to.

Just as I was thinking this, the metal door of the studio opened. Madame Sud and I faced each other, both of us surprised.

She recovered more quickly than I, and inclining her head slightly, said, "Ma'm'selle has lost her way, perhaps?"

"That would be difficult a hundred yards from the house," I answered. "The view interested me."

"*Sans doute*. For you, a place of great significance."

Her tone was wooden, expressionless, yet the remark was calculated to inflict the maximum pain possible. But instead, it aroused my anger. "Madame Sud, I have done you no injury. Yet you make it clear that you hate me."

The flat gaze met mine without flinching. "Why would I not hate you? I am only a servant, but I came to the Rising when François was only eleven years old. He was like a son to me. You are your father's daughter, that is reason enough."

"I pity you, Madame Sud. Such hatred will harm only yourself."

"Who will be harmed remains yet to be learned." She moved a step closer to me, then halted when I failed to yield ground.

"Are you threatening me, madame?"

"I am predicting that your blood will tell, that you will meet an unlucky end. You heard the reading of the cards."

"I am not bothered by such nonsense."

Nothing in her face was alive except the tiny black pupils of her lidded eyes, and they throbbed with malevolence. "Madame Dorothy is a dying woman. The dying are given special insights into what is to come. I was at River Rising before you were born, and I shall still be here when your life is over."

Then the duel of our locked eyes ended as she glanced over my shoulder in surprise.

"Good morning," said Morgan, coming onto the porch. "My studio is a popular place today."

"I have finished cleaning, m'sieur. All is in order."

Turning away, she reached inside the studio door, retrieved a broom, mop and pail.

Avoiding Morgan's eyes, I gazed across the river, trying to compose myself and to conceal the emotions Madame Sud had aroused.

"I'd offer to show you the studio," said Morgan, "but there's nothing in it now. After the burglary I moved everything to a safer place."

When I did not reply, he said, "I assume you've just had an unpleasant scene."

" 'Vicious' would be a better word."

"I'm sorry. She's an old servant and we're rather helpless to control her." He shook his head. "Well, Rochelle, you can't say I didn't warn you."

"Yes, you warned me."

And so had Madame Sud. The battle lines were drawn, and I could only wonder from what quarter the next attack would come.

In the days that followed I seemed to have braced myself for nothing. On the surface, life at the Rising began to flow as smoothly and evenly as the great river below us. But, also like the river, the house concealed deeper crosscurrents following their own hidden channels.

Regina and I were absorbed in preparations for the St. John the Baptist celebration. An elderly seamstress arrived, sent by a city agency, and was soon installed on the second floor, her machine humming as she created fancy-dress costumes which Regina had designed.

"Everyone, including the servants, is to appear in seventeenth- or eighteenth-century costumes. French, English or Canadian," Regina had announced at dinner.

Eunice clapped her hands like a child. "I want to be a Versailles lady disguised as a shepherdess."

Regina gave her a doubtful look.

Mr. and Mrs. Carlton, now occupying Chimney House, were such marvels at handling domestic chores that even Madame Sud was tolerant of them. Joseph Carlton was tall and bony, with an equine face. His wife, Marjory, seemed to match. Courteous and capable, they answered all of Regina's hopes. "If only they stay!" she remarked, looking heavenward imploringly.

Pierre took Thalia and me on another picnic, a completely happy occasion this time, and then for a long ride on the lake in a birchbark canoe he himself had made. He knew the lore of the forest and streams, stories of trappers and fur traders. Thalia was gradually losing her fear.

Madame Sud and I maintained a polite truce, and there came only one sharp reminder that I had closed my mind, too complacently, to events of the past.

I stood on a low stool in the sewing room, being fitted for my costume, an Evangeline outfit and a closely guarded secret, when Tante Emma rushed in exclaiming that I was wanted on the "instrument," which meant the telephone.

"New York is calling you, *poupée!*"

"Who on earth?" I said, and hurried downstairs.

The telephone crackled and buzzed while Tante Emma hovered a yard away. "If it is an admirer of yours, invite him to our celebration," she urged.

But it proved to be someone else's admirer, not mine.

"Rochelle, this is Brad Copeland in New York. Do you have any news of Deirdre?"

My heart sank. "No, I've heard nothing."

"I suppose I knew that, since you didn't call me," he said, sounding disappointed but not surprised. "I had to give up, to leave it to the police. Be sure you call me if you hear anything or even think of any possibility."

"I will, Brad. Meanwhile, we'll keep hoping."

"Thanks. Hope has become a little difficult."

For hours after Brad's call, thoughts of Deirdre dominated my mind and would not leave, although I knew that worrying was futile. I had retraced the same steps so many times that there was nothing more to be remembered, nothing new to learn. The police, I kept assuring myself, would soon find her, no doubt as well and as happy as Deirdre ever could be.

During those busy days there was little time for reflection, much less for brooding. Regina, a born executive, seemed to be everywhere at once, directing and organizing, planning menus, bargaining with caterers and cleaners from the city.

"She's burning hay as if the whole year were harvest," Tante Emma remarked, then had to explain that "hay" meant money to a Québecois.

Often we spoke of the forthcoming party as Midsummer Eve, but the same night was the eve of the great feast of St. John the Baptist, patron of the province, and the saint was the real cause for our celebration.

On the morning of June twenty-third, a few hours before

guests were expected, Regina inspected me as critically as if
she were a Paris *couturière* preparing for an international
show. "The Evangeline outfit is perfect," she declared.

"I hadn't realized Evangeline was the wealthiest girl in
Canada," I said. The full, ruffled skirt could indeed have
passed for homespun flax, but its richness and holiday effect
came from a dazzling rainbow of embroidery.

"Another thing," I remarked, "if Evangeline had been this
decollete, she would have been chased out of Grand Pre."
The neckline of the peasant blouse that no peasant could
have afforded plunged almost dangerously close to the top
of the laced bodice.

"Perfect," she repeated. "And the lace cap is like gossamer,
but push it back a bit. We don't want to hide your hair."

"You know, Aunt Regina, this is a party, not an exhibition."

"All parties are exhibitions. Never forget it! Didn't Charlotte teach you anything? Don't bother answering, I know
she didn't." Then Regina gave me a quick hug. "Forgive my
fussing. I want to show off my niece."

I changed into a modern beige and white suit, also Regina's design, in time to greet the first guests who were arriving for a garden-party luncheon. After Regina introduced
me to a dozen friends, I realized that one fear I had suppressed was groundless.

No one ogled me as the daughter of Jean-Paul Dumont,
even though everyone had surely heard about the famous
case, including guests too young to remember it themselves.

Several people spoke warmly of my mother, with no implications or questions. Then, during luncheon, a surprise
came.

I had not caught the name of the man seated on my right,
and our conversation had been only chat about the traditions
of St. John the Baptist. Then, smiling, he leaned toward me.
"I must tell you that your father and I were classmates and
great friends years ago. It is a pleasure to learn that his
daughter is charming. I would expect it."

I managed not to gasp. I had heard so much from my
father's critics and enemies, it never occurred to me that he
had even one friend.

"Thank you," I murmured. "You're very kind." At the
same time I silently thanked Regina, who had tactfully arranged this seating.

More guests arrived and soon the garden bubbled with holiday talk and laughter. Regina performed more introductions, and soon I had lost track of which name fitted which person in this curiously assorted group whose ages ranged from twenty to seventy-odd.

"Look over there," said Regina, lowering her voice. "The blonde with too much mascara is Sonia Kerr from Montréal. In wild pursuit of Pierre, as usual."

Sonia Kerr, svelte in a black sheath, talked animatedly with Pierre, tossing her golden head to make sure the sun caught its luster.

"She's standing so close, you couldn't put a knife between them," muttered Regina. "I never cared for that girl."

"Then why did you invite her?"

"So Pierre could bask in some feminine admiration for a change." She gave me a look which I ignored.

That evening, gay in our fancy-dress costumes and harlequin masks, we drove in a motor caravan to the village where a pageant was to be staged by torchlight. Afterwards we would return to the Rising for dancing and supper.

Julien Clouet, a young surgeon from Beauport who appointed himself my escort, seemed much too serious to be wearing the striped doublet and hose of a court dandy.

"I am not the type for costumes," he said. "But later, with enough cariboo inside me, I promise to be festive."

"Cariboo?"

"You do not know it? A mixture of red wine and white alcohol. Regina is sure to serve cariboo. It is the world's most delicious dynamite." He struggled to arrange his floppy lace collar. "Captain Lachance avoided the costume problem very cleverly. He is wearing buckskins, a style not changed in two centuries."

"I haven't seen him," I said, lying for no reason I could understand. "He seems occupied elsewhere." I thought of Sonia Kerr with a twinge of annoyance that I denied was jealousy.

The village pageant celebrated the founding of Ste. Marie du Lac and was performed with such gusto that I suspected the cariboo Julien Clouet had described was already flowing freely somewhere behind the makeshift stage. Almost everyone in the applauding crowd wore antique costumes, and even those in modern dress had donned the traditional Québecois red sash.

A bystander handed Julien a tall white cane and gave him an inviting nod.

"A wonderful cane, a miracle worker," Julien said. "Observe, I pull off the top and it becomes a four-foot drinking flask. *A votre sante!*" He lifted the cane to his lips and took a long swallow. *"C'est magnifique! Merci!"*

I shook my head when he offered me a drink. "I'll wait for the champagne at the Rising, thanks."

The cariboo seemed to have instant effect. He put his arm around my waist and sighed contentedly. "A beautiful night, a beautiful girl, a beautiful place. I am glad my father's plans did not succeed. Otherwise, I would not be here at this party."

"Your father's plans?"

"He is in the hotel business. Last year he and his partners tried to buy River Rising for a hotel."

"Isn't it too remote?"

"Not at all. The house would need much remodeling, but think of the view and of those slopes behind it! Perfect for skiers. Stacks of hay could be made here."

This time I knew what "hay" was. "Regina refused?"

He chuckled. "She ordered them out, and told them it was vulgar to discuss her home in such terms. A formidable lady!"

We laughed together as the formidable lady herself, stunning in a gold brocade dress that might have come from the court of the Sun King, moved regally through the crowd, her silver hair piled high like a perfectly powdered wig and crowned with a nest of jeweled larks.

"Several persons here lost fortunes because of that lady's refusal to sell," Julien said.

"How? I don't follow you."

"The land behind the Rising, the slopes and hills, are of little value now. But combined with the main house and gardens as a winter resort their worth would go up five times, maybe ten times."

"You mean Morgan's land?"

"Mostly Morgan's. But Madame Eunice Armitage owns land, too, and the older servants at River Rising have been given small pieces. Then there is the worthless Lachance farm, not so worthless if my father's plans had worked."

"Owned by Captain Lachance?"

"Yes, it belonged to his family."

I realized there must have been bitter resentment of Regina's stand against selling, yet no one had ever shown a trace of such feelings. It was typical of River Rising, I thought. Matters there were seldom what they appeared to be.

When we returned to the château, the sprawling building twinkled with candles and lanterns, an enchanted world. I was now delighted that Regina had not allowed me to be too demure an Evangeline, for I loved the flash of my skirt and the fire of the ruby pendant she had lent me.

In the ballroom, a buckskin-clad Pierre Lachance saluted me, Sonia Kerr still clinging to his arm. She wore the scanty garment of some Canadian dryad with scarlet maple leaves in her hair.

The small orchestra alternated folk tunes, to which we improvised steps, with more modern music, and I found myself whirled away first by Julien Clouet, then captured by a swarthy pirate afloat on cariboo. Morgan, transformed into a husky peasant in a Breton smock, rescued me.

Since the arrival of the first guests, Morgan had been the social lion of the party, the celebrated painter everyone wished to claim as an acquaintance. He was far too accustomed to adulation to let his pleasure in it show, but I had no doubt now that Morgan loved his own fame.

"Enjoying yourself?" he asked.

"Yes. I've never imagined a party like it. The Rising is beautiful tonight, the way it should always be."

My words must have tempted fate, for just as I spoke the ballroom doors banged shut, a hundred candles flickered in a sudden gust of wind, some of their flames vanishing, leaving behind wisps of smoke quickly carried away by the draft.

"I like this better," said Morgan, smiling. "Dim and romantic."

As the music quickened, he spun me away and I felt my skirt flare like a Spanish dancer's. Then, when I whirled back, Pierre Lachance had moved between us, was taking me in his arms.

"Permit me, Morgan. I must have this dance because it is the only one I know."

We had moved across the floor before Morgan had a chance to reply. "What caused this?" I asked. "Did Miss Kerr sprain an ankle?"

"Who cares what Miss Kerr sprains? At one time I found her fascinating, but now she seems insipid. Come, we are leaving here."

"Leaving? I certainly am not. I've just begun dancing."

"This is important. For once, believe me without an argument, please."

The urgency of his tone silenced me, and still pretending to dance we passed through the ballroom doors which two waiters, disguised as footmen, were now propping open. A moment later we hurried up the stairs.

"We have an experiment to perform," he said in a low voice. "I think I have been stupid. Now we shall find out."

"I don't understand. What . . . ?"

"Quickly! The wind is rising now, but if it dies, we must wait for it. Days could pass."

When we reached my room, he said, "Now go through the nursery and up the stairs to the Captain's Walk. Open the door and leave it open, but do not go outside."

I did as he asked, but felt gooseflesh rise on my arms as I mounted the steep stairway. When I opened the door at the top, the creaking hinges were a terrible reminder, and I was happy to move down a few steps and wait.

Outside the wind whistled, not so strong as on that other night but powerful enough to bang shutters and rattle windows. I waited, not knowing what to expect but suddenly apprehensive. Then I felt a rush of air that tugged my skirt, and the door in front of me slammed shut violently, striking with enough force to lock itself, even though I had left it off the latch.

I was still staring at it, unbelieving, when Pierre hurried up the stairs. He had removed the harlequin mask, and his face glowed with triumph.

"Again I have the right to call myself a sailing master," he said. "I do know something about winds and air currents, after all."

"How did you do it? The door was hardly moving at all, and then—"

"Not difficult, Rochelle, if one learns the secret, and the effect, you will agree, seems almost supernatural. I had only to open a second door, the one from your room to the corridor, and *voilà!* An updraft, a current of air strong enough to slam the door. Also, to lock it. The safety catch on the lock is old and worn. Or perhaps it has been loosened." He hesitated, his look of victory becoming grim. "Someone knows this little trick of drafts and doors, knows it and has put it to use."

"But I locked the door to the corridor earlier that evening," I protested.

Pierre gave a shrug of dismissal. "So our mischief-maker has a key. You told me that Viking raised an alarm at the door to the corridor."

"An alarm? I think he wanted to chew it off the hinges."

Taking my hand, Pierre led me through the nursery into my room. "Sit down, Rochelle. Do you understand now? Do you see what may have happened?"

I nodded slowly, not really accepting my own words as I spoke. "You think someone opened the door to the Captain's Walk, knowing the noise of the hinges would make me go to close it. Then he went to the corridor outside my room and . . ." I stopped, frowning. "No, there wasn't time. Whoever did it would have to scramble over the roof or climb that ladder, then find a way to my door."

He shook his dark head. "Then think of two mischief-makers, Rochelle, two working together. We do not know their names, so we will call them Rooftop and Corridor. They must have a way of signaling each other. Once Rooftop lures you onto the Captain's Walk, a sign is given and Corridor unlocks your door to create the draft. Then you are trapped outside."

"But why?" I demanded, shuddering at the memory of those hours of torment. "Who could hate me enough to do such a thing? Madame Sud might, and so would Madame Jeanette. But playing this trick was complicated. And what could anyone gain by locking me out? It was pointless and mad."

Pierre walked the length of the room and back, seeming undecided between speech and silence. Then he drew his chair close to mine. When at last he spoke, it was quietly. "As you say, this trick was mad. Yet perhaps not so pointless. I think the mischief-makers are very real, and I think they failed. The great harm intended for you did not take place."

I swallowed drily. "Great harm?" I asked. Blurring the truth with soft words was futile. "Do you mean someone intended my death?"

"Who can answer that?" he said slowly. "But you must at least suspect that was the plan, even though it alarms you. Then you will be watchful, you will be on guard."

His voice compelled belief, and for a moment I felt he was right. It was logical—he had shown how the stairway door could be manipulated and explained Viking's frantic barking at the corridor entrance. Yes, it could have taken place as he said, yet there was no evidence that it actually had. More important, my mind and emotions rebelled at the notion that at least two people hated me deeply enough to go to the lengths Pierre had described. He was talking about murder, and I refused to accept this.

Pierre leaned back in his chair and shrugged. "So you think I am mistaken, overly alarmed. I read this in your face."

I averted my eyes. "There is simply no reason for anyone to do me serious harm. Someone might want to make me uncomfortable enough to drive me away from River Rising, of course. But beyond that—"

"*Tabernac!* Must you be blind and stubborn? What if Regina decided to change her will? She is fond of you, she is rich. That would be a serious loss to Morgan and Eunice." His lips twisted in a saturnine smile. "And a loss to me, of course." He saw my blink of surprise. "She has said I am to have a small legacy. Maybe you endanger it, maybe it is worth protecting."

"That's ridiculous," I said. "Regina has no intention of giving me anything at the expense of people she has known and loved for years."

"You are quite sure of that, Rochelle? Certain that you do not stand between me and a fortune?"

He regarded me with cool amusement, and I could not tell where mockery stopped and seriousness began. Nor could I deny that he had planted a seed in my mind that might grow into a jungle of suspicions about everyone at River Rising.

"I expect nothing from Regina," I said, "and she's a long way from dying." I rose, wanting to shake off the doubts he had caused in me. "Maybe someone worked my entrapment on the Captain's Walk,' as you said. But it remains only a cruel trick, not a great danger. And there's still no explanation for the most frightening thing of all, that voice calling my name."

"I do not understand that," he admitted, "and I do not

understand Viking's behavior. But one thing is certain, we are changing the locks on both of those doors."

"I think that's wise."

"Wise?" He stepped toward me, a look of angry frustration on the taut gypsy-brown face. "Not to do so would be madness. Will you not understand that nothing more serious happened on the Captain's Walk because you were armed?"

"Armed? But I wasn't!"

"You had a powerful and unexpected weapon. Viking. No one knew he would be with you, and no man can stand against him except with a gun. But using a gun would spoil the effect of the accident that was planned for you that night. Rochelle, remember that ladder!"

"I never would have climbed it."

"It was not there for you to climb. The ladder was for someone else to descend."

For a moment I imagined myself on the Captain's Walk, alone in the darkness without Viking. I pictured a shape, a figure climbing quickly and silently down from the attic window, a shape moving toward me, the hands lifting, reaching out. It was unbearable.

"No," I said, "No." Faintly I heard the music of the orchestra. My voice trembled slightly as I said, "Should we go back to the party?"

"I am not sure," he answered. "In the ballroom are too many masks, too many strangers."

"That's ridiculous." I fluffed out the Evangeline skirt and brushed back my hair. "I intend to enjoy myself."

He stood between me and the doorway, his towering frame an impassable barrier. "I see I must protect you from your own rashness."

"And how will you do that?" I demanded.

Reaching out, he drew me close to him. "You will be with me every moment."

"And what will your friend Sonia say to that?"

"What does it matter? With Sonia, I was doing what one calls comparison shopping. I have decided not to buy. Come along, Rochelle. Tonight I will be your only danger."

I looked up at his hard, weathered features, the fullness of the firm mouth. The embrace brought a flush to my cheeks, yet I did not want to move, to draw away from him. And feeling the response of my blood, I knew Pierre was right, that I was certainly in danger, though perhaps not the kind of danger he had described.

The next day I proved little help to Regina in the task of directing the temporary servants as they packed away party decorations and returned the house to order.

Pierre's demonstration of how my entrapment on the roof might have been accomplished occupied my thoughts, and at times his word "mischief-makers" whirled in my mind. While trying to concentrate on other things, memories and suspicions of Madame Jeanette distracted me. More than ever I felt sure it was she and no other I had seen from the window that night. Madame Sud had said that the witch had not been inside River Rising then, but Dorothy, I decided, might tell the truth. I had to find out, and a little before noon I tapped on Dorothy's door.

"Come in, Madame Sud," she called.

"Not Madame Sud," I said, entering. "This is a busy day for her, but I suppose she'll be here a little later."

Dorothy sat propped against the white pillows, a writing board in her lap. I was shocked to see how wasted her features had become the hollowness of her face grotesquely emphasized by the luster of the blond wig she wore today. Only its dead tresses seemed healthy and alive.

I took the chair beside the bed. "Forgive me for not visiting you earlier," I said. "I was told that callers tire you."

"Some of them do," she answered with surprising sharpness. "Excuse me, I'm just finishing an important letter."

She added another line to the paper on the writing board, signed her name boldly, then folded the single sheet to fit into an envelope which lay beside her. She addressed it in a slightly shaky hand to Mr. Howard Palmer.

"I want Howard to see me today," she said. "I need his help. You, of course, know why."

"I'm afraid not."

"Oh, I think you do." Her expression was sly, feline. "They are planning to send me away."

"Who is?"

"Morgan, Regina . . . all of them," she said vaguely.

A glass of water and a bottle of yellow capsules stood on the bedside table. I wondered what the drug might be and how much she had taken, for although she spoke clearly, her eyes wandered the room, seemed not to focus. She stared in my direction, yet looked through me to something beyond.

"If you're sent away, it will be to a sanatorium for your own good," I said. "You need more care than you can be given here."

"You'd like to see me gone, it would give you a free hand with Morgan." When I ignored both her words and the malice in her voice, she went on, "I heard you met with an unfortunate experience on the roof."

"Yes." I decided to try a rather obvious trap. "It happened the night you had your special fortune told, the night Madame Jeanette called on you."

"I remember. She said it would be an unlucky night for you. Her dead daughter's spirit was here that night and spoke to Madame Jeanette through the tarot cards. She asked for vengeance."

"Vengeance on me?"

"Of course." Dorothy leaned forward so abruptly that the writing board slipped from the bed, falling to the floor at my feet. "You don't really believe in the ghosts of River Rising, do you, Rochelle? How absurd of you! The only reason Regina invited you here was because of the ghosts. She was afraid, she needed help."

"Tell me about it, Dorothy," I said softly. The airless room was stale with the scent of dead flowers and burned incense. Dorothy's voice fell to a whispered chant.

"Justine, Monique, Céleste. They were servants who left here because of the ghosts. Regina was faced with closing River Rising, and Morgan begged her to sell the house, but she still refused. How they battled about it! I could hear them shouting." Dorothy's whisper became almost inaudible. "If she sold the Rising, Morgan would be rich. His land, all the slopes toward Castaways . . . Pierre Lachance would be rich, too. He owns a farm there."

The thin voice trailed into silence. I remembered my conversation the night before with Julien Clouet, the young man from Beauport. I had paid no close attention when he talked about the value of the Rising and the land below it as a resort. Now I realized that a fortune was involved, and for the first time felt I understood the tension between Morgan and Regina.

Dorothy sensed what I was thinking. "At times Morgan and Regina hate each other, but I don't believe they realize it." Beneath the blanket she stirred impatiently. "Last year Regina saw herself for what she is. A helpless, lonely old woman. And frightened. What if Morgan had gone away and persuaded Madame Sud to leave? He could, you know. There would have been only Regina and Eunice and Tante Emma. Three old women alone in this house! Then she learned where you were. The long-lost niece."

When Dorothy ceased speaking, I prompted her. "So she invited me to River Rising."

"She thought you would change things. She talked about having a young person here, a member of the family. Always the family! Armitage pride. That's why she'll forgive Morgan anything, he brings fame to the family." She pressed gaunt hands against the yellow wig, struggling to concentrate. "Everyone knows Regina has promised you a fortune if you'll stay here. She needs you to lean on. But it won't succeed. River Rising will destroy you just as it destroyed your father." Dorothy lay back against the pillows, eyelids fluttering. "I'm tired, I want to be left alone. Will you take my letter to Howard?"

"Of course."

"Howard could make Morgan change his mind about sending me away to a hospital. Howard has great influence on Morgan." She must have seen my expression of disbelief, for she said, "You think Howard isn't important, don't you? How little you know, Rochelle. How very little!"

When I left, my feeling of pity was almost unbearable. Not just pity for Dorothy, but for Morgan and, above all, for Thalia.

Howard Palmer now had rooms somewhere on the second floor of the west wing, an area of the house not familiar to me. As I mounted the stairs on my way to deliver Dorothy's letter, I considered what I had just learned.

Madame Jeanette had been at the Rising on the night of the storm and I had not been mistaken. She might well have been making mischief, seeking the mad revenge Dorothy talked about. But Dorothy herself had no active role in any malicious trick played on me. She was too ill, too weak. Her talk of witchcraft and spirits could be disconcerting, but Dorothy was long past taking part in events at the Rising. She did not matter; Madame Jeanette did.

The second-floor corridor was deserted, and I hesitated, not sure which of the dozen doors led to Howard's rooms.

One door stood half open, and as I moved toward it, I heard voices.

Although I had no intention of eavesdropping, Howard Palmer's tone and words were so surprising that I stood silently listening.

"You're a fool, Morgan," he was saying. "Every day she stays here adds to the danger."

"I know. But what more can I do?"

"Stop being weak and indecisive!"

"I wonder if I can stand more of this?" said Morgan.

"You'll have to. I tell you she has to be taken care of before it's too late. Taken care of properly."

It seemed impossible that the speaker was Howard Palmer. His voice had a ring of command, almost contempt, while Morgan sounded defeated and submissive. So Dorothy was right, I thought. They were discussing a plan to send her away.

I must have taken an unconscious step backward, for a floorboard creaked loudly, and there was instant silence inside the room.

"Hello," I called quickly. "It's Rochelle."

The door ahead of me was flung wide. Howard Palmer, face white and shoulders tense, confronted me. Behind him, across the room, stood Morgan.

"I have a letter from Dorothy," I said, confused by his manner, awkward at having been caught listening. "I'm sorry. I couldn't help overhearing you."

"Yes?" Palmer's face was set, masklike.

"This letter is about what you were just saying," I told him. "Dorothy knows she is going to be sent away. I just came from her room."

"Really? Come in, my dear."

Palmer stepped aside and I moved past him. He had undergone an instant change of personality, had suddenly reverted to the genial, deferential man he always seemed. But Morgan, upset, stared at me blankly.

Palmer closed the door carefully. Turning, I handed him the envelope, which he took without speaking. The silence made me uneasy, and I gathered that Morgan felt embarrassed, even angry, at having been surprised in a moment of weakness.

"You're quite right about Dorothy's needing proper care,"

I said to Howard. "It's not my affair, but I was startled when I saw her."

For a moment neither man spoke, then Palmer nodded slowly. "I'm glad you agree. I was talking sternly to Morgan about the matter."

"I should go to Dorothy," said Morgan, and left quickly without glancing in my direction.

Palmer consulted his watch. "And you and I, my dear, are late for lunch. May I escort you?" He offered his arm with mock formality, and I had no choice but to take it. As I touched him, thinking how swiftly his whole manner could alter, I felt I was touching a chameleon.

Dorothy's words lingered with me. *"How little you know, Rochelle."* She was right. And of the people at River Rising the one I knew least was Howard Palmer.

10

———

I sat in a parlor at Clarendon Abbey, looking through the grille into the tranquil face of Dame Theresa Armitage.

At River Rising the interval of quiet had continued; Pierre's mischief-makers, if they really existed, remained invisible and inactive. But for me, although I had appeared outwardly calm, there had been little peace. Thoughts of two men created havoc with my feelings.

First, there was Pierre, whose effect upon me I could no longer deny. I at last admitted to myself that I longed to be near him, to see him, to hear his quietly firm voice. Yet when we were actually together, I found myself in turmoil, alarmed by the realization that he was fast acquiring the power to change my life, to reset its course if he chose.

No man had ever aroused such deep longings in me, and I felt myself walking the edge of a precipice. My mind told me that this attraction I felt, I would not call it love, drew me only toward unhappiness. Pierre was attracted to me, and perhaps, as a novelty, would enjoy an affair with a woman as inexperienced as I was in such matters. He could have his adventure and go his way, as he had done with so many others. I would be left lonely and wounded. Yet this is what I drifted toward. Drifting, I told myself, drifting as I had always done.

And there was more to be afraid of in this strange man. He himself had told me that I was as much a financial threat to him as I was to the others at the Rising. He had done nothing to conceal his wish to have me gone at the beginning.

Perhaps his recent concern for my welfare merely covered that old hostility to me, to Deirdre—wherever she now was.

Then there was my father, always present in the portrait which I still kept hidden. Now the secret of his escape and survival had become too much for me to contain. I had to talk to someone, to pour out the doubts that assailed me, so I had come to the Abbey.

"Aunt Theresa, this parlor is like a confessional, isn't it?" I asked haltingly. "I mean, things discussed here are private."

"Yes, things said in the parlors are privileged and secret," she answered. "But, dear child, even if they were not, I trust you would rely on me. You can, you know."

This, of course, was true. I felt I could trust her not only for silence but for wisdom as well.

"Jean-Paul Dumont did not die, as the authorities believed," I began, the words tumbling out. And as I told her the story, the bars between us seemed to vanish.

". . . So you see, Aunt Theresa," I said, nearing the end, "I cannot accept my father in the role of murderer. He was too kind, too gentle. I'll never rest until I know the truth."

Dame Theresa Armitage studied me thoughtfully. For a moment she bowed her head, then raised it, her features, framed by the white wimple and black veil, radiating the strength I needed.

"Are you searching for the truth," she asked, "or merely for the confirming of an illusion you cherish?"

The question took me by surprise. "Why, the truth. There isn't any illusion. I *knew* my father."

"Rochelle, you are very young. You have not had time to witness the miracle of conversion."

"Conversion? I don't understand."

Reaching through the grille, she took my hands in hers. "You must face facts. Jean-Paul, in his youth, was a violent man and often he could not control himself, especially when he had been drinking. He could be cruel even to Charlotte."

I tried to protest, but she silenced me. "Believe me. Your mother herself told me, sitting where you sit now. She forgave him because she knew he could never forgive himself. Often Jean-Paul did not realize what he was doing, did not even remember afterwards. He was sorry for what he sometimes did, truly sorry.

"To take the life of another human being is a fearful act.

Is it not possible that after François's death, remorse changed your father? That he became a different man?"

"People don't change that much," I said without great confidence. "For instance, my father never touched liquor, not even a glass of wine."

"That is precisely what I mean, Rochelle. Suffering altered his life. I assure you he drank in Ste. Marie du Lac. It happens that I was an eyewitness."

I glanced at her in surprise.

"Yes." She smiled faintly. "I know nothing about what happened on the night François was killed. At that time I was too ill to know anything. But I must tell you of something else that happened that summer. I avoided this matter when you visited me before, because it involves things which should be discussed only within the Abbey, in the Chapter or with the Lady Abbess.

"You see, it is the story of a nun who did not have enough strength . . ."

She had lived at the Abbey four and a half years, she told me, and the time for her Solemn Profession, her vows to remain for life, was rapidly approaching.

"I looked forward to that day with happiness that was mystical. Far too mystical, I realize now. Such fervor is unreliable, it gives a dangerous, shaky foundation."

Her troubles began quietly when she realized that the date was August thirteenth, her birthday. "In childhood I was always given elaborate presents and a party with cake and candles. The foolish notion of being a 'birthday girl' had somehow never quite left me, although I didn't know this. At the Abbey the day passed unnoticed, of course, and I felt neglected. Nothing serious, but it was the start of what we call 'monsoons,' a violent wind that shakes your emotions and won't stop blowing."

That night she was unable to sleep, unable to pray. The Abbey, which she had loved, became a prison. The next day brought no relief, and when evening came she was frantic, yet unable to speak of her suffering, unable to seek help.

"It was late and I should have been sleeping. Instead, I slipped out to pace in the garden." Memories of the outside world swept over her, tidal waves of loneliness that carried her almost unconsciously to a small postern at the rear of the garden. "Then I was outside and running, I can't remember stopping for breath, although I must have done so several times. The experience was like a dream, River Rising just ahead, standing tall in the moonlight. I thought, If only I can reach it, I will be well again."

As she entered the garden, the spell suddenly broke. "It was like coming out of a trance. I was horrified, I couldn't imagine why I had done what I had done. Completely bewildered. I started to turn back. It was then I saw your father. There used to be a long wooden bench. Is it still in the garden?"

"No," I said.

"Your father was lying on it. I recognized him at once, of course, and my position was dreadful, utterly mortifying. I would have fled as fast as I could, but he called out your mother's name. I thought he must be ill, so I went closer and spoke to him."

Already I saw the end of the story. "But he wasn't ill, after all," I said.

"No." Dame Theresa hesitated. "In charity we should call him ill. He seemed to be half awake, yet not really conscious. It seemed wrong to leave him there. Clouds were gathering, rain was going to come. I shook Jean-Paul's shoulder, but couldn't arouse him, even though he spoke your mother's name again. Oh, what a preposterous situation it was!" She paused, and a note of ironic humor came into her voice. "You might say I was saved by the bell. It was the eve of Assumption Day, and at that moment Mary Major, the huge bell here, rang for midnight to proclaim the feast. That bell was a command telling me where my duty lay. I started back to the Abbey, and a few minutes later rain began to pour, a rain like ice. I came down with pneumonia and I'm surprised Jean-Paul didn't. Perhaps the rain awakened him."

"You never saw him again?" I asked.

"No. I was ill for several months and couldn't return from the hospital in Québec City until almost Christmas. By then Charlotte had left, François was dead. It was all over."

"Not quite all over," I reminded her. "My father was very much alive." Unwillingly, I added, "A changed man, as you said. I have to recognize that. Aunt Theresa, should I tell the truth? Should I make it known that he survived?"

The nun hesitated, her face grave. "You raise a question of conscience, Rochelle. Duty does not require you to tell all you know merely for the sake of telling. And you might injure three men who, I begin to suspect, turned out to be very loyal friends to your mother and father."

"What men? I don't understand."

She leaned toward me. "Morgan, of course, and Morgan's friend, whose name I do not remember. Then there is Captain Lachance."

"But how should my speaking injure them?"

"They were the witnesses to your father's plunge to the river. I remember those cliffs at the Rising, and only a miracle could have saved Jean-Paul." She sat straight in her chair, lips now drawn in an ironic curve. "Naturally, I believe in miracles, they are part of my faith. But this particular miracle arouses my skepticism. Let me be the devil's advocate for a moment. Either Jean-Paul took wings and flew to the south shore, or three men lied to cover his escape. Which do you find easier to believe?"

Just then there came a sharp knock at the narrow door behind Dame Theresa. Turning in surprise, she called, *"Deo gratias."*

A frightened girl in the dress of a novice stepped in quickly. "Benedicite," she gasped. "Oh, Dame, forgive me, but you must come at once. The Lady Abbess is suddenly very ill and is calling your name."

"Mother is worse?" Dame Theresa's cheeks paled. "I'll come at once."

There was a carved stone bench outside the main portal of the Abbey, and pausing there, I considered my interrupted conversation with Dame Theresa.

Little as I liked admitting it, Jean-Paul Dumont had been no saint. I had to accept the nun's suggestion that his character had been changed by the horror he felt at his own crime, and I remembered Dame Theresa's words, "Your mother forgave him because she knew he could never forgive himself."

Dame Theresa, in her wisdom, had probably discerned the truth, a truth that reconciled wild young Jean-Paul Dumont with the gentle Paul LaFarge that I remembered.

Also, she had instantly seen the most reasonable explanation for my father's miraculous escape. Morgan, Pierre and Howard Palmer had all lied, all helped Jean-Paul escape.

The conversations of the last weeks suddenly took on new

irony. All three of them had known my father survived, and now I knew it, too. We all pretended to each other, although the four of us were part of the same conspiracy.

I heard the sound of a motor, and looking up, saw Pierre's jeep approaching, Viking sitting proudly upright in the rear seat behind his master.

Pierre halted near the bench. *"Bonjour!"* he called. "You had a long walk to get here. I thought you might prefer to ride back."

"Thank you," I said, taking the seat beside him, delighted he had thought of me, yet disturbed by something in his expression. I had a premonition that matters between us were going to be made clear, and I was not at all prepared.

"You are too quiet," he said after we had driven a few minutes. "What troubles you? Some words of Dame Theresa?"

I nodded. "Partly that. Tell me, Pierre, can a man's character change completely?"

"How many times?" he asked lightly.

"Please, I'm serious."

"So am I." He drove more slowly, and as he spoke I sensed that his almost jaunty manner was a mask for the depth of his feelings. "As a boy I was the village roughneck, the priest and the schoolteacher pointed me out as gallows-bait. Then I changed, or at least I changed for several years."

We were in the village now, and he stopped speaking. "You passed the turn to the Rising," I said.

"I know. We will go somewhere else first."

"Where?"

"Chez Pierre Lachance. I want you to see my house, my bit of land."

"I'd love to, but I think Aunt Regina is expecting me to be . . ." I felt and sounded like a schoolgirl, a very immature schoolgirl. Worse, I knew it.

"Your protest is too feeble and too cliché. I will ignore it." He glanced away from the road and for an instant his eyes seemed to bore through me. "This is difficult enough for me. Do not make things worse by being childish."

"Childish! I must say—"

"Ave Maria! Have you no emotions but anger and argument? Be quiet. Enjoy the scenery."

We crossed the covered bridge, drove a mile or two toward the river, then turned sharply left onto a side road hidden by birches. Ahead I saw another bridge, a small one of logs, spanning a narrow stream, and when we reached it he halted the jeep.

"Look upstream. That is my waterfall, not Niagara, but my own."

The water, only a few feet wide, cascaded to white foam over the darkness of granite boulders, then swirled in eddies below the bridge where willow fronds brushed the surface.

"There's a rainbow at the falls," I exclaimed.

"Yes, almost always, a small rainbow." He turned off the ignition key. "We will pause here. The house is just beyond." Turning in the seat, he gave Viking a quick command and the dog leaped to the ground, trotted across the bridge to vanish where the road turned among the trees.

"When Madame Gallet sees Viking, she will know I am coming soon and coffee will be ready."

"Madame Gallet is your housekeeper?"

"What else?" he asked, his expression elaborately innocent. Then we both fell silent again.

"You asked if a man changes," he said quietly after a moment. "When I fell in love with Giselle Massine, I must have been a different man, even though I was still a boy, only seventeen years old. Only seventeen . . ." He shook his head unbelievingly, as though what had happened to him was beyond comprehension.

"I knew she belonged to François Armitage, that she would marry him on her eighteenth birthday. I hated François and I hated myself for feeling as I did. He was good to me, I owed him much. Yet I repaid his kindness by secretly taking part of what was his."

"Did she love him?" I asked.

Pierre shrugged. "She loved the dream of the château, of being the wife of an important man. Does it matter whether she loved the man or loved the dream? They came to the same thing." He spoke softly, but the knuckles of his brown hands showed white as he gripped the steering wheel.

"It was a summer of agony. The joy of Giselle's kisses at night, then my guilt when I saw François. When he was killed I thought the guilt had ended, but it had only begun. Now I blamed myself for being pleased by his death, happy that my rival was gone and Giselle could belong only to me. *Mon dieu,* what a childish illusion! François was dead, but Giselle's dream did not die with him."

"Yet she married you," I said.

"Only when other ambitions had failed. Twice she left me, once for a man who promised to make her a film star and then with another man, rich, a prominent banker. I am not sure what his promises were, probably marriage. I endured this, I took her back when these hopes turned to smoke. But nothing I could do was enough, and in the end . . ." He did not need to finish. I knew the end.

Pierre turned his gaze full upon me, a small vein in his left temple throbbed, yet his features were the same unyielding flint I knew too well. "Does a man change? Would you not say that I have changed since then?"

"You were a boy, you were—"

"A boy at the beginning, very much a man at the end. When I look back I cannot recognize myself as the fool who wept openly at Giselle's funeral in the suicides' field."

Looking at his set face, I found no words for a moment, then I said what I felt deeply. "The fool you talk of, the young man who wept . . . I like him, and I'm sorry he has vanished. I wish we could meet one day."

He looked away from me, then nodded. "I wish so, too. It would be better if he, not I, were here with you today."

He started the jeep and drove ahead.

Pierre's house, built of sand-colored stone and heavy timbers, stood on a shelf of land above the broad river. The site was not the awesome command post of the heights at River Rising, for here the St. Lawrence and its north shore seemed at peace with each other, even as the comfortable house seemed at peace with the forest.

Madame Gallet, middle-aged and motherly, greeted me with a certain air of surprise that made me think young women were infrequent visitors here. If *Le Capitaine,* as Madame Gallet called him, had as many affairs as gossip claimed, they must be conducted away from home.

The living room, where she served us coffee and hearty slices of fresh-baked bread and butter, held the fragrance of pine smoke, and I liked the leathery comfort of the barrel chairs facing the hearth.

One wall was given over to shelves lined with books and displaying several hand-carved models of clipper ships. This was a man's room, yet it did not assert its maleness.

"I built part of the house myself," he told me. "Now I

wish I had built all of it. There is pleasure in living with what one has made for one's self."

"Your tenants keep it in beautiful condition," I said with a smile.

"Very good condition," he agreed, lifting an eyebrow.

After Madame Gallet had excused herself, Pierre said, "You must forgive me the scene at the bridge. I did not intend that your first visit here would have such a prelude. Usually I keep a firmer control of myself."

"Perhaps too much control is not wise."

He smiled at my remark. "Good advice, Rochelle. I give it back to you."

I ignored this and went on quickly. "Also, I think you brood too much about the past."

"More good advice. This time doubly returnable. With you, the past is an obsession that leaves you little time for the present."

"At River Rising the present and the past are always hand in hand." I put down my coffee cup, trusting him, despite myself, appealing to him. "Pierre, tell me about that night."

"The night François died? There is little to tell. I had been in the village. I walked back to the Rising very late. I lived there then, François had given me a room. There was some moonlight, but I carried my electric torch because I was near the cliff edge. I heard a terrible shout and a crash of wood. When I looked toward the studio porch, I saw Jean-Paul falling."

"How could you be sure?"

"Because I saw the flash of his yellow raincoat, a special coat for walking at night on the road. It reflected light, and there was no other like it in the village." He studied me, puzzled. "I do not understand. I speak of your father's death and it does not sadden you. Instead, you look relieved, even happy."

"I'm glad he didn't suffer."

Pierre accepted this without comment and his look was doubtful.

I could not explain yet that he had lifted a burden by telling the truth—for I believed him. I believed he had seen a falling raincoat, perhaps with something inside it, but nothing more. He had played no part in the scheme to help my father escape, and the truth, if it became known, could

not harm. Pierre. Only two witnesses left, Morgan and Howard Palmer. I knew, and accepted, that I was grateful that
Pierre might be eliminated.

"By the way," he said, "I have thought of another explanation for your entrapment on the Captain's Walk. I do
not believe it is the true one, but it remains possible."

"What is it?"

"The whole thing was the work of ghosts," he said, sar-
donic. "Ghosts who are bored with the Armitage family and
wish to see River Rising sold as a resort. They achieved
some success that night. After all, Angélique left."

"The maid? What can she have to do with it?"

"How do you make the Rising uninhabitable without actually burning it down? Quite simply. You frighten away the
servants and living there becomes impossible." He shrugged,
minimizing the matter.

And who would profit from such a situation? Several people, including Pierre himself. I pushed the notion from me; I
had to trust him.

"Come," he said, rising. "I will show you how a back-
woodsman lives."

I saw the cool, shadowy springhouse and looked at the
whirling windmill. The kitchen, where Madame Gallet pre-
sided, was a gleam of copper and brass, and in a storeroom
I inspected snowshoes, skates and skis.

"A beautiful house!" I exclaimed.

"At least it is the house I always wanted," he said. "I was
able to buy the land a few years ago, thanks to Regina."

"Regina?"

"I worked hard, I saved money, but it was Regina who
knew how to invest it. I owe her great gratitude."

As we were leaving to return to the Rising, Pierre was
called to the telephone. I could not hear the conversation
except Pierre's frequent explosions of provincial profanity.
He emerged from the rear of the house scowling, a very sub-
dued Viking trailing behind.

"*Sacrebleu! L'Etoile Filante!* Will I never be free of that
floating carnival? If Captain McCabe's pleurisy is to continue
until the ice sets in, he should find someone besides me to
take his place. *Ave Maria!*"

His boot heels slammed on the planks of the porch.

"Can't you refuse?" I asked.

"Not easily. Arthur McCabe is an old friend. He gave me my first command."

Viking, with a flying leap, took his accustomed place in the jeep. Getting in, I said, "It's a pity you feel that way about the ship. In spite of Deirdre, in spite of her leaving so abruptly and rudely, for me it was a beautiful voyage. One I'll always remember."

"It is not the ship but the people." He hesitated, his hand on the ignition key, then smiled. "If you enjoy the voyage so much, why not come with me?"

I froze, unable to say, "Because I am afraid of my own emotions, because you could hurt me deeply." I stared at him questioningly, wondering if he realized how vulnerable I was.

"Why not?" he repeated.

This time it was a challenge. I hesitated only a moment, but in that moment I saw myself with pitiless clarity. I put my suspicions of Pierre behind me with the past, which stretched as empty and trackless as a beach washed by the tide. I had belonged to no one, and no one, even for an hour, had been mine. I had known loneliness and fear, but love was an emotion strange to me.

"How can I go with you?" I said quietly. "You haven't asked me."

"*Chose jugee,*" he said, starting the motor. "It is settled. We start for Montréal at five tomorrow morning."

I felt light-headed, giddy, as though I had just won some magnificent and unexpected prize.

As we crossed the bridge I looked for the rainbow at the falls, but the sun was hidden and I saw only the whirlpool splitting against black rocks. And at that moment the great voice of Mary Major spoke, the solemn first tone of a passing bell, telling Ste. Marie du Lac and the farther villages of the river or forest that the Lady Abbess of Clarendon now rested in death.

11

That week I learned what it must be like to be sixteen years old—and happy.

As the ship skimmed the waters of the St. Lawrence like a giant swan, the winds billowing her royals and gallants seemed to sweep the shadows of River Rising from my mind.

I danced every night, and Pierre, to the utter astonishment of the crew, joined me. At first he remained stiff and formal with the other passengers, but finally yielded to the spirit of the voyage and actually shared their laughter.

On deck I found myself chatting, or perhaps chattering, with complete strangers, boasting of the beauties of Québec as if I had spent my life on this river.

"I've turned into a magpie," I confessed to Pierre, "but I can't help it. I have to make sure everyone realizes how glorious all this is."

He smiled. "It is well. You make me see things for the first time again."

We had one brief quarrel, a skirmish when he discovered me the first day out, dressed in jeans and a striped shirt, trying to climb to the crow's-nest.

"What possessed you?" he demanded.

"The devil," I answered.

"In the future you will keep that devil in his proper place. And another matter"—he stepped closer, glowering—"where did you find that tight shirt? You are distracting the crew. Change it at once before the helmsman steers us against a cliff."

I looked at him coolly, lifting my chin. "This shirt becomes me. I remind you, Captain Lachance, that I am not your private property." Yet only the night before I had felt that I belonged to him, completely, utterly.

His anger abated. "No, you are not my property, so I must let you endanger all our lives."

He took my hand and we stood together at the rail, gazing at the shore when River Rising loomed into view. Neither of us spoke, but a few minutes later he said, "Do you see the flag on shore? There among the trees."

"Yes. A fleur-de-lis."

"That is my house. Look just below—you'll see a patch of water where the stream joins the river. To me this is the most beautiful place in the world, and though it cannot contain me all of the time, much that I love is here."

The *Etoile Filante* skimmed past colorful fishing villages and the cliffs of the Gaspé, where rock and water met in shallows that Pierre said were shoal. We rounded the great cape, scudding into the vast Golfe Saint-Laurent, and speeded by a fresh breeze, made anchor in the ancient port of Gaspé.

That night Pierre said, "There is news from home."

"Home?" For a second I did not know where home was. I had lived so intensely in the present that the *Etoile Filante* seemed my whole world.

"I have talked with Regina on the ship-to-shore telephone. Dame Theresa Armitage has been elected Lady Abbess of Clarendon. You have another distinguished relative."

"The nuns chose wisely, I think. She's a woman of great strength. What else did Regina say?"

"Dorothy Armitage left the Rising yesterday. She has entered a private hospital."

"That's sad news. Or perhaps not, it's hard to judge."

"Not sad. Better for her, better for Morgan and, most important, better for Thalia."

New passengers boarded at Gaspé, and I felt uneasy when I noticed how watchful Pierre became in port, realizing this had also been true in Montréal and Québec City. What did he suspect? Surely there were no enemies here. But then I remembered Deirdre, her life and her disappearance, and I became less certain.

As the ship began her return voyage up the river, I was less interested in the other travelers than I had been when we were outward-bound. Pierre dominated my thoughts, my attention, and I struggled to suppress the knowledge that soon the voyage would end.

That night at supper in Pierre's cabin he said, "You are serious and very far away from me this evening."

"I was dreaming."

"Tell me your dream, Rochelle."

I flushed slightly. "I was wishing that these days would go on forever, that there would never be a harbor. Perhaps even that River Rising and everything connected with it would vanish."

"All voyages end," he told me gravely. "And I would be sad if Regina Armitage disappeared like a mirage. Besides, you know you must return."

I looked away from him, wondering if the inevitable words of farewell might come now.

But he said, "There will be no peace or safety until you are sure about certain matters."

"What do you mean?"

"You must know what happened to Deirdre Cameron."

"Deirdre!" I said sharply. "I've put her out of my mind, I want only to forget her."

He got up and stood beside my chair. "The night when I showed you how you might have been trapped on the Captain's Walk, you thought I was imagining enemies. Perhaps I am. But do you believe I invented tenants for my house and moved into River Rising without reasons?"

"I have never understood your reasons," I answered.

"The day we talked with Brad Copeland, I decided you had both courage and honesty. Also, I was very attracted to you, which makes me a wicked old man, although I do not feel very wicked and every day with you makes me younger."

"Pierre, I—"

"Listen to me. I came to the Rising because I believed you were in danger." He moved slowly to the door of the cabin, then back, his strides almost pantherlike in their smoothness. "No one in Ste. Marie du Lac has ever seen you except as a tiny child, no one could recognize your face. At the Montréal airport your name is spoken over a microphone—and who answers? A girl your age wearing a shawl Regina has sent to her niece. At the desk she claims a large, brightly colored envelope, an object anyone watching can see at a distance."

"I asked Regina about the envelope," I said. "She did not send it."

"No. Let me continue. Rochelle Dumont has been identified, recognized. And what happens to this supposed Rochelle? Within hours she nearly meets with a fatal accident. The next night she disappears without a trace." His voice hardened. "Do you still think I have no reason to fear for you? Early the next morning there is a burglary at River Rising, a thing that has never happened before. Do you not see that wherever Rochelle Dumont goes, the real girl or the supposed one, strange things take place?" Scowling, he shook his head again. "When Deirdre appears, alive and well, we will cease to be on guard. Until then . . ."

I stared at him, still fighting against belief. "But why? Why?"

"*Tabernac!* If that is the question, then ask, 'Why Deirdre?' "

Overhead, the creaking shrouds sounded different now, oddly menacing. I thought, *Monkshood. An enemy is near.*

Pierre bent over me, holding my shoulders, gazing into my face. "You must return to the Rising. One cannot run away from an unknown enemy and live forever in doubt, never sure when danger may come. At first I thought you were right to leave. When you changed your mind I saw the wisdom of staying. The ways of making mischief at the Rising are limited and there are only a few people in the household. But if you should leave, the possibilities for harm are endless."

For a moment fear and dread held me, then I broke free, summoning a strength I did not know I had, perhaps the strength of Regina, of Theresa, and even some of the steel that had enabled my mother to endure.

"I will not be afraid," I said. "And I will never run away."

Then his lips were pressed against mine.

The following week we returned to River Rising, and when I saw the old château, mellowed by the early-autumn sun, my apprehensions about this homecoming lessened. Aunt Regina welcomed me fondly and Tante Emma served me a huge slab of cake she had baked for my arrival.

"Have you become engaged?" Tante Emma hissed in my ear after Pierre had left us.

"No," I answered.

Tante Emma thinks you will be. It is the look in his eyes, the look of a trapped man."

"Trapped!" I exclaimed. "Really!"

"*Mais oui*. How else?"

Eunice greeted me with a vague kiss, then inquired, too coyly, about the voyage. When I proved unresponsive, she turned to the subject of Dorothy.

"Poor woman. At least she's where the care is excellent. An invalid simply can't remain in a place as remote as the Rising."

"Are Thalia and Morgan with her?"

"Thalia left for a school near Montréal yesterday. She said she'll write you a letter every week. Imagine, having to answer all those letters! Morgan's here, preparing for an exhibition in Ottawa. It's quite special, a great honor!"

I was relieved to learn that Morgan would be home tonight. It had become imperative now that I talk with him.

"Oh, Rochelle," Eunice said with a little shudder. "You missed the most hair-raising experience. Two nights after you left, all the service bells in the house began ringing all at once. And at the stroke of midnight!"

She paused, awaiting a horrified reaction, but I said, "Not so frightening, I think."

"But the timing!" she insisted. "It was the exact anniversary, down to the moment, of François's death. Uncanny! Regina was shaken, and even Morgan, who is quite fearless, seemed upset." She stopped abruptly, her hand fluttering to her lips. "Oh, I'm sorry. I've brought up a subject painful to you."

"Not at all," I said honestly. "The past no longer disturbs me."

But she left me then, embarrassed.

Later, when I had tea with Regina, the bell-ringing incident was mentioned, but calmly.

"It's what you expect from antique wiring," she said. "But I admit the oddity of timing. As Eunice told you, it was down to the very minute. Mr. Carlton, however, found the electrical short and stopped the ringing. That man is a jewel; he's ordered some modern gadgets from the city to replace the old bell system." Regina appeared to concentrate on her teacup, then said, "About Pierre Lachance. I hope you're behaving wisely."

"I am not."

She smiled thinly. "Then I hope you're behaving well." She shifted the subject. "I took the liberty of accepting an invitation for you. If it's not agreeable, you can invent an excuse and cancel."

"What invitation, Aunt Regina?"

"Theresa called. Or should I say the Lady Abbess? She hopes you will spend the weekend at the Abbey guest house. I have an impression that she's very fond of you and wants you to have a clearer idea of life at the Abbey." Regina's eyebrows lifted. "I hope to heaven she isn't trying to recruit you, or whatever they call it."

"Small danger," I said, smiling. "I'll be delighted to go. Should I telephone?"

"I told her you'd call only if you weren't coming. And I have another date for your calendar, an important one."

"What is it?"

"The first of October. It's an exhibition in Ottawa honoring Morgan. The Prime Minister is attending! I've reserved a suite for us and invited Henri Berthelot. A great honor for our family."

Regina's eyes glistened with pride. She might have her battles with Morgan, yet she gloried in his achievement, in the prestige he added to the Armitage name.

"Morgan must be delighted," I said.

"On the contrary, he tried to cancel the whole affair with an absurd excuse about Dorothy's health. But that was impossible. Now he pretends to be embarrassed at having his family attend." Regina closed the matter with a toss of her head, then pursing her lips thoughtfully, changed the subject. "I'm closing the Rising this winter and going to some warm climate. Would you come with me?" She added carefully, "I mean if there's nothing to keep you in Canada."

I thought of Pierre, of the curt way he had left when we reached home. All voyages, he'd said, had to end. There were no promises; we shared only a brief time that was too beautiful to last.

"Let me think about it at the Abbey," I said, forcing the words.

A weekend at the Abbey. Nothing could have sounded quieter, more serene. I looked forward to it with no worries, no suspicions.

Pierre did not return for supper nor did Morgan join us, but after the meal I found Morgan in the small library, a snack tray on the desk, where he was writing letters.

"I'm sorry I couldn't welcome you back from your trip,"

he said, putting down his pen. "With the exhibition coming up and Dorothy's troubles, I've been racing every minute."

When I expressed sympathy about Dorothy's health, he nodded somewhat absently. "Thank you, Rochelle. But this isn't a shock to me. We've known she couldn't stay here long."

There was silence, and he looked at me inquiringly.

"I want to ask about a miracle," I said.

"What miracle?"

"One that involves a man plunging over a cliff, being crushed on the rocks below and then carried away by the river. A little later he appears in Antigua, quite undamaged. In fact, he enjoyed perfect health for ten years."

Morgan crossed to the door, closed it, then returned to his chair at the desk to resume his seat, sighing.

"So you know," he said calmly. "Have you always known?"

"No. I learned it recently. I saw a picture of my father."

"Is that all?"

"All?" I stared at him, astonished, "Quite enough, isn't it?"

"I'm glad you've found out," he answered, thoughtful but unruffled. "I hope the truth will bring us closer together, Rochelle. Of course, you've guessed part of the story. Howard and I lied to the police, although we didn't want to. Jean-Paul was so horrified by what he'd done that he intended to stay and face his punishment."

"Then why did you lie?"

"For Charlotte. She heard the argument, arrived too late to prevent what happened. But nobody could have stopped Jean-Paul. It was over in an instant. Charlotte became hysterical. She said she wouldn't be parted from her husband, threatened suicide. She was in a terrible state, and at last we gave in. Charlotte, as usual, had her way." Morgan sighed again, this time with deep weariness. "We were foolish, I think. But remember, we were also very young and, in different ways, each of us loved Charlotte." He rose, rested against the desk, looking older than I had ever seen him. "We hid Jean-Paul in an attic, then lied our heads off. He waited until the police were satisfied. He had to, because there was a chance that Howard might be accused or I might be. In my case, it was a near thing."

"They suspected you?"

"They did indeed," he said bitterly. "You know that Andrew Armitage was my father by adoption. He was fond of me, but knew I wanted to be a painter and didn't think painters were to be trusted with money. In his will he gave François control of everything."

"So the police thought you had a motive and suspected you?"

"Yes, and I can tell you I was more than worried. But people knew Jean-Paul's character, they'd heard the threats and there were his fingerprints on the hammer. So he didn't have to come forward and rescue me. When it was safe, we helped smuggle your father out of the country. Canadian passports were easy to come by in those days. Paul La-Farge had no trouble."

Morgan's quiet voice, his simple manner of telling the story touched feelings deep within me. Once again I found myself admiring my mother, a woman able to command such loyalty.

"That isn't quite all," Morgan said. "I worried about them, so I saw Jean-Paul about two years later."

"You came to Antigua?" I asked, astonished.

"Oh, no. That would have been much too risky. We met on St. Kitts, and I learned that Jean-Paul was having a hard struggle. He was too proud to accept money from me, so I persuaded my Toronto dealer to take a few of his paintings, but it didn't work out. I wish I'd been able to help. There was no way."

For a moment Morgan stared at the unfinished letter on the desk, then said, "If the truth came out, I suppose it would cause trouble. It happened so long ago, I doubt there'd be any prosecution, but we'd have a scandal, of course. The papers would love a sensational tale about a well-known artist." He paused, gave me a questioning glance. "Charlotte and Jean-Paul are no longer living. Only three of us share the secret."

"Only three? What about Pierre Lachance?"

"Pierre was an accidental, and very convenient, witness. We saw his electric torch approaching and did a bit of quack trickery that worked. No, we are the only ones who know the truth."

Moving to him, I impulsively grasped his hand. "Thank you, Morgan. Thank you for giving my mother and father those added years, and for giving me a chance to know my father. The secret is safe with me."

I went quickly to my room, ashamed of the suspicions I had harbored about Morgan and Howard Palmer. I could never like Howard, but both he and Morgan had taken great risks for the sake of my parents. It was ironic that I had repaid such kindness with doubt and mental accusation. This, I thought, should be a lesson to me.

Only the three of us know, I told myself as I gazed down at the dark river before drawing the draperies. Then an annoying and pointless saying crossed my mind, an ancient adage that surely had nothing to do with the situation: "Three can keep a secret if two of them are dead."

12

———◆———

I was playing the harpsichord the next afternoon, rather melancholy music reflecting my own feelings. Viking lay on the carpet near me, his half-closed eyes reproachful, a reminder that I had hardly seen Pierre since coming back to River Rising.

Lost in the music, I did not hear Howard Palmer enter, and only realized he was in the room when the dog rose and growled a warning. As I turned on the bench, Howard said placatingly but rather feebly, "Nice boy. Nice fellow."

Viking, unconvinced by flattery, growled again and would not remain quiet until I smoothed his bristling fur and reassured him.

Howard carried a tape recorder. "How appropriate that I found you playing, Rochelle," he said. "I want you to listen to something."

Beaming, he turned on the machine and I heard the familiar notes of a Mozart gigue. After a few measures I realized this was a recording of my own playing made without my knowledge and on a day when I was certainly not at my best. The phrasing sounded stiff, the interpretation lifeless.

When it ended Howard nodded enthusiastic approval. "Brilliant! I caught exactly the right selection."

"When did you catch this? I didn't know you were interested in making tapes." The notion of a concealed recorder bothered me.

"I find electronics a fascinating but rather expensive hobby," he said. "I thought you would be more relaxed if you weren't aware a tape was being cut. The results are proof I was right. No doubt you have heard of Arturo Baroni?"

"No, I don't think so."

"His greatest reputation is in Europe. He's an outstanding impresario who handles concert bookings all over the world. I understand baroque music is his specialty, the harpsichord and so on."

Howard glanced at me expectantly, but I did not answer, being unable to imagine what all this had to do with me.

"When I heard you play, I thought at once of Baroni, who is an old friend of mine. So several weeks ago I made this recording and sent him a copy."

"Really, you shouldn't have!" I felt painfully embarrassed at the thought of an expert listening to the music I had just heard. What could the man, an old friend, possibly reply to Howard?

"Baroni telephoned me an hour ago!" exclaimed Howard, flushed with triumph. "He's very impressed and he wants you to come to New York to audition."

"But that's impossible!"

"Not impossible, not even difficult, my dear," he continued rapidly. "I'll drive you to Québec City, where you can take the New York plane. Baroni has guaranteed expenses."

I stared at him, dumbfounded. Anyone who plays music seriously longs to believe in the gift of a major talent; it is easy to succumb to self-flattery, to the delusion that impossible dreams will become realities. But I had heard the recording with my own ears, I knew its mediocrity. Mr. Baroni was either a swindler hoping to make money from naïve beginners or a devoted friend repaying Howard Palmer for some past favor.

"It's impossible," I repeated.

"I understand how you feel," Howard went on, undaunted. "You are afraid of failure. But there's no need for anyone at River Rising to know the reason for your New York trip. You could be visiting an old friend, or have a dozen other excuses. Then, if Baroni does not offer anything, only you and I——"

"Please! That is not what disturbs me. Howard, such miracles simply do not happen. It would take me weeks, probably months, of hard practicing to prepare. And that is assuming I have an ability that certainly does not show in that recording you made."

"Out of the question!" Palmer's smile faded. I felt he was controlling anger. "Baroni leaves for Europe at the end of the month. You must go tomorrow or the next day. You disappoint me, Rochelle. I thought you'd have the courage to seize an opportunity."

"It's not a matter of courage but of good sense," I told him. A bullying note that I resented had crept into his voice.

"I've presumed on an old friendship and gone to considerable trouble to arrange this," he went on, moving a step nearer to me.

"Not at my request!"

Apparently he realized he had chosen the wrong tactics, for his anger vanished in a smile. "This came as a surprise," he said. "You are not thinking clearly. I'm sure you'll reconsider your answer."

"Perhaps," I said. "And it was kind of you to make this effort."

"Don't delay too long, Rochelle. As I said, Baroni is leaving for Europe and you absolutely must make the trip before the end of the month. Such a chance may not come again."

After he had left I sat with my fingers resting on the silent keyboard, trying to understand my reactions to his unexpected news.

"I don't believe it," I said, half aloud. No doubt there was some person named Baroni who was connected with music, but the story Howard Palmer told seemed highly unlikely. Could Palmer, for a reason I could not fathom, want me to go to New York on a fool's errand?

I felt uncharitable. I knew from Morgan that Howard had been kind to my mother, had helped in my father's escape from Canada, and no doubt now he is trying to be kind to me. He probably did not understand the futility of such an attempt.

Howard had even offered to drive me to Québec City. I winced at the thought of traveling anywhere with him. My distrust of Howard was more instinctive than logical, but it persisted. I glanced down at Viking, realizing that the two of us shared this suspicion, although neither could tell why.

I heard a confusion of voices in the entrance hall, and then Regina calling my name. "Rochelle, come quickly!"

She met me at the living-room door. Two men from the village stood in the hall. "Your trunk has arrived from Antigua!" she exclaimed.

"There's no reason for excitement," I said, smiling. "It's only a few clothes, some books. Odds and ends."

"The men can take it to my sitting room and I'll help unpack it. No need for them to climb all those stairs if most things are for the storeroom."

Regina glided ahead, leading the way, looking astonishingly youthful and slender. She seemed to glow with new-found vitality these days and I wondered how much of it came from relief at Dorothy's departure from River Rising. Then, too, there was her pride in Morgan's forthcoming exhibition.

The afternoon had turned cool and a small fire burned brightly on the hearth in her sitting room. "Put the trunk near the couch where we can spread things out," she told the men, then dismissed them.

Unpacking took only a few minutes. The trunk was hardly half full, and its contents were unremarkable. I wondered why I had bothered to keep some of the worn clothing.

I thought Regina blinked back tears as she examined a photograph of my mother. I took a dozen treasured books from the trunk, then, like Regina, felt a tear in my eye as I touched two childhood gifts made for me by the man I now knew was my father.

Sandy-Panda, the garishly striped rag doll, had survived the years well, and when I placed him gently on the couch his painted grin seemed as friendly as ever. And I paused to examine the last item in the trunk, a child's coloring book filled with printed outlines of ducks, geese, rabbits and a score of other creatures. The book had been a birthday present. My fourth birthday? Or fifth? I had lacked the patience and skill to fill the outlines with crayon, so Jean-Paul Dumont had done the coloring for me as I sat at his side marveling. In the margins he had made small sketches of me, whimsical drawings of a little girl admiring a peacock, looking doubtfully at a tiger.

As I put the book beside Sandy-Panda, I realized that Regina was staring at the rag doll, a puzzled frown on her face.

"Where did you get that?" she asked. "Did it once belong to Charlotte?"

"No. It was made for me when I was about five years old," I told her.

Moving quickly past me, she seized Sandy-Panda, turning him in her hands, scrutinizing the cloth animal with a strange intensity. "It's a copy of another toy," she said at last. "It has to be!"

"Sandy is a complete original. In fact, an improvisation. I remember the day he was stitched together and painted."

She shook her head, seeming not to comprehend. "That's impossible . . ." Regina's voice trailed off as her glance fell on the coloring book. Picking it up, she leafed silently through the pages.

"Aunt Regina, dear, it was my father who drew the sketches for me, and he who made Sandy-Panda," I said. Regardless of my promise to Morgan, Regina had to know the truth. I could no longer keep the secret from her. "Jean-Paul did not die that night. He escaped, and lived in the islands near my mother for many years."

The color drained from Regina's face, leaving it chalky white. "How could he?" The words were whispered. "There were witnesses. Morgan and Howard swore that—" Regina suddenly raised her hands as though to ward off a blow. "Don't tell me any more. I don't want to know."

She took an uncertain step toward me, almost stumbled, and caught the back of a chair for support. "Who else knows this?" she demanded.

"Only Morgan and Howard."

"You must tell no one! I need time to think. I must have time, Rochelle!"

She was trembling and the whiteness of her face had been replaced by an alarming gray pallor. "Aunt Regina!" I started toward her, but she moved away, her balance unsteady.

"I have believed in honesty," she said, "believed in truth. Can an entire life be built on lies? It is horrible, unthinkable! I must be mistaken, I have to be mistaken."

"Aunt Regina, I don't understand. What do you . . . ?"

Her pale hands clutched at her throat, she staggered backward, then crumpled to the floor.

Dr. Dorlan arrived from the village in less than half an hour. That evening a specialist from Québec City, Dr. Real, had traveled by chartered plane and was also attending Regina. A nurse, Madame Corres, came with him.

"She has suffered a stroke," Dr. Dorlan told the assembled household, "but there is no cause for grave alarm. True, she cannot speak and there is paralysis of the right side. We are convinced this is temporary."

"She should be taken to a hospital," said Morgan.

"The lady must not be moved! She requires absolute quiet, complete rest. And for the present, no visitors."

"Who will care for her?" Tante Emma demanded. "That nurse is a stranger."

"Madame Corres is highly qualified. The patient is not to be disturbed by anyone." Dr. Dorlan was emphatic. "You can speed her recovery by going quietly about your usual activities."

During the last hours I had been questioned first by Dr. Dorlan, then by the others about any emotional shock that might have caused Regina's seizure.

"She found a photograph of my mother," I told them. "It brought painful mémories."

I felt I must not speak of her shock at learning of my father's escape. Regina had urged me, pleaded with me, to say nothing until she had time to think. I would give her that opportunity. Sandy-Panda and the coloring book were safely hidden in the chest with my father's self-portrait.

Regina's strange question came back to me: "Can an entire life be built on lies?" Whose life had she meant? In a few days, I felt sure, Regina herself would be able to tell me.

13

—◆—

Alone on the sun porch the next morning, I was finishing a late breakfast when Pierre entered.

"Good morning," he said. "I just saw Dr. Dorlan leaving. He tells me that Regina is doing well."

"Yes. Dr. Real returned to Québec City early this morning. He felt there was no danger."

"You look very tired," he said. "What happened after I left last night?"

"Eunice became hysterical about Regina and had to be taken to bed. Meanwhile, Morgan paced the living room and drank far too much. And Howard Palmer kept badgering me about an idiotic plan of his for me to go to New York, where I am to astonish the musical world."

Pierre scowled. "What plan?"

"Just sheer nonsense. And quite insulting for him to think I would go anywhere with Regina in such condition."

We fell silent, both of us strangely awkward. He stared at me absently, then said, "I must make a trip. The timing is unfortunate, but in a few minutes I must leave for Montréal."

"Really?" I took a quick sip of coffee, avoiding his eyes. My days of being protected, of his watching over me, had apparently come to an end. In the silence he must be composing the farewell speech I dreaded.

"There was a call at my house yesterday. A Montréal firm needs a sailing master this winter. It is for the Bahamas and Jamaica. They offer an unusual amount of money and I know the vessel. She is beautiful. And only a few passengers."

"How exciting for you," I told him, studying the coffee cup.

"I spent hours thinking. If my house had carpets, my paces would have worn a path."

"Is the decision so hard to make?"

"The decision may not be mine." He gave me an uncertain look. "This company may not want a married man. Also, a married man might not care to accept."

"There is no one less married than you," I said, lifting my chin defiantly.

Pierre studied me gravely. "With your help, I expect to change that, Rochelle." Rising, he moved to my side, his voice gruff. "I suppose you think I am saying this badly." His face darkened, he looked angry, but it did not matter. After what he had just said, nothing else mattered.

"Tabernac! Why should you expect me to talk drivel about love, although I am certain we love each other? I suppose we will have battles all the time. It is natural for me to give orders and natural for you to defy them. You are head-strong, impulsive and forever mutinous. I am quite mad to ask you to marry me, and you are mad if you accept! *Alors,* what do you say? I do not want to argue about this. Yes or no?"

I was in his arms, we held each other. I do not remember saying "Yes," but he understood.

My happiness filled the overcast morning with imaginary sunshine. Pierre had left Viking with me, and the dog, usually inclined to treat me with polite seriousness, seemed to catch my mood, capering like a puppy as I tossed a stick for him to retrieve.

Howard Palmer crossed the garden, went toward the kitchen door. The two unpleasant-looking hounds he had acquired gave Viking a wide berth. Hunting seemed his sole preoccupation now. I had only seen him with a sketchbook once.

Pierre's image passed through my mind a dozen times in a dozen forms—his stance as he dominated the deck of the *Etoile Filante,* the silent way he had led Thalia and me along the paths near the Rising, his boots as quiet as moccasins. Life might not always be tranquil with my rugged, often hot-tempered *coureur de bois,* but it would never be dull. The end of my drifting had come, and I wanted to shout the news, to make the old walls of the château ring with it, but we had agreed to say nothing until we talked to Regina.

Keeping a promise to Pierre, I moved the few things I would need from my room to a smaller but comfortable chamber on the ground floor just down a hall from Tante Emma's room.

"Stay there tonight," he had told me, issuing orders in his usual manner. "Then you will be at the Abbey until I return."

I did not argue, did not even give my customary ironic "Aye, aye, Captain." This moving, I thought, was unnecessary and I liked my own room, yet I loved Pierre even more for worrying about me, however needlessly.

As I was hanging clothes in the old-fashioned armoire, Mr. Carlton, correct and formal as always, came to the door. He carried a small black device that I took to be a radio.

"Pardon me, miss. The gadgets I ordered to replace the old service bells have arrived and you'll be needing one."

"It seems a waste to wire it into this room," I told him. "I'll be here only tonight."

"Oh, no wiring is required. Wiring is quite out of date since these were invented." He placed the plastic box on the dresser, plugged a cord into a nearby electrical outlet. "To call the kitchen, press the red button. The blue one calls Madame Sud's apartment. Now if you'll excuse me, I'll step to the kitchen and we'll test it."

The device, however it worked, would surely be an improvement over the antique service bells at the Rising. I looked at it idly, expecting a ring or some sort of buzzing sound.

"Can you hear me, Miss Dumont?" The words came loudly and plainly. Mr. Carlton's voice was slightly distorted but sounded nothing like the flat tone of a speaker on a telephone.

Then my hand flew to my mouth as I stifled a cry. Another voice came back to me, a voice human yet not human as it whispered, "Ro-chelle, Ro-chelle!"

"Miss Dumont, can you hear me, please?"

I paid no attention. My eyes moved to Viking, who lay quietly at my side, eyes half closed. The dog, always alert to any human speech, ignored the sound. He did not respond because his keen sense of smell told him that no person was actually present, and perhaps his ears, which could catch overtones inaudible to me, also reassured him. Viking, like most dogs, would have been equally uninterested in a radio or a recording. Such sounds were not really human and so they indicated no danger.

But the dog was instantly alert when Mr. Carlton appeared in person.

"No sound, miss? Must be something wrong with it."

"I heard you," I answered, keeping my voice calm. "I wasn't sure which button to press."

Patiently he explained again, and after he had gone I pressed the red button. A rattle of dishes in the kitchen was plainly audible, and the voice of Tante Emma, sounding far away yet distinct, speaking to Mr. Carlton in English, describing her shock the night the old bells had caused such a commotion.

I sat on the bed, staring at the black box that seemed at that moment like an infernal machine. It could have been concealed anywhere near the Captain's Walk, in the eaves, behind the chimney, even shifted and moved along a wire. And the whisperer, who could not only speak but hear me, might have been far away, for there was no need to watch. My cries of "Thalia" would have told where I was.

My watch said noon. Pierre had promised to call me in the evening, but now I could not wait, even though I did not think he could have yet arrived at the Seaway Inn in Montréal. At least I could leave a message for him.

I hurried to the telephone at the front of the house, my feelings a churning mixture of anger at whoever had played this appalling trick and a sense of relief that I had not imagined the voice. It had been real, as real as Mr. Carlton speaking from the kitchen.

When I picked up the telephone, there was no reassuring hum. The line was dead, as happened so often at Ste. Marie du Lac. Now there was nothing to do but wait. And wonder.

As I turned away from the telephone I heard a creaking sound on the stairway, and glancing up, caught a glimpse of a figure withdrawing quickly into the concealment of the landing.

"Who is it? Who's there?" I asked, speaking as loudly as I dared. Regina's need for quiet prohibited any calling or shouting in the house.

"Ro-chelle." It was a papery whisper. "Ro-chelle."

"Thalia?" I asked, incredulous.

"Yes. I'm here."

I hesitated, but Viking pushed past me, bounding up the stairs, his tail wagging. Then the girl herself stepped into view to greet him.

"Thalia!" I exclaimed. "What are you doing here?"

She raised a finger to her lips, indicating silence, gestured for me to follow and hurried up the stairs. A moment later we were in the Captain's Country, the door closed behind us.

"I've run away from the school," she said, her grave eyes staring into mine. "I'm never going back."

"Does your stepfather know you're here?"

"No. But why should he care? He doesn't like me, he never has."

"Thalia!" I started to protest, then stopped. There was a quality almost frightening in the girl's quiet voice. She was, as always, speaking the plain truth and both of us knew it.

"He doesn't care what happens to me, and neither does my mother."

"Your mother is ill, she's not responsible."

"She wasn't ill before, not ill when she left me and my father to marry Morgan." Thalia was pronouncing a final and considered judgment. Her tone carried no accusation, only a sad emptiness. "If she cared for me, why did she ask the witch to come to the house? I begged her not to. The witch frightens me."

I took Thalia's hand; her fingers were icy. "Madame Jeanette frightens me, too."

"After you were locked on the roof, Aunt Regina told my mother that the witch must never come here again. But she did come!" Thalia moved closer to me, her shoulders trembling. "You had gone away with Captain Pierre, and one night I heard her in my mother's room. I wanted the witch to be caught, but I couldn't tell on my mother. Do you know what I did, Rochelle?"

"What, Thalia?"

"I went to the kitchen and pinched two wires together, so all the bells rang and woke everyone up. But the witch hid somewhere. No one saw her."

"You couldn't have done that," I said, startled. "You wouldn't know how."

"Yes, I did. I heard Mr. Palmer tell my stepfather how the bells could be rung."

"Why would they have such a conversation, Thalia?"

"I think it was a kind of joke to play on Aunt Regina. This was long ago, before you came here. Aunt Regina and my stepfather were quarreling every day because she wouldn't sell River Rising. And the servants were frightened of ghosts, so nobody would work here."

Thalia moved away from me, going to the window, where she stared down at the sweep of the river. "Then you came and things were better. You and Captain Pierre came."

For a moment I sat in silence, pondering what Thalia had told me. She confirmed what Dorothy had said earlier. The supposed haunting had been a very effective way of halting operation of the house, of forcing Regina's hand. My presence and Pierre's had been inconvenient. Four watchful eyes to detect trickery. I could understand why Morgan had urged me to leave River Rising as quickly as possible.

But that did not explain Regina's violent reaction to Sandy-Panda and the coloring book. Something else was involved, some secret that still lay hidden from me.

The immediate problem, however, was Thalia. "The teachers at your school must be worried to death."

She shook her head. "I left a note saying I was going to visit my stepfather and I was traveling very safely by bus. They wouldn't worry much anyhow. It's a school for girls whose parents don't want them. Girls like me. So what does it matter?"

"Thalia, you mustn't feel this way," I said, going to her. "You have to realize your mother is ill and Morgan is pre-occupied with his painting. He hasn't time to—"

"That's not true, Rochelle. He goes to his studio, but he doesn't paint. There's an attic window in the south wing, and you can see through the studio skylight. He plays solitaire or sometimes just paces the floor. I've watched."

"That happens to an artist," I said. "Times come when he can't work. You should try to have sympathy, Thalia."

"Why? If he doesn't care about me, why should I care about him?" she answered with a terrible logic.

I turned away. "What on earth am I to do with you? Morgan has to be told you're here."

"Not until tomorrow! Please, Rochelle, let me stay with you tonight. Then you can tell him. Only Tante Emma knows I'm here and she won't say anything."

"I can't do that, Thalia."

"Then I'll run away again," she said calmly. "There's no way to stop me."

Looking at her pleading eyes, I suddenly thought of Dierdre Cameron. Running away, frightened. Running to . . . nowhere. I needed advice, I longed to talk to Regina or to Pierre.

"Very well," I said, yielding. "But just for tonight."

"Rochelle!" She threw her arms around me. "You're the only one who understands. You and Captain Pierre. I love you."

So Thalia stayed with me and I was glad for her companionship, although Tante Emma's stony look when she brought supper to the room downstairs informed me that she thought I was part of a schoolgirl conspiracy.

The house felt lonely and oppressive that night. Regina, the nurse told me, was resting quietly. But for me there was little sleep.

In the morning I learned that Thalia had won a temporary reprieve from seeing her stepfather. Morgan was not in the house and no one knew his whereabouts. Perhaps the studio, Mr. Carlton said, but the studio was sacrosanct even though I now knew that Morgan was not painting there.

I tried again to call Pierre but, maddeningly, telephone service had not resumed at the Rising, and as the morning wore on, my uneasiness increased. Yesterday I had not realized all the implications of what Thalia told me. Now the thought of Howard Palmer and Morgan discussing a way of alarming the house with bell-ringing struck me not as unpleasant but sinister.

The living room was chilly. I went to the small library, where Mr. Carlton had made a fire, and paced restlessly. Something about the ringing of the bells haunted me, some vital fact that lay just beyond the reach of my consciousness. Was it something Eunice said? Or Regina? Trying to bring some order to my confused thoughts, I took a pen and paper from the desk and wrote: "The bells. Midnight. August fourteenth."

Tante Emma entered. "I have brought your lunch. The fireplace is cheering on a gray day."

"Tante Emma," I said, "Eunice told me that the service bells rang here on the anniversary of François's death."

"That is so. To the very minute."

"But how is the minute known? Did Morgan or Howard look at a watch? It seems unlikely at such a moment."

"Why dwell on this?" she asked, annoyed. "It was in statements Monsieur Morgan and Monsieur Palmer made to the police. The midnight bell of the Abbey somehow enraged Jean-Paul. The sound triggered the attack, they said. Now leave this matter alone."

She returned to the kitchen, and I toyed with my lunch, troubled and unsatisfied.

Viking's ears lifted sharply, and I glanced over my shoulder to see Madame Sud hovering in the doorway, an envelope in her hand.

"A telegram for you," she said and gave it to me. I noticed the flap was open and looked at her. "It must have arrived like that. Monsieur Palmer accepted it. He asked me to bring it to you." And Palmer, I thought, had no doubt read the contents.

As soon as she was gone, I drew out the message, my pulse quickening as I read it:

WORST FEARS ABOUT DEIRDRE CONFIRMED ON RADIO. I MUST CONTACT POLICE. GO TO ABBEY AT ONCE. REPEAT AT ONCE. I WILL RETURN QUICKLY. LOVE. PIERRE.

This, I realized, was no time to hesitate or question. After a futile attempt to reach the Abbey by telephone and an equally useless try to summon Gagnon's taxi in the village, I hurried to my room to gather the few things I would need. I could take no more than my shoulder bag would hold. There was no way to get there but to walk.

Thalia sat on the bed, cross-legged, reading a book. Her smile faded when she saw my face. "What's happened, Rochelle?"

There was no time to explain. But suddenly every shadowed room of River Rising seemed filled with menace, and I could not leave Thalia here alone.

"Thalia, do you know where Captain Lachance lives?" She nodded, and I continued, "Take Viking and go to the village. Here's some money. Have Monsieur Gagnon's taxi drive you to the captain's house. Tell the housekeeper I sent you, and you are to wait there until the captain returns."

Thalia repeated my instructions carefully, asking no questions. Then she brushed her lips against my cheek and a moment later she and Viking were on their way, slipping quietly out the side door. I hesitated, watching her, silently resolving that Thalia's future would be happier than her past. At least she would always know that Pierre and I loved her, that she would never be alone. It was a promise.

Although the day was cool, even chilly, I did not take time to go upstairs for a coat. My salt-and-pepper wool dress, which had a matching cape and hood, would give adequate warmth. From the bureau I took a small transistor radio.

In the garden I passed Tante Emma, who gave me an inquiring look. "I'm visiting the Abbey," I said. "If Aunt Regina asks for me, tell her I'll return tomorrow."

"Impossible! The captain told me to keep you under my eye at all times. His orders were clear; he said it was important."

"He wants me to go. He sent a telegram."

She looked doubtful. "Walking? The sky is very overcast."

"I know the way. Please, Tante Emma, don't argue."

"Wait one moment." She hurried to the kitchen, then returned with a small paper bag. "Here is a candle, some matches and a tiny flashlight. Often the Abbey has no electricity. Also some soap. Their soap removes the skin and this will help you survive."

"Thank you." She was still shaking her head gloomily as I left her.

When I reached the firebreak, I tuned the radio to a Montréal station. The little receiver cracked with static, but eventually I heard the voice of a newscaster. There followed national and local announcements, but nothing that concerned Deirdre. Twisting the dial, I tried Québec City, then halted, standing completely still as I heard the first words.

". . . recovered from the river below Ile d'Orleans, has been identified as Miss Deirdre Cameron, daughter of a prominent Toronto family. She had been missing . . ." The radio faded, then returned. ". . . medical authorities . . . not a case of drowning, but apparently a victim of foul play."

When the announcer shifted to a weather report, I switched off the set.

Foul play. I shuddered at this description of her death, and more than ever I wanted to resist the belief that Deirdre had died in my place.

But she did. A voice deep in my mind spoke the words and would not be stilled. Who should have been wearing the yellow shawl? Rochelle Dumont, of course. Deirdre had been the victim in a tragedy in which she herself played no part, a girl who innocently borrowed a shawl, who answered, in my name, a summons to an airport desk. The terrible, growing conviction that Deirdre, by accident, had suffered a fate intended for me chilled my shivering shoulders as much as the wind that had turned coldly penetrating.

A storm was gathering; fortunately, Thalia would be safe in the village before it broke.

Now I regretted not wearing an overcoat. I had been foolhardy to trust the Québec weather even though it was only mid-September. I looked longingly toward the distant turrets of Clarendon Abbey, which seemed no closer than they had been five minutes before.

It would be easy to catch a chill; anyone venturing out too thinly clad was almost asking for pneumonia. After all, that had happened to Aunt Theresa all those years ago when—

I uttered a sharp exclamation. *When? Exactly when?*

Unexpectedly a few large flakes of snow swirled to the ground near me and vanished, but I paid no attention, standing transfixed, struggling to sort out a twisted pattern of events, striving to recall Aunt Theresa's exact words. And I was certain I remembered them.

On August thirteenth, twenty years ago, a young nun at Clarendon Abbey had been seized by emotional storms that she called "monsoons." The following day she lived in torment and that night, hardly knowing what she was doing, had briefly run away.

And what had called her back to the Abbey? The great bell, Mary Major, proclaiming Assumption Day, the bell she heard at midnight as she stood watching my father.

Midnight, August fourteenth, the date and hour when François Armitage was killed on the porch of the studio. But at that moment Jean-Paul Dumont was in the garden, his presence there confirmed by a witness no one had known about—Theresa Armitage, now Lady Abbess of Clarendon.

Why had she not spoken long ago, cleared my father of the crime? Even as I asked the question, I realized the answer. When news of the murder electrified Ste. Marie du Lac, the nun was being taken to a hospital in the city, and she only learned of the tragedy months later when the late Abbess told her of the death but spared her the details. Dame Theresa never suspected the importance of what she had seen. It seemed improbable that Aunt Theresa had ever mentioned my father to the Abbess, for this would have been repeating what seemed like pointless gossip, and as Aunt Theresa said, "You have no duty to tell all you know."

Lost in thought, I had ignored the snow which was thickening in the air around me. Startled by it now, I knew I must hurry, for although the path along the firebreak was plainly visible, the Abbey's towers had disappeared, enveloped in a cloud of whiteness.

I pressed ahead, astonished and rather frightened by this sudden, unexpected storm. At the Rising there had often been talk of snowstorms coming even in summer, but I had not imagined anything like this.

It's almost blinding, I thought, pulling the hood of my cape forward to protect my face against the sharpening wind. The sky was blotted out; nothing remained above me but tumultuous white, spiraling and whirling.

I kept my eyes on the path, gazing downward, trying not to worry about the cold, attempting instead to concentrate on what I had just discovered about the death of François Armitage, trying to frame the questions I would soon ask Aunt Theresa.

Was she certain of the date and hour when she had seen my father? There must be no possible error, for if she held fast to her story, Morgan and Howard Palmer would have difficult explaining to do.

The silver trunk of a birch tree loomed in front of me, blocking my path. I halted, astonished, knowing well that no trees grew in the firebreak. On the left stood another birch and to the right a high stump I had never seen before. Somehow I had left the main path, turned onto one of the many small trails that crossed the strip of cleared land on either side.

Against my will, I thought of Thalia and her father, how they had stumbled through a blind world where all directions seemed the same, just as I found now.

Don't remember them, I commanded myself. Don't!

But I could not help thinking of her story as, eyes to the ground, I now struggled to retrace my steps, and realized my footprints seemed to vanish instantly, blurred by the wind and quickly brushed over with new-fallen snow. Thalia and her father had stopped, had waited, and that I must not do.

Keep going, I thought. A little farther, only a little farther.

Then my confidence arose when I realized I was no longer surrounded by trees. It was still impossible to see more than a few feet ahead, yet the lack of forest indicated that I was once more safely on the firebreak. Surely I was somewhere not far from the Abbey. Besides, I assured myself, this storm must be only a snow flurry and could not last. Even now it seemed abating, the white less blinding; the flakes were not swarming so heavily.

Something, not a tree, stood just ahead of me. A tall fence? Part of the Abbey walls? No, it was clapboard, a cabin or a small house.

"Hello!" I shouted, but the wind swept my voice away.

There was no door in the cabin wall, only a gaping rectangular hole. I had stumbled upon an abandoned house, a ruin. This must be near the edge of the ghost village, Castaways. I had not moved nearer the Abbey but away from it.

Inside the ruined cabin I found shelter, but only a little. Most of the shingle roof had collapsed; the flooring, doors and window frames were stripped away. Only trash had been left behind—some empty, rusted cans and the remains of ticking and straw that had once been a mattress. But in one corner a brick fireplace, unused for years, gave promise of desperately needed warmth.

Although my fingers were almost numb, it was easy to start the fire. I found a heap of dry leaves in one corner of the room and plenty of loose shingles.

"Thank you, Tante Emma," I whispered, shivering as I ignited the pile on the hearth with a match from her little "survival kit" intended to save me from any small discomforts at the Abbey guest house. It was perhaps saving me from a good deal worse than discomfort.

A moment later I huddled near the roaring blaze, stretching out my hands, then jerking them back quietly as the fireplace spat a volley of sparks. Now I looked at the flames with sudden suspicion, not liking the way the old shingles behaved when heat touched them. The rotting wood consumed itself in a series of quick, small explosions. I backed away, quickly brushing tiny red coals from my cape.

The friendly fire I had counted on was acting more like an enemy, hissing, snapping and refusing to be contained by its bed. It was the chimney, I thought. Part of the chimney must have collapsed long ago and the draft was pushing sparks and smoke into the cabin instead of drawing them out.

I did not notice which shower of sparks reached the ticking and dry straw, but realized in alarm that the torn mattress was smoking. As I moved toward it, not knowing what I should do, the whole thing blazed up, sending a spiral of burning straws into the gray air.

Choking and coughing, I made my way outside, where the snowfall had slackened. Although I should have taken instant advantage of the lull, I felt compelled to turn back, to stand a moment, fascinated by the cabin I had unwittingly set afire.

It went like a matchbox, the licking flames almost smokeless except where they touched melting snow, sending up a hiss of steam. In a few minutes there would be only smoldering embers and the blackened chimney left.

Then I turned away from it, still feeling the heat on my back, and tried again to determine where I was. Near the Sawdust Desert, of course, on one edge of the ghost town. But the little I could see of the landscape told me nothing more.

A quick gust of wind momentarily cleared the view and I caught sight of a farmhouse standing among tall timbers not far away.

I hurried toward it, soon aware that my sense of distance had deceived me and the stone building was not as near as I had hoped. But a few minutes later I crossed a rutted road I could not remember seeing before and reached the doorway, my shoes and clothing now thoroughly wet where snow had melted.

I knocked twice and called loudly, but there was no answer. This was, I thought, a peculiar building, not really a house nor yet a barn. Another knock brought no response, so I pulled a latchstring dangling from a hole bored between two heavy planks. The door, not locked, swung silently open, revealing an apparently deserted interior, but as I entered, a deep-voiced, rather quizzical "Moo!" greeted me.

This was both a dwelling and a farm shed, one big room with an unpainted fence to divide human and animal occupants. Above it was a hayloft for storing fodder and, I supposed, a place used for sleeping, since I saw no beds. The dim room smelled of straw, stale smoke and animals.

"Is anyone here?" I asked loudly.

Only the cow replied from beyond the fence, and her calf

looked up from nursing but made no comment, remaining undisturbed as two black cats, hardly more than skins, eyes and skeletons, streaked through the room to race up the ladder to the loft, startling me.

I put my bag and radio on the round table near the fireplace and hung my wet cape over the back of a wooden chair. There was no blaze on the hearth, but the stones were hot and the ashes gave a warmth that comforted me.

It was not until I lighted a candle that I realized what a strange place I had wandered into. Overhead, almost above the ladder to the loft, was a rather large wooden box attached to ropes and pulleys. Examining it more closely, I discovered it was a hay trolley to carry fodder the length of the room from the loft to the pen housing the animals. The ropes to lower it, held by a hook in the wall, looked frayed. I stepped back, not caring to stand under it, and almost bumped into a set of open shelves lined with rows of peculiar containers.

There were bottles and stone flagons, oddly shaped apothecary jars. Carrying the candle from the table, I looked in better light and saw herbs and sprigs, some whole, others ground to powder. In one of the large glass jars something green and slimy either drifted or swam, seeming neither quite living nor yet dead. A second jar of clear liquid displayed a small skull, that of a dog or perhaps a cat, I could not tell. Containers on the lower shelves were obscured by thick, interlaced cobwebs.

I turned away from this unsettling collection, hoping the snow would cease quickly and I could leave without thanking my unknown host in person.

Two big cupboards stood against the opposite wall and I went to the first one hoping it might contain towels to chafe my face and arms or perhaps a blanket I could wrap around myself.

Success, I thought when I opened the door, for although the cupboard contained nothing else, there was a patched blanket draped over some square object leaning inside. I pulled the blanket away, then gasped at what I saw.

It was an oil painting, quite large and simply but perfectly framed. Even in the faint candlelight I felt certain of what I had discovered.

Taking the painting from its hiding place, I stood it against the wall, where the pale illumination from a window struck the brilliantly colored canvas.

"Wistful Child!" I exclaimed. This had to be the painting stolen from River Rising only hours before I had arrived there.

At first glance one hardly noticed that this was a portrait. What dazzled the eye was the riot of clashing colors, blue and orange, pink and green, softened and saddened by darker shadows. But it was also the lovingly painted picture of a little girl, the face turned partly away, yet her melancholy and loneliness poignantly shown in the droop of her thin shoulders, in the emptiness of her hand as she reached toward a rag doll.

Tears came to my eyes, tears brought not so much by the sheer beauty of the painting as by the way it spoke so personally to me.

The small girl who was the *Wistful Child* wore a white cotton dress with a hibiscus print; the floor on which she sat was covered with linoleum, a design of poppies. In the lower right corner I saw the M. Armitage signature I remembered from the museum in Montréal.

The squeak of wagon wheels outside snapped me from the spell cast by the painting. Running to the window, I wiped a small spot on the steamed glass and looked out cautiously.

The snow no longer fell, the ground seemed covered by a white sheet full of holes, and approaching the house only a few yards away was a familiar farm wagon, drawn by "Horse" and carrying two passengers bundled in heavy coats, Gilles and Madame Jeanette.

Madame Jeanette's house. Of course, it had to be, and in a flash I understood the sinister-looking jars and bottles which were surely the trappings of village witchcraft.

I blew out the candle. I thrust the painting into the darkest corner—no time to return it to the cupboard. Snatching up my cape, handbag and the radio, I looked about desperately for a way of escape, to find there was none. Voices were approaching the door as I scrambled up the ladder to the only hiding place I could see, the loft above.

The door of the house opened. I saw an increase of light, then a diminishing as it closed again. There was a stamping of Gilles's boots mixed with the softer footfalls of Madame

Jeanette as she moved quickly across the room. The scratch of a match, then pale candlelight.

"Cold," growled Gilles.

"I do not feel it," she answered, her voice harsh. "I have not felt cold or heat for many years."

"Only a body with blood feels things."

"Vraiment. My blood dried long ago." A chair creaked. "Put wood on the fire if you like."

"Merci."

After a long silence she said, "He is to meet you here, then?"

"So I was told. Have you cider? I'm thirsty."

Her laughter was thin, reedy. "Nervous, I think. Yes, I have cider to singe your eyebrows."

In the deep dusk of the loft four luminous eyes stared balefully at me. The cats, abandoning the soft hay, had both leaped to the top of a ricked bundle of straw, their black bodies merging with the darkness of the eaves. They sat poised, ready to spring.

Madame Jeanette said, "Drink up. No, my cider has no nightshade." With a chuckle, she added, "Not even monks-hood."

"What are you laughing at?"

"A small joke. Never mind." A hesitation, then, "Do you know what the plan *is?"*

"I am not paid to know. My job is to watch the path and make sure she does not reach the Abbey this way. Have you a rag? The window is steaming again."

Not reach the Abbey. The words reechoed in my mind with an icy certainty that they must be talking about me. Then Madame Jeanette spoke, and there remained no possible doubt.

"The murderer's daughter seeks sanctuary in the Abbey. Another joke, and a sour one. What if she is already there?"

"She is not. The Abbey gate is being watched."

Madame Jeanette's voice crackled with excitement. "So she might come down the path outside at any moment! What then, Gilles?"

"I take her to the place in Castaways. After that, I go home. I am not paid for what comes next. I know nothing of it."

"I do not believe you! Why do you carry a shotgun? Why is there a new rope coiled in the wagon?"

"That is not my part."

Her tone softened, became a velvet purr. "Ah, I wish it were mine. My poor Giselle would like to watch that—she would like to see the murderer's daughter die."

Horror at her words had unconsciously made me sit up, lean forward to listen, dreading to hear, yet knowing I must. Without realizing it, I moved my hand, then felt the touch of something which began to move, to roll down the sloping hay toward the edge of the loft. I tried to snatch the dark object, but it eluded me, dropping to the floor below with a muted thud.

"Tabernac! Is it raining pumpkins? Is someone in the loft?"

"Pumpkins and squash are stored up there. One dislodged itself, nothing more."

"Watch at the window, I will see."

As I heard the first sound of his moving boots, I drew back my arm, then threw it forward in the direction of the cats, pretending to hurl something at them. Leaping from their perch, they scampered down the rails of the ladder just as Gilles was starting to ascend. I held my breath, cringing back, praying that somehow I might be made invisible.

"Cats," he chuckled. "Only your devils of cats!"

I heard him recross the room, and I lay quietly, trying to still the pounding of my heart, which, madly, I felt they must be able to hear.

"Look toward Castaways," said Madame Jeanette. "Is that smoke?"

The burning cabin, I thought, and had the frantic hope that smoke from its smoldering embers might draw them out to investigate. If only Gilles would go outside, even for a moment, I could dart down the ladder, out the door.

"You are imagining it," he said, and my hope died.

In the ensuing silence a strange sensation took possession of me. I remained as alert and tense as a cornered animal, yet part of my mind seemed numb, seemed to drift to a far-away place and to a time long ago.

I felt I was sitting on the floor of my mother's kitchen with poppies scattered around me. No, not real poppies, something else. Then I recalled the ugly linoleum, the floral pattern Charlotte was eager to replace. *"Do not wiggle, lit-tle one."* It was Paul's voice, my father's voice, and those were not his words but that was his meaning. He bent over the table, deftly sketching with my crayons. Beside me on the floor lay Sandy-Panda.

The doll in the painting I had just seen! The doll the *Wistful Child* reached for so sadly. But Morgan Armitage had never seen that doll, never seen the floral linoleum. The painting in the room below was not a portrait of Charlotte, but of me. I was that child, and only one artist could have painted it—my father, Jean-Paul Dumont. What had Morgan said about trying to get a Toronto art dealer to show my father's work? "It didn't work out." But it had! It worked very well indeed—for Morgan.

Regina had discovered this. Her keen eye must have recognized Sandy-Panda at once, and no doubt she realized why *Wistful Child* had to be taken from River Rising before I could see it.

The coloring book, I supposed, had told her the rest of the story. Even in the sketches, she had identified the style of the artist and knew Morgan's career was built on lies. The exhibition in Ottawa to honor the name Armitage would be a fraud. No wonder Regina had crumpled under the shock.

"That is his car," said Madame Jeanette. "He is coming now."

Startled from my reverie, I tried to withdraw deeper into the loft, but found my back was touching the stone wall. The unknown *he* of whom they spoke so respectfully was clearly the man who paid them, the man who commanded, the man determined I would not reach the Abbey.

When he entered the house, no greetings were exchanged. His first words were "She did not come this way?"

"Non, monsieur." Madame Jeanette and Gilles answered together.

"She must have lost her way in the storm."

"C'est bon!" exclaimed Madame Jeanette. "Let her die in the forest, then. It saves trouble."

"No. We will hunt for her. People who lose their way find it again. She's to be taken care of properly."

I knew the man's voice well, but only once before had I heard him use this cold tone of command that had steel behind it. Howard Palmer had sounded like this when I overheard him talking with Morgan about Dorothy. Dorothy? The terrible realization came to me that I had been the subject of their conversation, not Morgan's wife. Palmer had even used the same words he spoke only a moment ago. "She's got to be taken care of properly." Now I knew what this meant.

Taken care of on a trip to New York, perhaps? One thing was certain. I must never be allowed to see the exhibition in Ottawa, where among dozens of paintings there would be at least one to prompt memories of my childhood, of my father's work. There was a time limit on my life.

"Monsieur Morgan watches near the Abbey?" Madame Jeanette asked.

"Yes. Another reason we must look for her. I am not sure of Morgan. He lacks nerve. What is the French word? *Le cran?*"

"You will not speak thus of Monsieur Morgan in my house! He is a man who understands honor and the duty of family. He is avenging François and Giselle. Do not insult him!"

"I was joking," Palmer answered, with a trace of his false geniality.

So this was how they were using Madame Jeanette. Palmer, and undoubtedly Morgan, intended my death. It was foolish not to recognize and face this fact. And the deluded madwoman thought they were doing it for revenge, a murder to satisfy some twisted sense of honor. She was mistaken. It was money they wanted. They had killed at least once for money and I knew with terrifying certainty that they would not hesitate to kill a second time.

"We should start looking," Palmer said. "You, madame, keep watch at the window here. I am leaving you the extra shotgun. Do you know how to fire it?"

"*Ave Maria!* Do you take me for a city idiot? Of course I know how."

"If you see her, fire it into the air. Fire first one barrel, then the other. Two shots. Do you understand?"

My mind raced ahead, planning my escape. Once the two men were gone, I would somehow outwit Madame Jeanette. Lure her to the loft, perhaps? Could I do anything with the hay trolley? From the edge of the loft near the ladder, I thought the heavy wooden box was within reach. Or did the ladder itself, which was not attached but simply leaning, offer some possibility of use? I had a weapon of sorts, I could swing my bag on its long leather strap and—

"What the devil!" Palmer exclaimed in English, then shifted into French, hard to follow because he seemed choked by rage. "Why did you bring out that picture? You are paid to keep it hidden!"

"Painting? *Sacrebleu!* I did not touch it, I swear. Someone has been here."

"And what's this mess on the floor? A pumpkin?"

"It rolled from the loft. The cats pushed it," said Gilles.

Utter silence followed, and I knew that Palmer had made some gesture to command the stillness. In a moment they would search the loft.

You are not finished yet, I told myself. Fight them, fight them back. Try anything, any trick.

Forcing back my fear, I called out, trying to sound like a sleeping person just awakened. "Hello? Has someone come back?"

I crawled quickly to the top of the ladder and looked down. Gilles stood below, his foot on the lowest rung.

"Gilles, please hold the ladder for me. It was very frightening climbing up, but I had to find a warm place to sleep."

Mouth agape, he obeyed me, and I descended awkwardly, clutching my cape and bag.

What, I wondered idly, had happened to the radio? Had I left it in the burning cabin? Somewhere in this room? I only knew that it was gone.

When I reached the floor, I forced my lips into a smile. "Howard, how nice to see you! Have you taken shelter from the storm? I was freezing when I found this place. The loft seemed the warmest spot and I fell asleep until just now!"

I had no illusions that my performance would convince them, but they might be confused by a show of confidence. I might win a little time, and time was the only thing I had on my side.

"The painting! Did you take it from the cupboard?" Madame Jeanette demanded.

"Yes, I did. I was looking for a blanket and I found it. Of course, the room was so dark I couldn't see it clearly. But I recognized your work, Howard. It's very pretty."

He stood tense, poised, ready for any false move, and there was a cruel gleam in his eyes, almost a look of amusement, when he said, "Yes. A sentimental thing I did for Madame Jeanette. A portrait of her dead daughter."

Madame Jeanette murmured a sigh, quiet yet packed with bitterness.

Pretending to yawn and stretch sleepily, I let my eyes dart over the room. Two guns leaned against the wall on the far side, but no one was carrying a weapon. Gilles's menacing bulk barred any rush to the door, and Palmer had moved dangerously close. Could I hurl one of the jars on the shelves? No, that was useless. The hook to release the hay trolley was only inches from my hand, but I could think of no way to make use of it.

Palmer came a step nearer. "My dear Rochelle, I've been searching for you. So has Morgan. We thought you had lost your way in the storm. And all the while you were safely here, admiring a work of art."

He was baiting me, taunting me, but I refused to take notice. It struck me that this was a game, a deadly one, but still the game of a man who had not grown up, the cruelty of an insensitive child. Howard Palmer, more intelligent than the backward Gilles, more plausible than Madame Jeanette, lived in illusions that were no less dangerous for being childish.

"How kind of you to worry about me," I went on quickly, and as I spoke, a desperate plan formed itself in my mind. "You shouldn't have worried. I was lost for a few minutes, then I met a man who guided me here."

"Indeed?" Howard was puzzled, almost convinced that I was lying, yet not quite sure. And he had to be sure, a small advantage to me.

"Who was this guide?" he asked.

"I didn't catch his name. We were both cold and exhausted. He brought me to the door and left at once. Deliberately, I glanced toward the loft in a furtive manner, then continued, "He was in a great hurry and had to leave at once. So of course I was all alone here." Again a quick look toward the loft. The nervous, high-pitched laugh I gave required no acting.

I saw a shadow of suspicion in his face, knew my plan might be starting to work, and I pressed on. "How silly of me to be afraid when my friend Howard Palmer was on his way. After all, you had read my telegram and knew I was going to the Abbey." I spoke his name in an unnaturally loud voice, as though to be sure that a concealed listener in the loft could not fail to hear it. "And Gilles from the village. And Madame Jeanette."

I glanced once more at the loft, then looked quickly away.

"What a relief to be among my friends—Howard Palmer and Gilles and Madame Jeanette."

Suddenly he believed my deception. "Gilles," he shouted. "Search the loft." Gilles looked at him, puzzled. "There's somebody else up there. She wasn't alone."

"No, no!" I protested, and moved to block the ladder. "I swear there's nobody, nobody—"

Gilles thrust me roughly aside, and I pretended to stumble, to catch the ropes of the hay trolley for support. In those few seconds every eye was riveted to the loft while Gilles raced up the ladder, cursing. The instant he stepped on the floor above, I jerked the ropes of the hay trolley from their hooks and let it crash down.

As I plunged toward the door, I saw the wooden box strike Palmer a heavy blow on the shoulder. He fell to the floor, seizing the loft ladder, bringing it down with him. I heard Gilles shout and the screech-owl cry of Madame Jeanette, and then I was outside, running desperately, dodging around the corner of the house, expecting to hear at any second the explosion of a shotgun.

Gasping for breath, I hurled myself into a tangle of brush and saplings, not feeling the scratch and sting of the branches, driven on by terror of the pursuers who must be only a few seconds behind.

14

I dropped to the ground in a tiny clearing, lungs bursting, the blood pounding in my ears.

For a few minutes I could only tremble as I gasped for breath. The matting of pine needles felt damp against my back, but the snow, except for large scattered patches, had melted, vanishing as quickly as it had come, and now that the storm had spent itself the air seemed almost warm.

I gazed at an overcast sky, wondering how much daylight was left. A branch had ripped away my watch and another low bough had torn my left sleeve from shoulder to elbow.

Gradually strength and clarity returned to me. Sitting up, I strained to hear sounds of pursuit, but the woods were silent, a quiet almost ominous. No branch rustled, no birds called.

I've lost them, I told myself, feeling a surge of joy and relief.

Then, much as I longed to believe this, I stifled the hope. Howard Palmer was a keen and experienced hunter, and Gilles must know every acre of the wilderness around the village. Why should I expect to hear them approaching? They would follow noiselessly, confident of the final outcome. So far I had merely blundered ahead in panic, now I must think, use caution.

How much head start did I have? The falling box must have given Palmer a painful blow, yet not one that would disable him more than momentarily. Gilles would have waited for the ladder to be replaced, although he might have lowered himself from the edge of the loft, then dropped to the floor. Yet I doubted he would risk a broken ankle no matter what Morgan and Palmer paid him. And they could pay a great deal, for the stakes were high. My life against theirs.

It had been that way from the beginning. Deirdre had died in my place because a girl named Rochelle Dumont could not be allowed to enter River Rising, go to the living room where she would see a famous painting and say, "That's my mother's kitchen, my doll. I am that child and I know who painted this."

I tried to take my bearings. Firs, maples and birches surrounded me, a world without directions. Where was the Abbey? The village? The woods gave no clue and I did not dare waste time in debating.

"There is a way out, there has to be," I whispered, reassuring myself, fighting against panic. One thing was certain, if I made my way south, I would eventually find the river. It did not matter where I reached it, I could follow its shore and come to the Rising, or even, and the hope welled in me, I might find Pierre's house.

But which way was south? The hidden sun told me nothing. Then, with new excitement and confidence, I remembered the picnics with Pierre and Thalia, the forest lore and woodcraft he had explained. Now I must recall everything, use what he had said. Of course I could find south! He had taught me.

Moving quietly to the nearest large pine, I knelt and studied the moss at its base. The moss was thicker on one side, cleaner and drier, not spongy. That side, I knew from Pierre, would be north. In the opposite direction branches of the trees seemed a little longer, more bushy. South, of course, although this was harder to detect. Now I knew the way to the river.

Losing no more time, I started out again, crouching low to disturb the foliage as little as possible, avoiding patches of snow that would hold telltale footprints. Yet, leaving some betraying tracks was inevitable. The ground was wet, often muddy, and some patches of snow could not be avoided. I did my best to obliterate such tracks, using a fallen branch as a whiskbroom, trying hard to do what Pierre had described. But my efforts were clumsy and progress became painfully slow.

I had at least one advantage over my pursuers, I told myself. They had to find me, while I had only to find any house, any party of hunters. Soon, perhaps even now, Pierre would be searching for me, and not alone, I was sure. After the news about Deirdre, he would turn out the whole village when he learned I had not reached the Abbey.

Breaking free of the brush, I found myself in another clearing, where I leaned against a birch, resting my back after the struggle of moving forward bent almost double to pass beneath the branches. Again I listened for any sound, a footfall, the breaking of a twig. And again there was only stillness.

Then I stiffened, poised for flight, when I saw the bushes a few yards away move quietly but in an unnatural way. There was a darker shape among the leaves, someone waiting in ambush.

I froze against the tree as a large black bear slouched into the clearing. It turned its head left, then right, puzzled. The small eyes fixed themselves on me.

Which kind of bear was dangerous, the black or the brown? Were both likely to attack if cubs were near? I could remember nothing Pierre had said, but knew I must remain motionless. The bear lowered its head as though to charge, then the nose lifted as the animal snuffled the air, ears cocked and listening.

Then it seemed to hurl itself straight toward me. Stifling a scream, I tried to dodge behind the birch trunk, but the bear veered away, plunged into the thickets and vanished.

I stared after it, baffled, unable to fathom its odd behavior. What had the animal heard, what scent had it caught? Then my question was answered, for the same sound that had frightened the bear now fell on my ears. Just ahead, I heard the baying of Howard Palmer's hounds.

Spurred by terror, I retreated the way I had come. Safety now lay only in flight, for I might elude the men but not the dogs. Panting, I came to a narrow thread of a path, a game trail, and turned onto it without thinking. Even in ill-controlled panic I remembered Pierre's talk about doubling back, moving in loops and almost in circles to throw off a scent. These were all the tricks of the hunted fox, but I had neither the strength nor skill to do such things. I could only flee and pray that the village or the Abbey lay just ahead of me.

The dogs were barking excitedly, on the scent now, yet still far away. Darkness would be here soon; the twilight was fading rapidly. Night was a friend to hunted creatures, but I did not know if for me it was a friend or enemy.

The woods thinned. I saw a broad, amost treeless opening just ahead. A pasture, I thought, a farm, thank God.

I ran into the open, heedless that I was no longer concealed, sure that my flight had come to an end. Then a chill feeling swept over me as I realized I stood not on ground, but on hard-packed sawdust, a long arm of the man-made desert at Castaways.

Dusk was now changing to darkness. I could no longer run, but I walked rapidly, drawing breath in quick gasps. Strangely, my fear had lessened. I believed that safety and shelter lay just ahead, believed it for no reason except that I had to. At any moment Pierre would meet me, Viking barking happily at his side. Yes, Pierre was coming quickly, and I felt this so strongly that I almost saw him, a wavering figure in the deep shadows, a figure I had seen in dreams.

I managed to run a few strides, then paused a second, casting an anxious look behind. No sign of Palmer or the dogs, yet I could hear them, closer now.

Stumbling ahead, I saw the ruins of a tumbledown house, then another behind it. I moved more slowly, almost mechanically. This was the edge of Castaways; now I knew where the Abbey lay.

Although the darkness was now almost complete, I recognized the old village square. A little farther on stood the building François Armitage had erected. It had caused me to quarrel with Pierre on our first picnic. We would not quarrel so foolishly again, I decided. We would be too happy, we would—

A beam of white light blazed in my face, blinding me, and at the same time bringing me to my senses.

"Who is it?" I cried.

I saw no face, but a heavy hand seized my arm, and as I began to struggle I heard Gilles cursing me. Then I screamed, screamed and shouted for help, kicking at him, striking and clawing his face with my nails.

For an instant I thought I had broken free; his grip relaxed. Suddenly a heavy cloth was thrown over me, stifling my cries and breath. Still I fought until something hard and painful struck my head and I knew no more.

Far away a light flickered dimly, a candle or a match in the distance, moving unsteadily closer. My head throbbed, I did not want to awaken, did not want to enter the world again. Muted voices were speaking and I wondered who was trying to arouse me by slapping my cheek lightly. Go away, I thought. Let me alone, let me sleep.

Then a voice spoke clearly and recognizably. "No, she's still out cold."

Morgan Armitage replied, "That's just as well."

Consciousness returned to me rapidly, but some instinct told me not to move, not to open my eyes. I sat half propped, half sprawled in the corner of a room, my back against a wall that felt like rough stone. Again, for a moment, staying awake seemed too much struggle; the desire to retreat from reality into dream became an almost irresistible compulsion.

Fighting against this feeling of lassitude, I forced my mind to concentrate on what was happening. Covertly, I opened my eyes just enough to learn where I had been taken.

We were in a large room lit by the glaring white brilliance of two gasoline lanterns. I had never seen this interior, yet I knew it was the building François Armitage had built in Castaways. I recognized the steel doors and shutters, the long, narrow shape. In my flight I had come to the very place where they wanted me.

I remembered the struggle with Gilles, but Gilles himself seemed to have left. Perhaps, as he had said earlier, what was to come now was not part of his job. The thought made me shudder inwardly. Madame Jeanette sat on a stool near the closed metal door, the shotgun Palmer had given her leaning against the wall within her reach. The black shawl was wound about her like a shroud and the wizened face, blanched by the harshness of the lanterns, had an empty, entranced expression.

Morgan and Palmer stood near her, their features tense with anger.

"Madame, I tell you to go home. You already know too much for your own good!" Morgan did not shout, yet he seemed to control his voice with difficulty.

"I stay until the end!" she flung back. "My Giselle is dead. You promised me vengeance if I would help you, and I will now see it done."

"You'll see nothing," said Palmer.

Instead of answering, she spat at him. Morgan turned away, moved to a table in the center of the room and took a swallow from a half-empty whiskey bottle that stood there. When he looked in my direction, I closed my eyes, but not before I had glimpsed a man in sheer torment. I heard him take several unsteady steps toward me.

"There's got to be some other way," he muttered. "Some reasonable way out of this." He seemed to have forgotten Madame Jeanette's presence.

"You're a coward, Morgan," Howard Palmer told him, the words seeming to bite. "You don't mind paying to have a risky job done, like the one I arranged in Montréal—"

"Bungled!" Morgan retorted. "Five thousand dollars paid to a stupid thug who made matters worse, not better. And now the Cameron girl's body is found!"

"Which is why you're a fool to delay any longer."

Palmer's calm, untroubled tone was even more terrifying than his words. What they intended to do to me seemed a matter of complete indifference to him. He was mad, I thought. There was some terrible lack in his mind or emotions.

"If we could have chosen our own time when she was away from here, when there'd be no connection with the Rising, then—"

"Will you get it through your head that it's too late for that? We're no longer dealing with a suspicious girl and that interfering Lachance. This morning it became a police matter. Time ran out."

I controlled my trembling, forced myself to remain as still as one already dead.

"The thing to do now," Palmer was saying, "is to get this over fast." He hesitated, then his voice rose. "Morgan, are you listening to me?"

"Yes."

"Put down that bottle and pay attention. We have to have a straight story. She must have been lost in the storm. You didn't see her today, I didn't see her after she left River Rising. Nobody saw her. There are hundreds of miles of wilderness out there. She'll never be found, and that's the end of our worries."

For a long time Morgan did not answer, and when he did, he sounded numb and listless. "Is that the end? It seems a lifetime since we went to the islands and saw Jean-Paul."

"You've always had a squeamish conscience," said Palmer.

"Not conscience. When I brought those first paintings of his back to Canada, I knew they were good. It was hard to believe Jean-Paul had painted them, they were so completely different, he'd changed so much."

"Well, he had plenty to make him change!"

"When I changed his signature to my own, I almost believed I had done the painting myself. It was what I wanted to do, it had everything I felt. I had no idea what it would lead to."

"A bloody fortune is what it led to! Will you shake off this heartbreaking self-pity so we can get on with business?"

Morgan seemed not to hear him. "A lifetime of lies. Always afraid that some stranger would tap me on the shoulder and tell me he'd seen a painting before or he recognized a style. But it wasn't a stranger who came. It was Jean-Paul's daughter!"

"You make me cry, Morgan," Palmer answered. "You weren't too worried to pocket the money and hog the fame." He added with a sneer, "Jean-Paul's dear friend, his secret Canadian dealer who kept him going. A little hungry, maybe, and too poor to travel where he might see some of his own work with your name on it. Jean-Paul was always a trusting fool."

"His daughter," Morgan repeated, then the pitch of his voice lifted, grew shrill. "Isn't there something else we can do? Some kind of explanation . . ."

I knew the moment had come when I must act quickly and forcefully, move before they did, make any attempt, however desperate, to confuse them. Delay was on my side, my only weapon. Someone would find us soon, Pierre would come, I had to believe that.

"Yes, there's another way out of this," I said loudly. My voice was not as calm as I had hoped, but it would have to pass, to get by. Both men whirled toward me as I struggled to my feet.

"I'm tired, Morgan," I told him with as much authority as I could muster. "Help me to a chair, please. We have to talk business."

Astonished, Morgan stared at me blankly, then came forward, took my arm.

"Thank you, Morgan. I've had a difficult day, thanks to the stupidity of your friend Mr. Palmer. You take foolish risks in trusting Howard, but I suppose you have no choice, have you?"

Howard Palmer made a threatening move, his small eyes glinting, but I ignored him and took a seat at the table. I kept my hands folded in my lap so I would not be given away by their involuntary trembling.

"If your blackmailing acquaintance had had his way, I might be dead by now, and that would have left you with no escape." I glanced at Morgan. "By the way, he is a black-mailer, isn't he? I think that's become obvious even to Regina."

Neither man spoke, but the look of defeat on Morgan's face gave the answer. I dared not glance at Howard Palmer. His flushed features, the barely repressed violence in his eyes were more than I could endure, and I must not risk shattering the façade of calm upon which my life depended.

"We can come to an agreement, Morgan," I continued quickly. "I'm afraid it will be expensive for you, but really, you have no choice."

Morgan lifted the whiskey bottle, swallowed a heavy drink. "What the devil are you talking about?"

"First of all, there's Deirdre Cameron. You're an accomplice in her murder." I was improvising frantically to gain time, yet now I was sure my voice would not betray me. Further, Morgan was a frightened, broken man, not thinking clearly. Howard Palmer remained the real threat, but I could imagine no way of dealing with him. No, it was Morgan I must confuse.

"Eventually the police will find your trail. Pierre Lachance will see to that. But of course, I can probably invent some story about Deirdre to keep the police away from you."

Palmer spoke, his mild tone carrying a deadly threat. "The police? I'm afraid you won't be around to tell the police anything."

"You are mistaken, Mr. Palmer, as you'll soon see. But what you think doesn't matter. My business is with Morgan." I almost managed a smile.

Looking directly at Morgan, I said, "When I saw your painting in the Montréal museum, Morgan, I suspected it was my father's work. Then, when *Wistful Child* was described to me, I remembered the day it was painted. My father worked constantly, as you well know. There must be a great many canvases that you've held back for the future, pictures still unsold. And I know what they are worth."

I glanced around the room at crated paintings, carefully wrapped in heavy brown paper. Several more, not wrapped, leaned against the wall.

I gambled on displaying my pretended confidence still further. Rising, I moved calmly toward the pictures. Howard Palmer stepped quickly between me and the door, but I paid him no attention.

"I don't recognize this abstract," I said. Then I swallowed hard, finding it almost impossible to go on. On the floor near the paintings was a coil of new rope, rope too strong and heavy to be used to tie the crated paintings. It had to be the rope that had been in Gilles's wagon, the coil Madame Jeanette had spoken of.

"It's cold in here," I said, shuddering, then made myself continue playing the desperate game. Gesturing toward the next painting, I went on, "I remember that landscape very well. I used to play among those trees. It's more realistic than most of my father's work." Turning back, I went to the table and resumed my seat. "Now shall we talk about my price?" I said.

Morgan stared at me blankly, seeming not to comprehend my words.

"Your price!" Palmer rested his thick hands on the table, leaning toward me. Now his face was twisted in a sneer. "You're not setting any prices, and you're not bluffing us, either. Oh, I'll admit you're a cool one, but it won't work."

The contempt in his voice almost defeated me. I had to struggle to go on, but had no choice. Why didn't someone come? Surely Pierre had returned by now. Surely he knew I was missing. A little time, I thought wildly. Only a little more time.

Then, unaccountably, my mind went blank. I could not remember what I had said, what point I was trying to make.

My unexpected rescue came from Morgan, who prompted me without realizing it. "So what is your price?" he asked. He was rubbing his hands together, clenching and unclenching the fingers.

"Yes," said Palmer. "Come to the point and get this waiting game finished."

"I will forget the past, forget today. I'll even ignore the

torments you've caused me while trying to drive me away from the Rising."

"How generous," Palmer jeered.

"Besides, I'll add a bonus. I agree to make up some story about Deirdre to keep the police away." Leaning back in the chair, I pretended to relax. "It's a good bargain, one you can't refuse."

"And for this you expect us to let you walk out of here?"

I hated and feared Palmer's contorted smile as he mocked me. "I expect a great deal more than that, and I'll get it, too," I retored angrily. "My price is one half the value of all the paintings you sell in the future."

Morgan raised his head, he was understanding me now, but I could read nothing in his face.

"What an interesting proposal," said Howard Palmer. He crossed the room to a tool rack that hung on the far wall.

I watched in horror and fascination as he lifted his hand, moving it past the framing hammer, a screwdriver, a pair of pliers.

The hand halted; his fingers closed around the handle of a mat knife. I could not speak, my throat seemed constricted, choked.

He turned back but did not come toward me. My eyes darted toward the door, although I knew I could never reach it in time. Madame Jeanette sat quietly on her stool, she had not moved, but now her gaze was intent on the knife in Palmer's hand and there was a demented look of triumph on her face.

"Really, my dear," said Palmer softly. "You sell too cheaply. Why take just half the value of the paintings? All of them belong to you. You are the artist's daughter and heiress. I assure you there's quite a fortune in this room." He paused, smiling. "But of course, one must be able to claim it."

"Yes, that's it!" I exclaimed. Hysteria was creeping into my voice, but I could not prevent it. My nerves, held taut for so long, were now breaking. In a moment the battle would be lost. "How am I to prove who did these paintings?" I said. "It would be my word against Morgan's. Years could go by before I had all the evidence. You understand that, don't you, Morgan? Morgan!"

His lips were slack, his eyes glassy, and when he spoke, it was not in reply to my question. "I thought Jean-Paul or

Charlotte would learn the truth one day. But I felt safe. What could she have done? And he was dead, he couldn't come back to claim anything."

Morgan's voice fell to a whisper. "Why did all the bells at the Rising ring that way? At midnight. Was it Jean-Paul? Charlotte? But they're dead!"

"Come to your senses, Morgan!" said Howard Palmer.

He walked slowly toward the coil of rope. His footfalls seemed unnaturally loud and every step seemed to pound in my ears.

Kneeling, but still watching me closely, Palmer cut off a length of the heavy line, the mat knife, razor-sharp, slicing through it easily.

A rope to bind my hands, I thought. Or a rope to strangle?

"Are you accepting my bargain?" I demanded, my tone too shrill. "There's no other way, you know."

"I think we have a better solution," said Palmer, then he frowned, taking a slow step toward me. "But of course, what you said is worth considering."

His tone was reassuring, velvet-soft. He was trying to calm me, trying to delay any screams or struggle until the last second, until it was too late.

I rose from my chair, not to retreat but to attempt one last show of defiance. "Dame Theresa has a letter. I wrote everything I suspected, everything I knew to her. It's to be opened only upon my death or disappearance. The letter explains all about the paintings."

I paused, then spoke directly to Morgan, playing my final card. "It also reminds her of the night she left the Abbey, the night when she saw my father helpless in the garden at the moment you were killing François Armitage. For you killed him, Morgan. You're a murderer, and worse than that. You convinced an innocent man that he was guilty. A man who couldn't remember, who didn't know what had happened. You pressed the hammer into his hand, you made sure his fingerprints would show. Howard helped you, and has blackmailed you ever since. You're guilty, Morgan, and Dame Theresa will soon know it."

Morgan's face crumpled, the knuckles of the clenched fists went dead-white. "It was an accident, I didn't mean it to happen!" he shouted, the strained emotions suddenly breaking. "François was squandering my inheritance, and he joked about it. He made fun of me, ridiculed my painting.

The hammer was there on the table, and I . . . yes, I hit him. Who could blame me? I tell you he drove me to it." He pressed his hands against his temples, as though there was a pounding pain inside his head. "Jean-Paul threatened to kill him; it was in Jean-Paul's mind, not mine. Why shouldn't Jean-Paul be guilty? He believed it himself!"

Morgan halted abruptly, astonished at the horror his own words evoked. He stood in silence, wide-eyed, seeming to relive the night of his crime.

Howard Palmer spoke, cursing. "You're a babbling fool, Morgan. She's driven you into admitting it. Now we'll get this over."

His expression told me that my last bluff had failed. He did not believe I had written a letter, and the game was lost. He moved slowly toward me, holding the rope loosely and easily in his extended hands.

I could not retreat, but stood paralyzed, riveted by terror, knowing the long-delayed moment had come, yet still not quite believing that this was the end.

An explosion ripped the air. Howard Palmer shied back, turned toward Morgan, who gave a strangled cry of pain and surprise before his knees buckled. He reeled, half falling against the table. I saw blood on his shirt as he slipped slowly and helplessly to the floor.

Madame Jeanette stood near the door, the gun cradled in her arms, her face dazed. She had heard Morgan's confession, she had given final judgment.

Now she spoke in a hoarse, mindless whisper, the dry lips hardly moving: *"Giselle . . . Giselle . . . Giselle . . ."*

I moved toward the door, strangely unafraid, and I realized as I passed Madame Jeanette that she did not see me. Her glazed eyes were fixed on Howard Palmer.

Quickly I slid back the bolt, hardly hearing Palmer speaking in a whining, desperate voice: "I swear I didn't know. It wasn't my fault . . ."

I opened the door, stepped outside, no longer a prisoner. Behind me, Howard Palmer's pleading, now shrill, frantic: "You must believe me, madame! You must understand!"

The night was cold, but although my dress was torn, I had no feeling of chill, no more than I had any real sense of hearing the blast of the second gunshot behind me.

Cloudy moonlight bathed the landscape, softening its

edges, luminous pools, pale but radiant, merging with the shadows of the Québec forest.

Ahead, not far away, I saw lights. Torches and lanterns carried by the men who were searching for me flickered in the darkness.

Then a voice called my name, a beloved voice ringing through the night, even as I had imagined it.

"Rochelle, Rochelle!"

Not drifting, not uncertain or afraid, I moved across the Sawdust Desert toward him and toward the future.

About the Author

JESSICA NORTH is the pseudonym of a prize-winning author whose books, short stories, and essays have appeared in many languages and on every continent. She was born in the United States but has spent most of her life abroad. She has, most recently, been living and working in the locale of the St. Lawrence River, the setting of this book.

More Big Bestsellers from SIGNET

☐ **THE GREEK TREASURE by Irving Stone.**
(#E7211—$2.25)

☐ **THE KITCHEN SINK PAPERS by Mike McGrady.**
(#J7212—$1.95)

☐ **THE GATES OF HELL by Harrison Salisbury.**
(#E7213—$2.25)

☐ **SAVAGE EDEN by Constance Gluyas.** (#J7171—$1.95)

☐ **ROSE: MY LIFE IN SERVICE by Rosina Harrison.**
(#J7174—$1.95)

☐ **THE FINAL FIRE by Dennis Smith.** (#J7141—$1.95)

☐ **SOME KIND OF HERO by James Kirkwood.**
(#J7142—$1.95)

☐ **THE HOMOSEXUAL MATRIX by C. A. Tripp.**
(#E7172—$2.50)

☐ **CBS: Reflections in a Bloodshot Eye by Robert Metz.**
(#E7115—$2.25)

☐ **'SALEM'S LOT by Stephen King.** (#J7112—$1.95)

☐ **CARRIE by Stephen King.** (#E6410—$1.75)

☐ **FATU-HIVA: Back to Nature by Thor Heyerdahl.**
(#J7113—$1.95)

☐ **THE DOMINO PRINCIPLE by Adam Kennedy.**
(#J7058—$1.95)

☐ **IF YOU COULD SEE WHAT I HEAR by Tom Sullivan and Derek Gill.** (#W7061—$1.50)

☐ **THE PRACTICE OF PLEASURE by Michael Harris.**
(#E7059—$1.75)